SHORT STORIES OF THE PAST

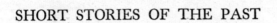

THOMAS HARDY
*from the pencil drawing by William
Strang in the National Portrait Gallery*

SHORT STORIES
OF THE PAST

EDITED BY
C. H. LOCKITT

LONGMANS, GREEN AND CO.
LONDON · NEW YORK · TORONTO

LONGMANS, GREEN AND CO LTD
6 & 7 CLIFFORD STREET LONDON W 1

ALSO AT MELBOURNE AND CAPE TOWN

LONGMANS, GREEN AND CO INC
55 FIFTH AVENUE NEW YORK 3

LONGMANS, GREEN AND CO
215 VICTORIA STREET TORONTO 1

ORIENT LONGMANS LTD
BOMBAY CALCUTTA MADRAS

First published 1949

PRINTED IN GREAT BRITAIN BY
NORTHUMBERLAND PRESS LIMITED
GATESHEAD ON TYNE

CONTENTS

		PAGE
INTRODUCTION		vii
1. DR. HEIDEGGER'S EXPERIMENT. *Nathaniel Hawthorne*		1
2. THE MASQUE OF THE RED DEATH. *Edgar Allan Poe*		14
3. THE SEXTON'S STORY. *Mrs. Gaskell*		22
4. THE ITALIAN PRISONER. *Charles Dickens*		35
5. THE JOURNEY TO PANAMA. *Anthony Trollope*		48
6. BROTHER MORGAN'S STORY OF THE DEAD HAND. *Wilkie Collins*		74
7. TENNESSEE'S PARTNER. *Bret Harte*		101
8. A RESUMED IDENTITY. *Ambrose Bierce*		113
9. THE SIRE DE MALÉTROIT'S DOOR. *R. L. Stevenson*		120
10. THE THREE STRANGERS. *Thomas Hardy*		146
11. THE HOUSE OF EULALIE. *Henry Harland*		174
12. THE HEADSWOMAN. *Kenneth Grahame*		185
13. BROOKSMITH. *Henry James*		208
NOTES		229

ACKNOWLEDGMENTS

ACKNOWLEDGMENT is due to the following for permission to reproduce copyright material:

Messrs. Jonathan Cape Ltd. for " A Resumed Identity " from *Can Such Things Be* by Ambrose Bierce; Messrs. John Farquharson, acting on behalf of the estate of the late Henry James, for " Brooksmith " from *The Lesson of the Master* by Henry James; the Trustees of the Hardy Estate and Messrs. Macmillan & Co. Ltd. for " The Three Strangers " from *Wessex Tales* by Thomas Hardy; the Houghton Mifflin Company of Boston for " Tennessee's Partner " by Bret Harte; Messrs. John Lane (The Bodley Head) Ltd. for " The Headswoman " by Kenneth Grahame, from *The Yellow Book*, Vol. 3, October 1894, and " The House of Eulalie " from *Comedies and Errors* by Henry Harland.

INTRODUCTION

THE purpose of this book is to illustrate, so far as limitations of space permit, the development of the technique of short story writing from the days when Maria Edgeworth wrote her dreary sentimental tales for eighteenth-century readers to those of Kipling and Stevenson. To-day the short story is regarded as a definite form of art, possessing its own technique: it is not a novel cut short; it has grown up alongside the novel but is not derived from it. Some of the best writers of short stories have not been very successful with their novels, nor have great novelists—Trollope, for instance—always succeeded in writing effective short stories. As a rough critical test of the merits of a short story, a reader might ask himself, as he lays it down, whether he is completely satisfied or whether he feels that he has been left in mid-air, so to speak; for the subject of a good short story should be so chosen as to be readable in whatever time-limit we decide, say, half an hour, should be imposed on any story classified as such. A short story should be a rounded whole: it may take a few hours or a few days or many years for the wheel to come full circle, but full circle it must come without a sense of overcrowding. This involves what has been called " the essential unity " of the short story: a principle to which Poe gave dogmatic expression in a review of Hawthorne's *Twice-Told Tales*. " A skilful literary artist," he wrote, " having conceived, with deliberate care, a certain unique or single effect to be wrought out, he then invents such incidents as may best aid him. If his initial sentence tend not to the bringing of this effect, then he has failed in his first steps. In the whole composition there should be no word written, of which the tendency, direct or indirect, is not to one established whole." Only one idea, in fact, must underlie the story and in studying any story one must look for this idea. It may be a situation, it may be the embodiment of a thought, or some idle fancy, or it may be the expression of some conception of beauty or of terror or of surprise. In " Dr. Heidegger's Experiment " it is the thought of the irrevocableness of one's actions; everything in the " Masque of the Red Death " is subordinated to the description of a moment of terror. Hawthorne actually kept a note-book in which he jotted down any curious fancy or idea which he might eventually make the basis of a story. It was their employment of this essential unity and their insistence upon it that made Poe and Hawthorne the creators of a new form of literary art.

If the business of writing short stories had remained where Poe and Hawthorne left it, it would have been but a barren affair—timeless and placeless, beautifully symmetrical, it is true, but limited in theme and devoid of human interest. Fortunately other influences were at work, notably a growing interest in other people's way of living. In Ireland Carleton and the Banims were busy describing in not very well constructed stories the life of the Irish people, and Mrs. Gaskell in England, as " The Sexton's Hero " shows, was applying what she had learnt from contact with Hawthorne to interest the readers of *Household Words* with pictures of her own Lancashire. This is the beginning of what American critics have christened the " local colour " school, a school of short story writers who laid the emphasis not so much on situation as on atmosphere. The leaders of the movement in America were Bret Harte and, to a lesser degree, Ambrose Bierce, both being influenced by the American Civil War, Harte because the civil convulsion had excited a widespread interest in the remote parts of the Union, Bierce because, after himself playing his part as a soldier of the North, he was determined to bring home to his readers a sense of the horrors of war. The popularity of " local colour " stories was at its height in the eighties of last century, when their authors first began to issue their stories in volumes of tales, such as Kipling's pictures of India in *Soldiers Three* and *In Black and White*, or, in America, Mary Wilkins Freeman's *New England Nun*, by some regarded as the most perfect product of the school. Robert Louis Stevenson, in a talk with his biographer, Graham Balfour, declared that there were only three ways of writing a story : " You may take a plot," he said, " and fit character to it; you may take a character and choose incidents and situations to develop it; or, lastly, you may take a certain atmosphere and get actions and persons to express and realize it." If, however, we, for convenience, speak of the story of plot, the story of character, and the story of atmosphere, we should include all the local colour stories in the last class, while remembering that like all classifications it may simplify too much. It is out of the question to say that Hardy's *Wessex Tales* are all atmosphere or all character : in sober truth there is a bit of both; and Stevenson's own tales of medieval France, of which an example is included in this volume, though admittedly inspired by the atmosphere of old France that surrounded him on his repeated visits to Barbizon and its district between 1875 and 1879, are, like all his stories, rich in plot. The three elements, plot, character, and atmosphere are in fact necessary ingredients of the best short stories as indeed they are of the novel.

Most of the stories in this selection first appeared in a magazine: without the magazines the short story would have had little chance of finding readers. The history of the modern magazine begins with the foundation of *Blackwood's* and the *London* in the early years of the nineteenth century and carries on with a succession of ever cheaper and cheaper magazines—*Fraser's Magazine*, Dickens's *Household Words* and *All the Year Round*, and Thackeray's *Cornhill*; but their editors were more inclined to find space for long novels in serial form than for short stories. That is why when Wilkie Collins produced short stories for his friend Dickens, as he did in *After Dark* and in *Queen of Hearts* from which "Brother Morgan's Story" is drawn, he allowed them to masquerade as novels by fitting a whole group of stories inside a framework which linked them together, just as Chaucer had done five hundred years earlier. The superiority of American short stories in the middle of the century is due to the fact that their cheap popular magazines—*Harper's* (1850), *Putnam's* (1853), and the *Atlantic Monthly* (1857)—freely offered the hospitality of their columns to the writer of short stories: the *Atlantic Monthly* is said to have printed three in each number during its first year. Not till the coming of the *Strand Magazine*, a monthly, and the *Yellow Book*, a not very successful quarterly, did the English author obtain an equally generous opportunity, and that was in the nineties. When the *Strand Magazine* printed the Conan Doyle stories of Sherlock Holmes, it not only ensured its own success but introduced what was to prove a very popular form of short story, the detective story. The stories in the *Yellow Book* under the guidance of its editor, Henry Harland, showed signs, not of American, but of French influence. French story-writing was marked by a stern uncompromising realism and often, as in Harland's own stories, by a light and airy touch, adorned by delicate humour. The band of young writers, whom Harland gathered round him, included some of the men who were to be the leading men of letters in the twentieth century and the *Yellow Book*, short-lived though it was, contains many clever and sometimes powerful short stories. Kenneth Grahame's tale of " The Headswoman " which appeared in the number of October 1894 has been selected for inclusion in this volume, partly because it has affinities with Stevenson's " The Sire de Malétroit's Door," and partly because it is an admirable example of the French influence free from the sentimentalism which often marred Harland's own work. Both it and " The House of Eulalie " remind one of the paintings of Watteau, graceful and gay: they make little attempt to develop either plot or character drawing or atmosphere but remain pictures and pictures only.

When Stevenson talked of the story of atmosphere, he was thinking of a purely imaginative process by which the writer peopled his chosen scene with appropriate creatures of his imagination. The scientific age in which we live has demanded more than this and the growing study of psychology has induced the more thoughtful writers to link atmosphere, or, if you prefer it, environment with character. Though this is primarily a development of the twentieth century and so outside the scope of this volume, it has its roots in the past and owes much to the work of Henry James, whose " Brooksmith " is included as an admirable example of what we may call the " psychological story," that is, one in which the writer endeavours to trace the effect of environment on character and so on destiny. Yet " Brooksmith " was written in the nineteenth and not in the twentieth century.

Out of a wide choice, we have necessarily been compelled to omit many excellent stories: those we have chosen have been chosen in an endeavour to illustrate the broad outlines of the development of short story-writing, and in conclusion we can only hope that this little volume will spur its readers to make themselves acquainted with some of those writers of distinction, both American and English, who have been excluded solely by reasons of space.

DR. HEIDEGGER'S EXPERIMENT

THAT very singular man, old Dr. Heidegger, once invited four venerable friends to meet him in his study. There were three white-bearded gentlemen, Mr. Medbourne, Colonel Killigrew, and Mr. Gascoigne, and a withered gentlewoman, whose name was the Widow Wycherly. They were all melancholy old creatures, who had been unfortunate in life, and whose greatest misfortune it was that they were not long ago in their graves. Mr. Medbourne, in the vigour of his age, had been a prosperous merchant, but had lost his all by a frantic speculation, and was now little better than a mendicant. Colonel Killigrew had wasted his best years, and his health and substance, in the pursuit of sinful pleasures which had given birth to a brood of pains, such as the gout, and divers other torments of soul and body. Mr. Gascoigne was a ruined politician, a man of evil fame, or at least had been so, till time had buried him from the knowledge of the present generation, and made him obscure instead of infamous. As for the Widow Wycherly, tradition tells us that she was a great beauty in her day; but, for a long while past, she had lived in deep seclusion, on account of certain scandalous stories which had prejudiced the gentry of the town against her. It is a circumstance worth mentioning, that each of these three old gentlemen, Mr. Medbourne, Colonel Killigrew, and Mr. Gascoigne, were early lovers of the Widow Wycherly, and had once been on the point of cutting each other's throats for her sake. And before proceeding farther, I will merely hint that Dr. Heidegger and all his four guests were sometimes thought to be a little beside themselves; as is not unfrequently the case with old people, when worried either by present troubles or woeful recollections.

"My dear old friends," said Dr. Heidegger, motioning them to be seated, "I am desirous for your assistance in one of those little experiments with which I amuse myself here in my study."

If all stories were true, Dr. Heidegger's study must have been a very curious place. It was a dim, old-fashioned chamber, festooned with cobwebs, and besprinkled with antique dust. Around the walls stood several oaken bookcases, the lower shelves of which were filled with rows of gigantic folios and black-letter quartos, and the upper with little parchment-covered duodecimos. Over the central bookcase was a bronze bust of Hippocrates, with which, according to some authorities, Dr. Heidegger was accustomed to hold consultations in all difficult cases of his practice. In the obscurest corner of the room stood a tall and narrow oaken closet, with its door ajar, within which doubtfully appeared a skeleton. Between two of the bookcases hung a looking-glass, presenting its high and dusty plate within a tarnished gilt frame. Among many wonderful stories related of this mirror, it was fabled that the spirits of all the doctor's deceased patients dwelt within its verge, and would stare him in the face whenever he looked thitherward. The opposite side of the chamber was ornamented with the full-length portrait of a young lady, arrayed in the faded magnificence of silk, satin, and brocade, and with a visage as faded as her dress. Above half a century ago, Dr. Heidegger had been on the point of marriage with this young lady; but, being affected with some slight disorder, she had swallowed one of her lover's

2

prescriptions, and died on the bridal evening. The greatest curiosity of the study remains to be mentioned; it was a ponderous folio volume, bound in black leather, with massive silver clasps. There were no letters on the back, and nobody could tell the title of the book. But it was well known to be a book of magic; and once, when a chambermaid had lifted it, merely to brush away the dust, the skeleton had rattled in its closet, the picture of the young lady had stepped one foot upon the floor, and several ghastly faces had peeped forth from the mirror; while the brazen head of Hippocrates frowned, and said —" Forbear! "

Such was Dr. Heidegger's study. On the summer afternoon of our tale, a small round table, as black as ebony, stood in the centre of the room, sustaining a cut-glass vase of beautiful form and elaborate workmanship. The sunshine came through the window, between the heavy festoons of two faded damask curtains, and fell directly across this vase; so that a mild splendour was reflected from it on the ashen visages of the five old people who sat around. Four champagne glasses were also on the table.

" My dear old friends," repeated Dr. Heidegger, " may I reckon on your aid in performing an exceedingly curious experiment? "

Now Dr. Heidegger was a very strange old gentleman, whose eccentricity had become the nucleus for a thousand fantastic stories. Some of these fables, to my shame be it spoken, might possibly be traced back to mine own veracious self; and if any passages of the present tale should startle the reader's faith, I must be content to bear the stigma of a fiction-monger.

When the doctor's four guests heard him talk of his proposed experiment, they anticipated nothing more wonderful than the murder of a mouse in an air-pump, or the examination of a cobweb by the microscope, or some similar nonsense, with which he was constantly in the habit of pestering his intimates. But without waiting for a reply, Dr. Heidegger hobbled across the chamber, and returned with the same ponderous folio, bound in black leather, which common report affirmed to be a book of magic. Undoing the silver clasps, he opened the volume, and took from among its black-letter pages a rose, or what was once a rose, though now the green leaves and crimson petals had assumed one brownish hue, and the ancient flower seemed ready to crumble to dust in the doctor's hands.

"This rose," said Dr. Heidegger, with a sigh, "this same withered and crumbling flower, blossomed five-and-fifty years ago. It was given me by Sylvia Ward, whose portrait hangs yonder; and I meant to wear it in my bosom at our wedding. Five-and-fifty years it has been treasured between the leaves of this old volume. Now, would you deem it possible that this rose of half a century could ever bloom again?"

"Nonsense!" said the Widow Wycherly, with a peevish toss of her head. "You might as well ask whether an old woman's wrinkled face could ever bloom again."

"See!" answered Dr. Heidegger.

He uncovered the vase, and threw the faded rose into the water which it contained. At first it lay lightly on the surface of the fluid, appearing to imbibe none of its moisture. Soon, however, a singular change began to be visible. The crushed and dried petals stirred, and assumed a deepening tinge of crimson, as if the flower were reviving from a death-like slumber; the slender stalk and twigs of foliage became green; and there was the rose of half a century, looking as fresh as when Sylvia Ward had first given it to her lover. It was scarcely full blown; for some of its delicate red leaves curled modestly around its moist bosom, within which two or three dewdrops were sparkling.

"That is certainly a very pretty deception," said the doctor's friends; carelessly, however, for they had witnessed greater miracles at a conjurer's show; "pray how was it effected?"

"Did you never hear of the 'Fountain of Youth'?" asked Dr. Heidegger, "which Ponce de Leon, the Spanish adventurer, went in search of, two or three centuries ago?"

"But did Ponce de Leon ever find it?" said the Widow Wycherly.

"No," answered Dr. Heidegger, "for he never sought it in the right place. The famous Fountain of Youth, if I am rightly informed, is situated in the southern part of the Floridian peninsula, not far from Lake Macaco. Its source is over-shadowed by several gigantic magnolias, which, though numberless centuries old, have been kept as fresh as violets by the virtues of this wonderful water. An acquaintance of mine, knowing my curiosity in such matters, has sent me what you see in the vase."

"Ahem!" said Colonel Killigrew, who believed not a word of the doctor's story; "and what may be the effect of this fluid on the human frame?"

"You shall judge for yourself, my dear Colonel," replied Dr. Heidegger; "and all of you, my respected friends, are welcome to so much of this admirable fluid as may restore to you the bloom of youth. For my own part, having had much trouble in growing old, I am in no hurry to grow young again. With your permission, therefore, I will merely watch the progress of the experiment."

While he spoke, Dr. Heidegger had been filling the four champagne glasses with the water of the Fountain of Youth. It was apparently impregnated with an effervescent gas, for little bubbles were continually ascending from the depths of the glasses, and bursting in silvery spray at the surface. As the liquor diffused a pleasant perfume, the old people doubted not that it possessed cordial and comfortable properties; and, though utter sceptics as to its rejuvenescent power, they were inclined to swallow it at once. But Dr. Heidegger besought them to stay a moment.

"Before you drink, my respectable old friends," said he, "it would be well that, with the experience of a lifetime to direct you, you should draw up a few general rules for your guidance, in passing a second time through the perils of youth. Think what a sin and a shame it would be, if with your peculiar advantages, you should not become patterns of virtue and wisdom to all the young people of the age!"

The doctor's four venerable friends made him no answer, except by a feeble and tremulous laugh; so very ridiculous was the idea, that, knowing how closely repentance treads behind the steps of error, they should ever go astray again.

"Drink, then," said the doctor, bowing: "I rejoice that I have so well selected the subjects of my experiment."

With palsied hands they raised the glasses to their lips. The liquor, if it really possessed such virtues as Dr. Heidegger imputed to it, could not have been bestowed on four human beings who needed it more woefully. They looked as if they had never known what youth or pleasure was, but had been the offspring of Nature's dotage, and always the grey, decrepit, sapless, miserable creatures, who now sat stooping round the doctor's table, without life enough in their souls or bodies to be animated even by the prospect of growing young again.

They drank off the water, and replaced their glasses on the table.

Assuredly, there was an almost immediate improvement in the aspect of the party, not unlike what might have been produced by a glass of generous wine, together with a sudden glow of cheerful sunshine, brightening over all their visages at once. There was a healthful suffusion on their cheeks, instead of the ashen hue that had made them look so corpse-like. They gazed at one another, and fancied that some magic power had really begun to smooth away the deep and sad inscription which Father Time had been so long engraving on their brows. The Widow Wycherly adjusted her cap, for she felt almost like a woman again.

"Give us more of this wondrous water!" cried they, eagerly. "We are younger—but we are still too old! Quick—give us more!"

"Patience, patience!" quoth Dr. Heidegger, who sat watching the experiment with philosophic coolness. "You have been a long time growing old. Surely you might be content to grow young in half an hour! But the water is at your service."

Again he filled their glasses with the liquor of youth, enough of which still remained in the vase to turn half the old people in the city to the age of their own grand-children. While the bubbles were yet sparkling on the brim, the doctor's four guests snatched their glasses from the table, and swallowed the contents at a single gulp. Was it delusion? even while the draught was passing down their throats, it seemed to have wrought a change on their whole systems. Their eyes grew clear and bright; a dark shade deepened among their silvery locks; they sat around the table, three gentlemen of middle age, and a woman hardly beyond her buxom prime.

7

"My dear widow, you are charming!" cried Colonel Killigrew, whose eyes had been fixed upon her face, while the shadows of age were flitting from it like darkness from the crimson daybreak.

The fair widow knew, of old, that Colonel Killigrew's compliments were not always measured by sober truth; so she started up and ran to the mirror, still dreading that the ugly visage of an old woman would meet her gaze. Meanwhile, the three gentlemen behaved in such a manner as proved that the water of the Fountain of Youth possessed some intoxicating qualities; unless, indeed, their exhilaration of spirits were merely a lightsome dizziness, caused by the sudden removal of the weight of years. Mr. Gascoigne's mind seemed to run on political topics, but whether relating to the past, present, or future, could not easily be determined, since the same ideas and phrases have been in vogue these fifty years. Now he rattled forth full-throated sentences about patriotism, national glory, and the people's rights; now he muttered some perilous stuff or other, in a sly and doubtful whisper, so cautiously that even his own conscience could scarcely catch the secret; and now again he spoke in measured accents, and a deeply deferential tone, as if a royal ear were listening to his well-turned periods. Colonel Killigrew all this time had been trolling forth a jolly bottle-song, and ringing his glass in symphony with the chorus, while his eyes wandered towards the buxom figure of the Widow Wycherly. On the other side of the table, Mr. Medbourne was involved in a calculation of dollars and cents, with which was strangely intermingled a project for supplying the East Indies with ice, by harnessing a team of whales to the polar icebergs.

As for the Widow Wycherly, she stood before the mirror curtsying and simpering to her own image, and greeting it as the friend whom she loved better than all the world beside. She thrust her face close to the glass, to see whether some long-remembered wrinkle or crow's-foot had indeed vanished. She examined whether the snow had so entirely melted from her hair, that the venerable cap could be safely thrown aside. At last, turning briskly away, she came with a sort of dancing step to the table.

"My dear old doctor," cried she, "pray favour me with another glass!"

"Certainly, my dear madam, certainly!" replied the complaisant doctor; "see! I have already filled the glasses."

There, in fact, stood the four glasses, brimful of this wonderful water, the delicate spray of which, as it effervesced from the surface, resembled the tremulous glitter of diamonds. It was now so nearly sunset that the chamber had grown duskier than ever; but a mild and moon-like splendour gleamed from within the vase, and rested alike on the four guests, and on the doctor's venerable figure. He sat in a high-backed, elaborately carved, oaken arm-chair, with a grey dignity of aspect that might have well befitted that very Father Time whose power had never been disputed save by this fortunate company. Even while quaffing the third draught of the Fountain of Youth, they were almost awed by the expression of his mysterious visage.

But, the next moment, the exhilarating gush of young life shot through their veins. They were now in the happy prime of youth. Age, with its miserable train of cares, and sorrows, and diseases, was remembered only as the trouble of a dream from which they had joyously awoke. The fresh gloss of the soul, so early lost, and without which the world's successive scenes had been but a gallery of faded pictures, again threw its enchantment over all their prospects. They felt like new-created beings, in a new-created universe.

"We are young! We are young!" they cried, exultingly.

Youth, like the extremity of age, had effaced the strongly marked characteristics of middle life, and mutually assimilated them all. They were a group of merry youngsters, almost maddened with the exuberant frolicsomeness of their years. The most singular effect of their gaiety was an impulse to mock the infirmity and decrepitude of which they had so lately been the victims. They laughed loudly at their old-fashioned attire, the wide-skirted coats and flapped waistcoats of the young men, and the ancient cap and gown of the blooming girl. One limped across the floor, like a gouty grandfather; one set a pair of spectacles astride of his nose, and pretended to pore over the black-letter pages of the book of magic; a third seated himself in an arm-chair, and strove to imitate the venerable dignity of Dr. Heidegger. Then all shouted mirthfully, and leaped about the room. The Widow Wycherly—if so fresh a damsel could be called a widow—tripped up to the doctor's chair, with a mischievous merriment in her rosy face.

"Doctor, you dear old soul," cried she, "get up and dance with me!" And then the four young people laughed louder than ever, to think what a queer figure the poor old doctor would cut.

"Pray excuse me," answered the doctor, quietly. "I am old and rheumatic, and my dancing days were over long ago. But either of these gay young gentlemen will be glad of so pretty a partner."

"Dance with me, Clara!" cried Colonel Killigrew.

"No, no, I will be her partner!" shouted Mr. Gascoigne.

"She promised me her hand, fifty years ago!" exclaimed Mr. Medbourne.

They all gathered round her. One caught both her hands in his passionate grasp—another threw his arm about her waist—the third buried his hand among the glossy curls that clustered beneath the widow's cap. Blushing, panting, struggling, chiding, laughing, her warm breath fanning each of their faces by turns, she strove to disengage herself, yet still remained in their triple embrace. Never was there a livelier picture of youthful rivalship, with bewitching beauty for the prize. Yet, by a strange deception, owing to the duskiness of the chamber, and the antique dresses which they still wore, the tall mirror is said to have reflected the figures of the three old, grey, withered grandsires, ridiculously contending for the skinny ugliness of a shrivelled grandam.

But they were young: their burning passions proved them so. Inflamed to madness by the coquetry of the girl-widow, who neither granted nor quite withheld her favours, the three rivals began to interchange threatening glances. Still keeping hold of the fair prize, they grappled fiercely at one another's throats. As they struggled to and fro, the table was overturned, and the vase dashed into a thousand fragments. The precious Water of Youth flowed in a bright stream across the floor, moistening the wings of a butterfly, which, grown old in the decline of summer, had alighted there to die. The insect fluttered lightly through the chamber, and settled on the snowy head of Dr. Heidegger.

"Come, come, gentlemen!—come, Madame Wycherly," exclaimed the doctor, "I really must protest against this riot."

They stood still, and shivered; for it seemed as if grey Time were calling them back from their sunny youth, far down into the chill and darksome vale of years. They looked at old Dr. Heidegger, who sat in his carved arm-chair, holding the rose of half a century, which he had rescued from among the fragments of the shattered vase. At the motion of his hand, the four rioters resumed their seats; the more readily, because their violent exertions had wearied them, youthful though they were.

"My poor Sylvia's rose!" ejaculated Dr. Heidegger, holding it in the light of the sunset clouds; "it appears to be fading again."

And so it was. Even while the party were looking at it, the flower continued to shrivel up, till it became as dry and fragile as when the doctor had first thrown it into the vase. He shook off the few drops of moisture which clung to its petals.

"I love it as well thus, as in its dewy freshness," observed he, pressing the withered rose to his withered lips. While he spoke, the butterfly fluttered down from the doctor's snowy head, and fell upon the floor.

His guests shivered again. A strange chillness, whether of the body or spirit they could not tell, was creeping gradually over them all. They gazed at one another, and fancied that each fleeting moment snatched away a charm, and left a deepening furrow where none had been before. Was it an illusion? Had the changes of a lifetime been crowded into so brief a space, and were they now four aged people, sitting with their old friend, Dr. Heidegger?

"Are we grown old again, so soon?" cried they, dolefully.

In truth, they had. The Water of Youth possessed merely a virtue more transient than that of wine. The delirium which it created had effervesced away. Yes! they were old again. With a shuddering impulse, that showed her a woman still, the widow clasped her skinny hands before her face, and wished that the coffin-lid were over it, since it could be no longer beautiful.

"Yes, friends, ye are old again," said Dr. Heidegger; "and lo! the Water of Youth is all lavished on the ground. Well—I bemoan it not; for if the fountain gushed at my very doorstep, I would not stoop to bathe my lips in it—no, though its delirium were for years instead of moments. Such is the lesson ye have taught me!"

But the doctor's four friends had taught no such lesson to themselves. They resolved forthwith to make a pilgrimage to Florida, and quaff at morning, noon, and night, from the Fountain of Youth.

Nathaniel Hawthorne—*Twice Told Tales.*

THE MASQUE OF THE RED DEATH

The " Red Death " had long devastated the country. No pestilence had ever been so fatal, or so hideous. Blood was its Avatar and its seal—the redness and horror of blood. There were sharp pains, and sudden dizziness, and then profuse bleeding at the pores, with dissolution. The scarlet stains upon the body and especially upon the face of the victim, were the pest ban which shut him out from the aid and from the sympathy of his fellow-men. And the whole seizure, progress, and termination of the disease, were the incidents of half an hour.

But the Prince Prospero was happy and dauntless and sagacious. When his dominions were half-depopulated, he summoned to his presence a thousand hale and light-hearted friends from among the knights and dames of his court, and with these retired to the deep seclusion of one of his castellated abbeys. This was an extensive and magnificent structure, the creation of the prince's own eccentric yet august taste. A strong and lofty wall girdled it in. This wall had gates of iron. The courtiers, having entered, brought furnaces and massy hammers and welded the bolts. They resolved to leave means neither of ingress nor egress to the sudden impulses of despair or of frenzy from within. The abbey was amply provisioned. With such precautions the courtiers might bid defiance to contagion. The external world could take care of itself. In the meantime it was folly to grieve, or to think. The prince had provided all the appliances of pleasure. There were buffoons, there were improvisatori, there were ballet-dancers, there were musicians, there was Beauty, there was wine. All these and security were within. Without was the " Red Death."

It was toward the close of the fifth or sixth month of his seclusion, and while the pestilence raged most furiously abroad, that the Prince Prospero entertained his thousand friends at a masked ball of the most unusual magnficence.

It was a voluptuous scene, that masquerade. But first let me tell of the rooms in which it was held. These were seven—an imperial suite. In many palaces, however, such suites form a long and straight vista, while the folding doors slide back nearly to the walls on either hand, so that the view of the whole extent is scarcely impeded. Here the case was very different, as might have been expected from the duke's love of the *bizarre*. The apartments were so irregularly disposed that the vision embraced but little more than one at a time. There was a sharp turn at every twenty or thirty yards, and at each turn a novel effect. To the right and left, in the middle of each wall, a tall and narrow Gothic window looked out upon a closed corridor which pursued the windings of the suite. These windows were of stained glass whose colour varied in accordance with the prevailing hue of the decorations of the chamber into which it opened. That at the eastern extremity was hung, for example, in blue—and vividly blue were its windows. The second chamber was purple in its ornaments and tapestries, and here the panes were purple. The third was green throughout, and so were the casements. The fourth was furnished and lighted with orange—the fifth with white—the sixth with violet. The seventh apartment was closely shrouded in black velvet tapestries that hung all over the ceiling and down the walls, falling in heavy folds upon a carpet of the same material and hue. But in this chamber only, the colour of the windows failed to correspond with the decorations. The panes here were scarlet—a deep blood colour. Now in no one of the seven apartments was there any lamp or candelabrum, amid the profusion of golden ornaments that lay scattered to and fro or depended from the roof. There was no light of any kind emanating from lamp or candle within the suite of chambers. But in the corridors that followed the suite there stood, opposite to each window, a heavy tripod, bearing a brazier of fire, that projected its rays through the tinted glass and so glaringly illumined the room. And thus were produced a multitude of gaudy and fantastic appearances. But in the western or black chamber the effect of the fire-light that streamed upon the dark hangings through the blood-tinted panes was ghastly in the extreme, and produced so wild a look upon the countenances of those who entered, that there were few of the company bold enough to set foot within its precincts at all.

It was in this apartment, also, that there stood against the western wall, a gigantic clock of ebony. Its pendulum swung to and fro with a dull, heavy, monotonous clang; and when the minute-hand made the circuit of the face, and the hour was to be stricken, there came from the brazen lungs of the clock a sound which was clear and loud and deep and exceedingly musical, but of so peculiar a note and emphasis that, at each lapse of an hour, the musicians of the orchestra were constrained to pause, momentarily, in their performance, to hearken to the sound; and thus the waltzers perforce ceased their evolutions; and there was a brief disconcert of the whole gay company; and, while the chimes of the clock yet rang, it was observed that the giddiest grew pale, and the more aged and sedate passed their hands over their brows as if in confused reverie or meditation. But when the echoes had fully ceased, a light laughter at once pervaded the assembly; the musicians looked at each other and smiled as if at their own nervousness and folly, and made whispering vows, each to the other, that the next chiming of the clock should produce in them no similar emotion; and then, after the lapse of sixty minutes (which embrace three thousand and six hundred seconds of the Time that flies), there came yet another chiming of the clock, and then were the same disconcert and tremulousness and meditation as before.

But, in spite of these things, it was a gay and magnificent revel. The tastes of the duke were peculiar. He had a fine eye for colours and effects. He disregarded the *decora* of mere fashion. His plans were bold and fiery, and his conceptions glowed with barbaric lustre. There are some who would have thought him mad. His followers felt that he was not. It was necessary to hear and see and touch him to be *sure* that he was not.

He had directed, in great part, the movable embellishments of the seven chambers, upon occasion of this great *fête*; and it was his own guiding taste which had given character to the masqueraders. Be sure they were grotesque. There were much glare and glitter and piquancy and phantasm—much of what has been since seen in *Hernani*. There were arabesque figures with unsuited limbs and appointments. There were delirious fancies such as the madman fashions. There were much of the beautiful, much of the wanton, much of the *bizarre*, something of the terrible, and not a little of that which might have excited disgust. To and fro in the seven chambers there stalked, in fact, a multitude of dreams. And these—the dreams—writhed in and about, taking hue from the rooms, and causing the wild music of the orchestra to seem as the echo of their steps. And, anon, there strikes the ebony clock which stands in the hall of the velvet. And then, for a moment, all is still, and all is silent save the voice of the clock. The dreams are stiff-frozen as they stand. But the echoes of the chime die away—they have endured but an instant—and a light, half-subdued laughter floats after them as they depart. And now again the music swells, and the dreams live, and writhe to and fro more merrily than ever, taking hue from the many-tinted windows through which stream the rays from the tripods. But to the chamber which lies most westwardly of the seven there are now none of the maskers who venture; for the night is waning away; and there flows a ruddier light through the blood-coloured panes; and the blackness of the sable drapery appals; and to him whose foot falls upon the sable carpet, there comes from the near clock of ebony a muffled peal more solemnly emphatic than any which reaches *their* ears who indulged in the more remote gaieties of the other apartments.

But these other apartments were densely crowded, and in them beat feverishly the heart of life. And the revel went whirlingly on, until at length there commenced the sounding of midnight upon the clock. And then the music ceased, as I have told; and the evolutions of the waltzers were quieted; and there was an uneasy cessation of all things as before. But now there were twelve strokes to be sounded by the bell of the clock; and thus it happened, perhaps, that more of thought crept, with more of time, into the meditations of the thoughtful among those who revelled. And thus too, it happened, perhaps, that before the last echoes of the last chime had utterly sunk into silence, there were many individuals in the crowd who had found leisure to become aware of the presence of a masked figure which had arrested the attention of no single individual before. And the rumour of this new presence having spread itself whisperingly around, there arose at length from the whole company a buzz, or murmur, expressive of disapprobation and surprise—then, finally, of terror, of horror, and of disgust.

In an assembly of phantasms such as I have painted, it may well be supposed that no ordinary appearance could have excited such sensation. In truth the masquerade licence of the night was nearly unlimited; but the figure in question had out-Heroded Herod, and gone beyond the bounds of even the prince's indefinite decorum. There are chords in the hearts of the most reckless which cannot be touched without emotion. Even with the utterly·lost, to whom life and death are equally jests, there are matters of which no jest can be made. The whole company, indeed, seemed now deeply to feel that in the costume and bearing of the stranger neither wit nor propriety existed. The figure was tall and gaunt, and shrouded from head to foot in the habiliments of the grave. The mask which concealed the visage was made so nearly to resemble the countenance of a stiffened corpse that the closest scrutiny must have had difficulty in detecting the cheat. And yet all this might have been endured, if not approved, by the mad revellers around. But the mummer had gone so far as to assume the type of the Red Death. His vesture was dabbled in *blood*—and his broad brow, with all the features of the face, was sprinkled with the scarlet horror.

When the eyes of Prince Prospero fell upon this spectral image (which, with a slow and solemn movement, as if more fully to sustain its *rôle*, stalked to and fro among the waltzers) he was seen to be convulsed in the first moment with a strong shudder either of terror or distaste; but, in the next, his brow reddened with rage.

" Who dares "—he demanded hoarsely of the courtiers

who stood near him—"who dares insult us with this blasphemous mockery? Seize him and unmask him—that we may know whom we have to hang, at sunrise, from the battlements!"

It was in the eastern or blue chamber in which stood the Prince Prospero as he uttered these words. They rang throughout the seven rooms loudly and clearly, for the prince was a bold and robust man, and the music had become hushed at the waving of his hand.

It was in the blue room where stood the prince, with a group of pale courtiers by his side. At first, as he spoke, there was a slight rushing movement of this group in the direction of the intruder, who at the moment was also near at hand, and now, with deliberate and stately step, made closer approach to the speaker. But from a certain nameless awe with which the mad assumptions of the mummer had inspired the whole party, there were found none who put forth hand to seize him; so that, unimpeded, he passed within a yard of the prince's person; and, while the vast assembly, as if with one impulse, shrank from the centres of the rooms to the walls, he made his way uninterruptedly, but with the same solemn and measured step which had distinguished him from the first, through the blue chamber to the purple—through the purple to the green—through the green to the orange—through this again to the white—and even thence to the violet, ere a decided movement had been made to arrest him. It was then, however, that the Prince Prospero, maddening with rage and the shame of his own momentary cowardice, rushed hurriedly through the six chambers, while none followed him on account of a deadly terror that had seized upon all. He bore aloft a drawn dagger, and had approached, in rapid impetuosity, to within three or four feet of the retreating figure, when the latter, having attained the extremity of the velvet apartment, turned suddenly and confronted his pursuer. There was a sharp cry—and the dagger dropped gleaming upon the sable carpet, upon which, instantly afterward, fell prostrate in death the Prince Prospero. Then, summoning the wild courage of despair, a throng of the revellers at once threw themselves into the black apartment, and, seizing the mummer, whose tall figure stood erect and motionless within the shadow of the ebony clock, gasped in unutterable horror at finding the grave cerements and corpse-like mask, which they handled with so violent a rudeness, untenanted by any tangible form.

And now was acknowledged the presence of the Red Death. He had come like a thief in the night. And one by one dropped the revellers in the blood-bedewed halls of their revel, and died each in the despairing posture of his fall. And the life of the ebony clock went out with that of the last of the gay. And the flames of the tripods expired. And Darkness and Decay and the Red Death held illimitable dominion over all.

EDGAR ALLAN POE—*Tales of Mystery and Imagination.*

THE SEXTON'S HERO

THE afternoon sun shed down his glorious rays on the grassy churchyard, making the shadow cast by the old yew-tree under which we sat, seem deeper and deeper by contrast. The everlasting hum of myriads of summer insects made luxurious lullaby.

Of the view that lay beneath our gaze, I cannot speak adequately. The foreground was the grey-stone wall of the vicarage garden; rich in the colouring made by innumerable lichens, ferns, ivy of most tender green and most delicate tracery, and the vivid scarlet of the crane's-bill, which found a home in every nook and crevice— and at the summit of that old wall flaunted some unpruned tendrils of the vine, and long flower-laden branches of the climbing rose-tree, trained against the inner side. Beyond, lay meadow green and mountain grey, and the blue dazzle of Morecambe Bay, as it sparkled between us and the more distant view.

For a while we were silent, living in sight and murmuring sound. Then Jeremy took up our conversation where, suddenly feeling weariness, as we saw that deep green shadowy resting-place, we had ceased speaking a quarter of an hour before.

It is one of the luxuries of holiday-time that thoughts are not rudely shaken from us by outward violence of hurry and busy impatience, but fall maturely from our lips in the sunny leisure of our days. The stock may be bad, but the fruit is ripe.

"How would you then define a hero?" I asked.

There was a long pause, and I had almost forgotten my question in watching a cloud-shadow floating over the far-away hills, when Jeremy made answer:

" My idea of a hero is one who acts up to the highest idea of duty he has been able to form, no matter at what sacrifice. I think that by this definition, we may include all phases of character, even to the heroes of old, whose sole (and to us, low) idea of duty consisted in personal prowess."

" Then you would even admit the military heroes? " asked I.

" I would; with a certain kind of pity for the circumstances which had given them no higher ideas of duty. Still, if they sacrificed self to do what they sincerely believed to be right, I do not think I could deny them the title of hero."

" A poor, unchristian heroism, whose manifestation consists in injury to others! " I said.

We were both startled by a third voice.

" If I might make so bold, sir "—and then the speaker stopped.

It was the Sexton, whom, when we first arrived, we had noticed, as an accessory to the scene, but whom we had forgotten, as much as though he were as inanimate as one of the moss-covered headstones.

" If I might be so bold," said he again, waiting leave to speak. Jeremy bowed in deference to his white, uncovered head. And, so encouraged, he went on.

" What that gentleman " (alluding to my last speech) " has just now said, brings to my mind one who is dead and gone this many a year ago. I, may be, have not rightly understood your meaning, gentlemen, but as far as I could gather it, I think you'd both have given in to thinking poor Gilbert Dawson a hero. At any rate," said he, heaving a long, quivering sigh, "I have reason to think him so."

"Will you take a seat, sir, and tell us about him?" said Jeremy, standing up until the old man was seated. I confess I felt impatient at the interruption.

"It will be forty-five year come Martinmas," said the Sexton, sitting down on a grassy mound at our feet, "since I finished my 'prenticeship, and settled down at Lindal. You can see Lindal, sir, at evenings and mornings across the bay; a little to the right of Grange; at least, I used to see it, many a time and oft, afore my sight grew so dark: and I have spent many a quarter of an hour a-gazing at it far away, and thinking of the days I lived there, till the tears came so thick to my eyes, I could gaze no longer. I shall never look upon it again, either far-off or near; but you may see it, both ways, and a terrible bonny spot it is. In my young days, when I went to settle there, it was full of as wild a set of young fellows as ever were clapped eyes on: all for fighting, poaching, quarrelling, and such-like work. I were startled myself when I first found what a set I were among, but soon I began to fall into their ways, and I ended by being as rough a chap as any on 'em. I'd been there a matter of two year, and were reckoned by most the cock of the village, when Gilbert Dawson, as I was speaking of, came to Lindal. He were about as strapping a chap as I was (I used to be six feet high, though now I'm so shrunk and doubled up), and as we were like in the same trade (both used to prepare osiers and wood for the Liverpool coopers, who get a deal of stuff from the copses round the bay, sir), we were thrown together, and took mightily to each other. I put my best leg foremost to be equal with Gilbert, for I'd had some schooling, though since I'd been at Lindal I'd lost a good part of what I'd learnt; and I kept my rough ways out of sight for a time, I felt so ashamed of his getting to know them. But that did not last long. I began to think he fancied a girl I dearly loved, but who had always held off from me. Eh! but she was a pretty one in those days! There's none like her, now. I think I see her going along the road with her dancing tread, and shaking back her long yellow curls, to give me or any other young fellow a saucy word; no wonder Gilbert was taken with her, for all he was grave, and she so merry and light. But I began to think she liked him again; and then my blood was all afire. I got to hate him for everything he did. Aforetime I had stood by, admiring to see him, how he leapt, and what a quoiter and cricketer he was. And now I ground my teeth with hatred whene'er he did a thing which caught Letty's eye. I could read it in her look that she liked him, for all she held herself just as high with him as with all the rest. Lord God forgive me! how I hated that man."

He spoke as if the hatred were a thing of yesterday, so clear within his memory were shown the actions and feelings of his youth. And then he dropped his voice, and said:

"Well! I began to look out to pick a quarrel with him, for my blood was up to fight him. If I beat him (and I were a rare boxer in those days), I thought Letty would cool towards him. So one evening at quoits (I'm sure I don't know how or why, but large doings grow out of small words) I fell out with him, and challenged him to fight. I could see he were very wroth by his colour coming and going—and, as I said before, he were a fine active young fellow. But all at once he drew in, and said he would not fight. Such a yell as the Lindal lads, who were watching us, set up! I hear it yet. I could na' help but feel sorry for him, to be so scorned, and I thought he'd not rightly taken my meaning, and I'd give him another chance: so I said it again, and dared him, as plain as words could speak, to fight out the quarrel. He told me then, he had no quarrel against me; that he might have said something to put me up; he did not know that he had, but that if he had, he asked pardon; but that he would not fight no-how.

"I was so full of scorn at his cowardliness, that I was vexed I'd given him the second chance, and I joined in the yell that was set up, twice as bad as before. He stood it out, his teeth set, and looking very white, and when we were silent for want of breath, he said out loud, but in a hoarse voice, quite different from his own:

"'I cannot fight, because I think it is wrong to quarrel, and use violence.'

"Then he turned to go away; I were so beside myself with scorn and hate, that I called out:

"'Tell truth, lad, at least; if thou dare not fight, dunnot go and tell a lie about it. Mother's moppet is afraid of a black eye, pretty dear. It shannot be hurt, but it munnot tell lies.'

"Well, they laughed, but I could not laugh. It seemed such a thing for a stout young chap to be a coward and afraid!

"Before the sun had set, it was talked of all over Lindal, how I had challenged Gilbert to fight, and how he'd denied me; and the folks stood at their doors, and looked at him going up the hill to his home, as if he'd been a monkey or a foreigner—but no one wished him good e'en. Such a thing as refusing to fight had never been heard of afore at Lindal. Next day, however, they had found voice. The men muttered the word 'coward' in his hearing, and kept aloof; the women tittered as he passed, and the little impudent lads and lasses shouted out, 'How long is it sin' thou turned Quaker?' 'Goodbye, Jonathan Broad-brim,' and such-like jests.

"That evening I met him, with Letty by his side, coming up from the shore. She was almost crying as I came upon them at the turn of the lane; and looking up in his face, as if begging him something. And so she was, she told me it after. For she did really like him, and could not abide to hear him scorned by every one for being a coward; and she, coy as she was, all but told him that very night that she loved him, and begged him not to disgrace himself, but fight me as I'd dared him to. When he still stuck to it he could not, for that it was wrong, she was so vexed and mad-like at the way she'd spoken, and the feelings she'd let out to coax him, that she said more stinging things about his being a coward than all the rest put together (according to what she told me, sir, afterwards), and ended by saying she'd never speak to him again, as long as she lived; she did once again, though—her blessing was the last human speech that reached his ear in his wild death-struggle.

"But much happened afore that time. From the day I met them walking, Letty turned towards me; I could see a part of it was to spite Gilbert, for she'd be twice as kind when he was near, or likely to hear of it; but by-and-by she got to like me for my own sake, and it was all settled for our marriage. Gilbert kept aloof from every one, and fell into a sad, careless way. His very gait was changed; his step used to be brisk and sounding, and now his foot lingered heavily on the ground. I used to try and daunt him with my eye, but he would always meet my look in a steady, quiet way, for all so much about him was altered; the lads would not play with him; and, as soon as he found he was to be slighted by them whenever he came to quoiting or cricket, he just left off coming.

"The old clerk was the only one he kept company with; or perhaps, rightly to speak, the only one who

27

would keep company with him. They got so thick at last that old Jonas would say Gilbert had gospel on his side, and did no more than gospel told him to do; but we none of us gave much credit to what he said, more by token our vicar had a brother a colonel in the army; and, as we threeped it many a time to Jonas, would he set himself up to know the gospel better than the vicar? that would be putting the cart afore the horse, like the French radicals. And, if the vicar had thought quarrelling and fighting wicked, and again the Bible, would he have made so much work about all the victories, that were as plenty as blackberries at that time of day, and kept the little bell of Lindal church for ever ringing; or would he have thought so much of 'my brother the colonel,' as he was always talking on?

"After I was married to Letty I left off hating Gilbert. I even kind of pitied him—he was so scorned and slighted; and, for all he'd a bold look about him, as if he were not ashamed, he seemed pining and shrunk. It's a wearying thing to be kept at arm's length by one's kind; and so Gilbert found it, poor fellow. The little children took to him, though; they'd be round about him like a swarm of bees—them as was too young to know what a coward was, and only felt that he was ever ready to love and to help them, and was never loud or cross, however naughty they might be. After a while we had our little one, too; such a blessed darling she was, and dearly did we love her; Letty in especial, who seemed to get all the thought I used to think sometimes she wanted, after she had her baby to care for.

"All my kin lived on this side the bay, up above Kellet. Jane (that's her that lies buried near yon white rose-tree) was to be married, and nought would serve her but that Letty and I must come to the wedding; for all my sisters loved Letty, she had such winning ways with

28

her. Letty did not like to leave her baby, nor yet did I
want her to take it; so, after a talk, we fixed to leave it
with Letty's mother for the afternoon. I could see her
heart ached a bit, for she'd never left it till then, and she
seemed to fear all manner of evil, even to the French
coming and taking it away. Well! we borrowed a
shandry, and harnessed my old grey mare, as I used in
th' cart. and set off as grand as King George across the
sands about three o'clock, for you see it were high-water
about twelve. and we'd to go and come back same tide,
as Letty could not leave her baby for long. It were a
merry afternoon were that; last time I ever saw Letty
laugh heartily; and, for that matter, last time I ever
laughed downright hearty myself. The latest crossing-
time fell about nine o'clock, and we were late at starting.
Clocks were wrong; and we'd a piece of work chasing a
pig father had given Letty to take home; we bagged him
at last, and he screeched and screeched in the back part
o' the shandry, and we laughed and they laughed; and
in the midst of all the merriment the sun set, and that
sobered us a bit, for then we knew what time it was. I
whipped the old mare, but she was a deal beener than
she was in the morning, and would neither go quick up
nor down the brows, and they're not a few 'twixt Kellet
and the shore. On the sands it were worse. They were
very heavy, for the fresh had come down after the rains
we'd had. Lord! how I did whip the poor mare, to
make the most of the red light as yet lasted. You, may
be, don't know the sands, gentlemen. From Bolton side,
where we started from, it is better than six mile to Cart
Lane, and two channels to cross, let alone holes and
quicksands. At the second channel from us the guide
waits, all during crossing time from sunrise to sunset;
but for the three hours on each side high-water he's
not there, in course. He stays after sunset if he's fore-

spoken, not else. So now you know where we were that awful night. For we'd crossed the first channel about two mile, and it were growing darker and darker above and around us, all but one red line of light above the hills, when we came to a hollow (for all the sands look so flat, there's many a hollow in them where you lose all sight of the shore). We were longer than we should ha' been in crossing the hollow, the sand was so quick; and when we came up again, there, again the blackness, was the white line of the rushing tide coming up the bay! It looked not a mile from us; and when the wind blows up the bay it comes swifter than a galloping horse. 'Lord help us!' said I; and then I were sorry I'd spoken, to frighten Letty; but the words were crushed out of my heart by the terror. I felt her shiver up by my side, and clutch my coat. And as if the pig (as had screeched himself hoarse some time ago) had found out the danger we were all in, he took to squealing again, enough to bewilder any man. I cursed him between my teeth for his noise; and yet it was God's answer to my prayer, blind sinner as I was. Ay! you may smile, sir, but God can work through many a scornful thing, if need be.

"By this time the mare was all in a lather, and trembling and panting, as if in mortal fright; for, though we were on the last bank afore the second channel, the water was gathering up her legs; and she so tired out! When we came close to the channel she stood still, and not all my flogging could get her to stir; she fairly groaned aloud, and shook in a terrible quaking way. Till now Letty had not spoken: only held my coat tightly. I heard her say something, and bent down my head.

"'I think, John—I think—I shall never see baby again!'

"And then she sent up such a cry—so loud, and shrill, and pitiful! It fairly maddened me. I pulled out my knife to spur on the old mare, that it might end one way or the other, for the water was stealing sullenly up to the very axle-tree, let alone the white waves that knew no mercy in their steady advance. That one quarter of an hour, sir, seemed as long as all my life since. Thoughts and fancies, and dreams, and memory ran into each other. The mist, the heavy mist, that was like a ghastly curtain, shutting us in for death, seemed to bring with it the scents of the flowers that grew around our own threshold; it might be, for it was falling on them like blessed dew, though to us it was a shroud. Letty told me at after, she heard her baby crying for her, above the gurgling of the rising waters, as plain as ever she heard anything; but the sea-birds were skirling, and the pig shrieking; I never caught it; it was miles away at any rate.

"Just as I'd gotten my knife out, another sound was close upon us, blending with the gurgle of the near waters, and the roar of the distant (not so distant though); we could hardly see, but we thought we saw something black against the deep lead colour of wave, and mist, and sky. It neared and neared: with slow, steady motion, it came across the channel right to where we were.

"Oh, God! it was Gilbert Dawson on his strong bay horse.

"Few words did we speak, and little time had we to say them in. I had no knowledge at that moment of past or future—only of one present thought—how to save Letty, and, if I could, myself. I only remembered afterwards that Gilbert said he had been guided by an animal's shriek of terror; I only heard when all was over, that he had been uneasy about our return, because of the depth of fresh, and had borrowed a pillion, and saddled his horse early in the evening, and ridden down to Cart Lane to watch for us. If all had gone well, we should ne'er have heard of it. As it was, old Jonas told it, the tears down-dropping from his withered cheeks.

"We fastened his horse to the shandry. We lifted Letty to the pillion. The waters rose every instant with sullen sound. They were all but in the shandry. Letty clung to the pillion handles, but drooped her head as if she had yet no hope of life. Swifter than thought (and yet he might have had time for thought and for temptation, sir—if he had ridden off with Letty, he would have been saved, not me), Gilbert was in the shandry by my side.

"'Quick!' said he, clear and firm. 'You must ride before her, and keep her up. The horse can swim. By God's mercy I will follow. I can cut the traces, and if the mare is not hampered with the shandry, she'll carry me safely through. At any rate, you are a husband and a father. No one cares for me.'

"Do not hate me, gentlemen. I often wish that night was a dream. It has haunted my sleep ever since like a dream, and yet it was no dream. I took his place on the saddle, and put Letty's arms around me, and felt her head rest on my shoulder. I trust in God I spoke some word of thanks; but I can't remember. I only recollect Letty raising her head, and calling out:

"'God bless you, Gilbert Dawson, for saving my baby from being an orphan this night.' And then she fell against me, as if unconscious.

"I bore her through; or, rather, the strong horse swam bravely through the gathering waves. We were dripping wet when we reached the banks in-shore; but we could have but one thought—where was Gilbert? Thick mists and heaving waters compassed us round. Where was he? We shouted. Letty, faint as she was, raised her voice and shouted clear and shrill. No answer came, the sea boomed on with ceaseless sullen beat. I rode to the guide's house. He was a-bed, and would not get up, though I offered him more than I was worth. Perhaps he knew it, the cursed old villain! At any rate, I'd have paid it if I'd toiled my life long. He said I might take his horn and welcome. I did, and blew such a blast through the still, black night, the echoes came back upon the heavy air; but no human voice or sound was heard—that wild blast could not awaken the dead!

"I took Letty home to her baby, over whom she wept the livelong night. I rode back to the shore about Cart Lane; and to and fro, with weary march, did I pace along the brink of the waters, now and then shouting out into the silence a vain cry for Gilbert. The waters went back and left no trace. Two days afterwards he was washed ashore near Flukeborough. The shandry and poor old mare were found half-buried in a heap of sand by Arnside Knot. As far as we could guess, he had dropped his knife while trying to cut the traces, and so had lost all chance of life. Any rate, the knife was found in a cleft of the shaft.

"His friends came over from Garstang to his funeral. I wanted to go chief mourner, but it was not my right, and I might not; though I've never done mourning him to this day. When his sister packed up his things, I begged hard for something that had been his. She would give me none of his clothes (she was a right-down saving woman), as she had boys of her own, who might grow up into them. But she threw me his Bible, as she said they'd gotten one already, and his were but a poor used-up thing. It was his, and so I cared for it. It were a black leather one, with pockets at the sides, old-fashioned-wise; and in one were a bunch of wild flowers, Letty said she could almost be sure were some she had once given him.

"There were many a text in the Gospel, marked broad with his carpenter's pencil, which more than bore him out in his refusal to fight. Of a surety, sir, there's call enough for bravery in the service of God, and to show love to man, without quarrelling and fighting.

"Thank you, gentlemen, for listening to me. Your words called up the thoughts of him, and my heart was full to speaking. But I must make up; I've to dig a grave for a little child, who is to be buried to-morrow morning, just when his playmates are trooping off to school."

"But tell us of Letty; is she yet alive?" asked Jeremy.

The old man shook his head, and struggled against a choking sigh. After a minute's pause he said:

"She died in less than two year at after that night. She was never like the same again. She would sit thinking—on Gilbert, I guessed; but I could not blame her. We had a boy, and we named it Gilbert Dawson Knipe: he that's stoker on the London railway. Our girl was carried off in teething; and Letty just quietly drooped, and died in less than a six week. They were buried here; so I came to be near them, and away from Lindal, a place I could never abide after Letty was gone."

He turned to his work; and we, having rested sufficiently, rose up, and came away.

MRS. GASKELL—*Lizzie Leigh and Other Tales.*

THE ITALIAN PRISONER

THE rising of the Italian people from under their unutterable wrongs, and the tardy burst of day upon them
after the long long night of oppression that has dark-
ened their beautiful country, have naturally caused my
mind to dwell often of late on my own small wanderings
in Italy. Connected with them, is a curious little drama,
in which the character I myself sustained was so very
subordinate that I may relate its story without any fear
of being suspected of self-display. It is strictly a true
story.

I am newly arrived one summer evening, in a certain
small town on the Mediterranean. I have had my dinner
at the inn, and I and the mosquitoes are coming out into
the street together. It is far from Naples; but a bright
brown plump little woman-servant at the inn is a
Neapolitan, and is so vivaciously expert in pantomimic
action, that in the single moment of answering my request to have a pair of shoes cleaned which I have left
upstairs, she plies imaginary brushes, and goes completely through the motions of polishing the shoes up,
and laying them at my feet. I smile at the brisk little
woman in perfect satisfaction with her briskness; and
the brisk little woman, amiably pleased with me because
I am pleased with her, claps her hands and laughs
delightfully. We are in the inn yard. As the little
woman's bright eyes sparkle on the cigarette I am smoking I make bold to offer her one; she accepts it none the
less merrily, because I touch a most charming little

dimple in her fat cheek, with its light paper end. Glancing up at the many green lattices to assure herself that the mistress is not looking on, the little woman then puts her two little dimple arms a-kimbo, and stands on tiptoe to light her cigarette at mine. " And now, dear little sir," says she, puffing out smoke in a most innocent and cherubic manner, " keep quite straight on, take the first to the right, and probably you will see him standing at his door."

I have a commission to " him," and I have been inquiring about him. I have carried the commission about Italy several months. Before I left England, there came to me one night a certain generous and gentle English nobleman (he is dead in these days when I relate the story, and exiles have lost their best British friend), with this request: " Whenever you come to such a town, will you seek out one Giovanni Carlavero, who keeps a little wine-shop there, mention my name to him suddenly, and observe how it affects him? " I accepted the trust, and am on my way to discharge it.

The sirocco has been blowing all day, and it is a hot unwholesome evening with no cool sea-breeze. Mosquitoes and fire-flies are lively enough, but most other creatures are faint. The coquettish airs of pretty young women in the tiniest and wickedest of dolls' straw hats, who lean out at opened lattice blinds, are almost the only airs stirring. Very ugly and haggard old women with distaffs, and with a grey tow upon them that looks as if they were spinning out their own hair (I suppose they were once pretty, too, but it is very difficult to believe so), sit on the footway leaning against house walls. Everybody who has come for water to the fountain, stays there, and seems incapable of any such energetic idea as going home. Vespers are over, though not so long but that I can smell the heavy resinous incense as I pass the church.

No man seems to be at work, save the coppersmith. In an Italian town he is always at work, and always thumping in the deadliest manner.

I keep straight on, and come in due time to the first on the right: a narrow dull street, where I see a well-favoured man of good stature and military bearing, in a great cloak, standing at a door. Drawing nearer to this threshold, I see it is the threshold of a small wine-shop; and I can just make out, in the dim light, the inscription that it is kept by Giovanni Carlavero.

I touch my hat to the figure in the cloak, and pass in, and draw a stool to a little table. The lamp (just such another as they dig out of Pompeii) is lighted, but the place is empty. The figure in the cloak has followed me in, and stands before me.

"The master?"

"At your service, sir."

"Please to give me a glass of the wine of the country."

He turns to a little counter, to get it. As his striking face is pale, and his action is evidently that of an enfeebled man, I remark that I fear he has been ill. It is not much, he courteously and gravely answers, though bad while it lasts: the fever.

As he sets the wine on the little table, to his manifest surprise I lay my hand on the back of his, look him in the face, and say in a low voice: "I am an Englishman, and you are acquainted with a friend of mine. Do you recollect——?" and I mentioned the name of my generous countryman.

Instantly, he utters a loud cry, bursts into tears, and falls on his knees at my feet, clasping my legs in both his arms and bowing his head to the ground.

Some years ago, this man at my feet, whose over-fraught heart is heaving as if it would burst from his breast, and whose tears are wet upon the dress I wear, was a galley-slave in the North of Italy. He was a political offender, having been concerned in the then last rising, and was sentenced to imprisonment for life. That he would have died in his chains, is certain, but for the circumstance that the Englishman happened to visit his prison.

It was one of the vile old prisons of Italy, and a part of it was below the waters of the harbour. The place of his confinement was an arched under-ground and under-water gallery, with a grill-gate at the entrance, through which it received such light and air as it got. Its condition was insufferably foul, and a stranger could hardly breathe in it, or see in it with the aid of a torch. At the upper end of this dungeon, and consequently in the worst position, as being the furthest removed from light and air, the Englishman first beheld him, sitting on an iron bedstead to which he was chained by a heavy chain. His countenance impressed the Englishman as having nothing in common with the faces of the malefactors with whom he was associated, and he talked with him, and learnt how he came to be there.

When the Englishman emerged from the dreadful den into the light of day. he asked his conductor, the governor of the jail, why Giovanni Carlavero was put into the worst place?

"Because he is particularly recommended," was the stringent answer.

"Recommended, that is to say, for death?"

"Excuse me; particularly recommended," was again the answer.

"He has a bad tumour in his neck, no doubt occasioned by the hardship of his miserable life. If he continues to be neglected, and he remains where he is, it will kill him."

38

"Excuse me, I can do nothing. He is particularly recommended."

The Englishman was staying in that town, and he went to his home there; but the figure of this man chained to the bedstead made it no home, and destroyed his rest and peace. He was an Englishman of an extraordinarily tender heart, and he could not bear the picture. He went back to the prison grate; went back again and again and again, and talked to the man and cheered him. He used his utmost influence to get the man unchained from the bedstead, were it only for ever so short a time in the day, and permitted to come to the grate. It took a long time, but the Englishman's station, personal character, and steadiness of purpose, wore out opposition so far, and that grace was at last accorded. Through the bars, when he could thus get light upon the tumour, the Englishman lanced it, and it did well, and healed. His strong interest in the prisoner had greatly increased by this time, and he formed the desperate resolution that he would exert his utmost self-devotion and use his utmost efforts, to get Carlavero pardoned.

If the prisoner had been a brigand and a murderer, if he had committed every non-political crime in the Newgate Calendar and out of it, nothing would have been easier than for a man of any court or priestly influence to obtain his release. As it was, nothing could have been more difficult. Italian authorities, and English authorities who had interest with them, alike assured the Englishman that his object was hopeless. He met with nothing but evasion, refusal, and ridicule. His political prisoner became a joke in the place. It was especially observable that English Circumlocution, and English Society on its travels, were as humorous on the subject as Circumlocution and Society may be on any subject without loss of caste. But, the Englishman possessed (and proved it well in his life) a courage very uncommon among us: he had not the least fear of being considered a bore, in a good humane cause. So he went on persistently trying, and trying, and trying, to get Giovanni Carlavero out. That prisoner had been rigorously rechained, after the tumour operation, and it was not likely that his miserable life could last very long.

One day, when all the town knew about the Englishman and his political prisoner, there came to the Englishman, a certain sprightly Italian Advocate of whom he had some knowledge; and he made this strange proposal. "Give me a hundred pounds to obtain Carlavero's release. I think I can get him a pardon, with that money. But I cannot tell you what I am going to do with the money, nor must you ever ask me the question if I succeed, nor must you ever ask me for an account of the money if I fail." The Englishman decided to hazard the hundred pounds. He did so, and heard not another word of the matter. For half a year and more, the Advocate made no sign, and never once "took on" in any way, to have the subject on his mind. The Englishman was then obliged to change his residence to another and more famous town in the North of Italy. He parted from the poor prisoner with a sorrowful heart, as from a doomed man for whom there was no release but Death.

The Englishman lived in his new place of abode another half-year and more, and had no tidings of the wretched prisoner. At length, one day, he received from the Advocate a cool concise mysterious note, to this effect. "If you still wish to bestow that benefit upon the man in whom you were once interested, send me fifty pounds more, and I think it can be ensured." Now, the Englishman had long settled in his mind that the Advocate was a heartless sharper, who had preyed upon his credulity and his interest in an unfortunate sufferer. So, he sat down and wrote a dry answer, giving the Advocate to understand that he was wiser now than he had been formerly, and that no more money was extractable from his pocket.

He lived outside the city gates, some mile or two from the post office, and was accustomed to walk into the city with his letters and post them himself. On a lovely spring day, when the sky was exquisitely blue, the sea divinely beautiful, he took his usual walk, carrying his letter to the Advocate in his pocket. As he went along, his gentle heart was much moved by the loveliness of the prospect, and by the thought of the slowly dying prisoner chained to the bedstead, for whom the universe had no delights. As he drew nearer and nearer to the city where he was to post the letter, he became very uneasy in his mind. He debated with himself, was it remotely possible, after all, that this sum of fifty pounds could restore the fellow-creature whom he pitied so much, and for whom he had striven so hard, to liberty? He was not a conventionally rich Englishman—very far from that—but, he had a spare fifty pounds at the banker's. He resolved to risk it. Without doubt, God has recompensed him for the resolution.

He went to the banker's, and got a bill for the amount, and enclosed it in a letter to the Advocate that I wish I could have seen. He simply told the Advocate that he was quite a poor man, and that he was sensible it might be a great weakness in him to part with so much money on the faith of so vague a communication; but, that there it was, and that he prayed the Advocate to make a good use of it. If he did otherwise no good could ever come of it, and it would lie heavy on his soul one day.

Within a week, the Englishman was sitting at his breakfast, when he heard some suppressed sounds of agitation on the staircase, and Giovanni Carlavero leaped into the room and fell upon his breast, a free man!

Conscious of having wronged the Advocate in his own thoughts, the Englishman wrote him an earnest and grateful letter, avowing the fact, and entreating him to confide by what means and through what agency he had succeeded so well. The Advocate returned for answer through the post, " There are many things, as you know, in this Italy of ours, that are safest and best not even spoken of—far less written of. We may meet some day, and then I may tell you what you want to know; not here, and now." But, the two never did meet again. The Advocate was dead when the Englishman gave me my trust; and how the man had been set free, remained as great a mystery to the Englishman, and to the man himself, as it was to me.

But, I knew this: here was the man, this sultry night, on his knees at my feet, because I was the Englishman's friend; here were his tears upon my dress; here were his sobs choking his utterance; here were his kisses on my hands, because they had touched the hands that had worked out his release. He had no need to tell me it would be happiness to him to die for his benefactor; I doubt if I ever saw real, sterling, fervent gratitude of soul, before or since.

He was much watched and suspected, he said, and had had enough to do to keep himself out of trouble. This, and his not having prospered in his worldly affairs, had led to his having failed in his usual communications to the Englishman for—as I now remember the period— some two or three years. But, his prospects were brighter, and his wife who had been very ill had recovered, and his fever had left him, and he had bought a little vineyard, and would I carry to his benefactor the first of its wine? Ay, that I would (I told him with enthusiasm), and not a drop of it should be spilled or lost!

He had cautiously closed the door before speaking of himself, and had talked with such excess of emotion, and in a provincial Italian so difficult to understand, that I had more than once been obliged to stop him, and beg him to have compassion on me and be slower and calmer. By degrees he became so, and tranquilly walked back with me to the hotel. There, I sat down before I went to bed and wrote a faithful account of him to the Englishman: which I concluded by saying that I would bring the wine home, against any difficulties, every drop.

Early next morning when I came out at the hotel door to pursue my journey, I found my friend waiting with one of those immense bottles in which the Italian peasants store their wine—a bottle holding some half-dozen gallons—bound round with basket-work for greater safety on the journey. I see him now, in the bright sunlight, tears of gratitude in his eyes, proudly inviting my attention to this corpulent bottle. (At the street-corner hard by, two high-flavoured able-bodied monks—pretending to talk together, but keeping their foul evil eyes upon us.)

How the bottle had been got there, did not appear; but the difficulty of getting it into the ramshackle vetturino carriage in which I was departing, was so great, and it took up so much room when it was got in, that I elected to sit outside. The last I saw of Giovanni Carlavero was his running through the town by the side of the jingling wheels, clasping my hand as I stretched it down from the box, charging me with a thousand last loving and dutiful messages to his dear patron, and finally looking in at the bottle as it reposed inside, with an admiration of its honourable way of travelling that was beyond measure delightful.

And now, what disquiet of mind this dearly beloved and highly treasured Bottle began to cost me, no man knows. It was my precious charge through a long tour, and, for hundreds of miles, I never had it off my mind by day or by night. Over bad roads—and they were many—I clung to it with affectionate desperation. Up mountains, I looked in at it and saw it helplessly tilting over on its back, with terror. At innumerable inn doors when the weather was bad, I was obliged to be put into my vehicle before the Bottle could be got in, and was obliged to have the Bottle lifted out before human aid could come near me. The Imp of the same name, except that his associations were all evil and these associations were all good, would have been a less troublesome travelling companion. I might have served Mr. Cruikshank as a subject for a new illustration of the miseries of the Bottle. The National Temperance Society might have made a powerful Tract of me.

The suspicions that attached to this innocent Bottle, greatly aggravated my difficulties. It was like the apple-pie in the child's book. Parma pouted at it, Modena mocked it, Tuscany tackled it, Naples nibbled it, Rome refused it, Austria accused it, Soldiers suspected it, Jesuits jobbed it. I composed a neat Oration, developing my inoffensive intentions in connection with this Bottle, and delivered it in an infinity of guard-houses, at a multitude of town gates, and on every drawbridge, angle, and rampart, of a complete system of fortifications. Fifty times a day, I got down to harangue an infuriated soldiery about the Bottle. Through the filthy degradation of the abject and vile Roman States, I had as much difficulty in working my way with the Bottle, as if it had bottled up a complete system of heretical theology. In the Neapolitan country, where everybody was a spy, a soldier, a priest, or a lazzarone, the shameless beggars of all four denominations incessantly pounced on the Bottle and made it a pretext for extorting money from me. Quires—quires do I say? Reams—of forms illegibly printed on whity-brown paper were filled up about the Bottle, and it was the subject of more stamping and sanding than I had ever seen before. In consequence of which haze of sand, perhaps, it was always irregular, and always latent with dismal penalties of going back or not going forward, which were only to be abated by the silver crossing of a base hand, poked shirtless out of a ragged uniform sleeve. Under all discouragements, however, I stuck to my Bottle, and held firm to my resolution that every drop of its contents should reach the Bottle's destination.

The latter refinement cost me a separate heap of troubles on its own separate account. What corkscrews did I see the military power bring out against that Bottle; what gimlets, spikes, divining rods, guages, and unknown tests and instruments! At some places, they persisted in declaring that the wine must not be passed, without being opened and tasted; I, pleading to the contrary, used then to argue the question seated on the Bottle lest they should open it in spite of me. In the southern parts of Italy more violent shrieking, face-making, and gesticulating, greater vehemence of speech and countenance and action, went on about that Bottle, than would attend fifty murders in a northern latitude. It raised important functionaries out of their beds, in the dead of night. I have known half a dozen military lanterns to disperse themselves at all points of a great sleeping Piazza, each lantern summoning some official creature to get up, put on his cocked hat instantly, and come and stop the Bottle. It was characteristic that while this innocent Bottle had such immense difficulty in getting from little town to town, Signor Mazzini and the fiery cross were traversing Italy from end to end.

Still, I stuck to my Bottle, like any fine old English gentleman all of the olden time. The more the Bottle was interfered with, the stauncher I became (if possible) in my first determination that my countryman should have it delivered to him intact, as the man whom he had so nobly restored to life and liberty had delivered it to me. If ever I had been obstinate in my days—and I may have been, say, once or twice—I was obstinate about the Bottle. But, I made it a rule always to keep a pocket full of small coin at its service, and never to be out of temper in its cause. Thus, I and the Bottle made our way. Once we had a breakdown; rather a bad breakdown, on a steep high place with the sea below us, on a tempestuous evening when it blew great guns. We were driving four wild horses abreast, Southern fashion, and there was some little difficulty in stopping them. I was outside, and not thrown off; but no words can describe my feelings when I saw the Bottle—travelling inside, as usual—burst the door open, and roll obesely out into the road. A blessed Bottle with a charmed existence, he took no hurt, and we repaired damage, and went on triumphant.

A thousand representations were made to me that the Bottle must be left at this place, or that, and called for again. I never yielded to one of them, and never parted from the Bottle, on any pretence, consideration, threat, or entreaty. I had no faith in any official receipt for the Bottle, and nothing would induce me to accept one. These unmanageable politics at last brought me and the Bottle, still triumphant, to Genoa. There, I took a tender and reluctant leave of him for a few weeks, and consigned him to a trusty English captain, to be conveyed to the Port of London by sea.

While the Bottle was on his voyage to England, I read

the Shipping Intelligence as anxiously as if I had been an underwriter. There was some stormy weather after I myself had got to England by way of Switzerland and France, and my mind greatly misgave me that the Bottle might be wrecked. At last to my great joy, I received notice of his safe arrival, and immediately went down to Saint Katharine's Docks, and found him in a state of honourable captivity in the Custom House.

The wine was mere vinegar when I set it down before the generous Englishman—probably it had been something like vinegar when I took it up from Giovanni Carlavero —but not a drop of it was spilled or gone. And the Englishman told me, with much emotion in his face and voice, that he had never tasted wine that seemed to him so sweet and sound. And long afterwards, the Bottle graced his table. And the last time I saw him in this world that misses him, he took me aside in a crowd, to say, with his amiable smile: " We were talking of you only to-day at dinner, and I wished you had been there, for I had some Claret up in Carlavero's Bottle."

CHARLES DICKENS—*The Uncommercial Traveller.*

THE JOURNEY TO PANAMA

THERE is perhaps no form of life in which men and women of the present day frequently find themselves for a time existing, so unlike their customary conventional life, as that experienced on board the large ocean steamers. On the voyages so made, separate friendships are formed and separate enmities are endured. Certain lines of temporary politics are originated by the energetic, and intrigues, generally innocent in their conclusions, are carried on with the keenest spirit by those to whom excitement is necessary; whereas the idle and torpid sink into insignificance and general contempt—as it is their lot to do on board ship as in other places. But the enjoyments and activity of such a life do not display themselves till the third or fourth day of the voyage. The men and women at first regard each with distrust and ill-concealed dislike. They by no means anticipate the strong feelings which are to arise, and look forward to ten, fifteen, or twenty days of gloom or sea-sickness. Sea-sickness disappears, as a general condition, on the evening of the second day, and the gloom about noon on the fourth. Then the men begin to think that the women are not so ugly, vulgar, and insipid; and the women drop their monosyllables, discontinue the close adherence to their own niches, which they first observed, and become affable, perhaps even beyond their wont on shore. And alliances spring up among the men themselves. On their first entrance to this new world, they generally regard each other with marked aversion, each thinking that those nearest to him are low fellows, or perhaps worse; but by the fourth day, if not sooner, every man has his two or three intimate friends with whom he talks and smokes, and to whom he communicates those peculiar politics, and perhaps intrigues, of his own voyage. The female friendships are slower in their growth, for the suspicion of women is perhaps stronger than that of men; but when grown they also are stronger, and exhibit themselves sometimes in instances of feminine affection.

But the most remarkable alliances are those made between gentlemen and ladies. This is a matter of course on board ship quite as much as on shore, and it is of such an alliance that the present tale purports to tell the story. Such friendships, though they may be very dear, can seldom be very lasting. Though they may be full of sweet romance—for people become very romantic among the discomforts of a sea voyage—such romance is generally short-lived and delusive, and occasionally is dangerous.

There are several of these great ocean routes, of which, by the common consent, as it seems, of the world, England is the centre. There is the Great Eastern line, running from Southampton across the Bay of Biscay and up the Mediterranean. It crosses the Isthmus of Suez, and branches away to Australia, to India, to Ceylon, and to China. There is the great American line, traversing the Atlantic to New York and Boston with the regularity of clockwork. The voyage here is so much a matter of every-day routine, that romance has become scarce upon the route. There are one or two other North American lines, perhaps open to the same objection. Then there is the line of packets to the African coast— very romantic as I am given to understand; and there is the great West-Indian route, to which the present little history is attached—great, not on account of our poor West Indian Islands, which cannot at the present moment make anything great, but because it spreads itself out from thence to Mexico and Cuba, to Guiana and the republics of Grenada and Venezuela, to Central America, the Isthmus of Panama, and from thence to California, Vancouver's Island, Peru and Chili.

It may be imagined how various are the tribes which leave the shores of Great Britain by this route. There are Frenchmen for the French sugar islands, as a rule not very romantic; there are old Spaniards, Spaniards of Spain, seeking to renew their fortunes amidst the ruins of their former empire; and new Spaniards—Spaniards, that is, of the American republics, who speak Spanish, but are unlike the Don both in manners and physiognomy—men and women with a touch perhaps of Indian blood, very keen after dollars, and not much given to the graces of life. There are Dutchmen too, and Danes, going out to their own islands. There are citizens of the stars and stripes, who find their way everywhere—and, alas! perhaps, now also citizens of the new Southern flag, with the palmetto leaf. And there are Englishmen of every shade and class, and Englishwomen also.

It is constantly the case that women are doomed to make the long voyage alone. Some are going out to join their husbands, some to find a husband, some few peradventure to leave a husband. Girls who have been educated at home in England, return to their distant homes across the Atlantic, and others follow their relatives who have gone before them as pioneers into a strange land. It must not be supposed that these females absolutely embark in solitude, putting their feet upon the deck without the aid of any friendly arm. They are generally consigned to some prudent elder, and appear as they first show themselves on the ship to belong to a party. But as often as not their real loneliness shows itself after a while. The prudent elder is not, perhaps, congenial; and by the evening of the fourth day a new friendship is created.

Not a long time since such a friendship was formed under the circumstances which I am now about to tell. A young man—not very young, for he had turned his thirtieth year, but still a young man—left Southampton by one of the large West Indian steam-boats, purposing to pass over the Isthmus of Panama, and thence up to California and Vancouver's Island. It would be too long to tell the cause which led to these distant voyagings. Suffice to say, it was not the accursed hunger after gold— *auri sacra fames*—which so took him; nor had he any purpose of permanently settling himself in those distant colonies of Great Britain. He was at the time a widower, and perhaps his home was bitter to him without the young wife whom he had early lost. As he stepped on board he was accompanied by a gentleman some fifteen years his senior, who was to be the companion of his sleeping apartment as far as St. Thomas. The two had been introduced to each other, and therefore appeared as friends on board the *Serrapiqui*; but their acquaintance had commenced in Southampton, and my hero, Ralph Forrest by name, was alone in the world as he stood looking over the side of the ship at the retreating shores of Hampshire.

"I say, old fellow, we'd better see about our places," said his new friend, slapping him on his back. Mr. Matthew Morris was an old traveller, and knew how to become intimate with his temporary allies at a very short notice. A long course of travelling had knocked all bashfulness out of him, and when he had a mind to do so he could make any man his brother in half an hour, and any woman his sister in ten minutes.

"Places? what places?" said Forrest.

"A pretty fellow you are to go to California. If you don't look sharper than that you'll get little to drink and nothing to eat till you come back again. Don't you know the ship's as full as ever she can hold?"

Forrest acknowledged that she was full.

"There are places at table for about a hundred, and we have a hundred and thirty on board. As a matter of course those who don't look sharp will have to scramble. However I've put cards on the plates and taken the seats. We had better go down and see that none of these Spanish fellows oust us." So Forrest descended after his friend, and found that the long tables were already nearly full of expectant dinner-eaters. When he took his place a future neighbour informed him, not in the most gracious voice, that he was encroaching on a lady's seat; and when he immediately attempted to leave that which he held, Mr. Matthew Morris forbade him to do so. Thus a little contest arose, which, however, happily was brought to a close without bloodshed. The lady was not present at the moment, and the grumpy gentleman agreed to secure for himself a vacant seat on the other side.

For the first three days the lady did not show herself. The grumpy gentleman, who, as Forrest afterwards understood, was the owner of stores in Bridgetown, Barbadoes, had other ladies with him also. First came forth his daughter, creeping down to dinner on the second day, declaring that she would be unable to eat a morsel, and prophesying that she would be forced to retire in five minutes. On this occasion, however, she agreeably surprised herself and her friends. Then came the grumpy gentleman's wife, and the grumpy gentleman's wife's brother—on whose constitution the sea seemed to have an effect quite as violent as on that of the ladies; and lastly, at breakfast on the fourth day, appeared Miss Viner, and took her place as Mr. Forrest's neighbour at his right hand.

He had seen her before on deck, as she lay on one of the benches, vainly endeavouring to make herself comfortable, and had remarked to his companion that she was very unattractive and almost ugly. Dear young ladies, it is thus that men always speak of you when they first see you on board ship! She was disconsolate, sick at heart, and ill at ease in body also. She did not like the sea. She did not in the least like the grumpy gentleman, in whose hands she was placed. She did not especially like the grumpy gentleman's wife; and she altogether hated the grumpy gentleman's daughter, who was the partner of her berth. That young lady had been very sick and very selfish; and Miss Viner had been very sick also, and perhaps equally selfish. They might have been angels, and yet have hated each other under such circumstances. It was no wonder that Mr. Forrest thought her ugly as she twisted herself about on the broad bench, vainly striving to be comfortable.

"She'll brighten up wonderfully before we're in the tropics," said Mr. Morris. "And you won't find her so bad then. It's she that is to sit next you."

"Heaven forbid!" said Forrest. But, nevertheless, he was very civil to her when she did come down on the fourth morning. On board the West Indian Packets, the world goes down to its meals. In crossing between Liverpool and the States, the world goes up to them.

Miss Viner was by no means a very young lady. She also was nearly thirty. In guessing her age on board the ship the ladies said that she was thirty-six, but the ladies were wrong. She was an Irish woman, and when seen on shore, in her natural state, and with all her wits about her, was by no means without attraction. She was bright-eyed, with a clear dark skin, and good teeth; her hair was of a dark brown and glossy, and there was a touch of feeling and also of humour about her mouth, which would have saved her from Mr. Forrest's ill-considered criticism, had he first met her under more favourable circumstances.

"You'll see a good deal of her," Mr. Morris said to him, as they began to prepare themselves for luncheon, by a cigar immediately after breakfast. "She's going across the Isthmus and down to Peru."

"How on earth do you know?"

"I pretty well know where they're all going by this time. Old Grumpy told me so. He has her in tow as far as St. Thomas, but knows nothing about her. He gives her up there to the captain. You'll have a chance of making yourself very agreeable as you run across with her to the Spanish main."

Mr. Forrest replied that he did not suppose he should know her much better than he did now; but he made no further remark as to her ugliness. She had spoken a word or two to him at table, and he had seen that her eyes were bright, and had found that her tone was sweet.

"I also am going to Panama," he said to her, on the morning of the fifth day. The weather at that time was very fine, and the October sun as it shone on them, while hour by hour they made more towards the South, was pleasant and genial. The big ship lay almost without motion on the bosom of the Atlantic, as she was driven through the waters at the rate of twelve miles per hour. All was as pleasant now as things can be on board a ship, and Forrest had forgotten that Miss Viner had seemed so ugly to him when he first saw her. At this moment, as he spoke to her, they were running through the Azores, and he had been assisting her with his field-glass to look for orange-groves on their sloping shores, orange-groves they had not succeeded in seeing, but their failure had not disturbed their peace.

" I also am going to Panama."

" Are you, indeed? " said she. " Then I shall not feel so terribly alone and disconsolate. I have been looking forward with such fear to that journey on from St. Thomas."

" You shall not be disconsolate, if I can help it," he said. " I am not much of a traveller myself, but what I can do I will."

" Oh, thank you! "

" It is a pity Mr. Morris is not going on with you. He's at home everywhere, and knows the way across the Isthmus as well as he does down Regent Street."

" Your friend, you mean? "

" My friend, if you call him so; and indeed I hope he is, for I like him. But I don't know more of him than I do of you. I also am as much alone as you are. Perhaps more so."

" But," she said, " a man never suffers in being alone."

" Oh! does he not? Don't think me uncivil, Miss Viner, if I say that you may be mistaken in that. You feel your own shoe when it pinches, but do not realize the tight boot of your neighbour."

" Perhaps not," said she. And then there was a pause, during which she pretended to look again for the orange-groves. " But there are worse things, Mr. Forrest, than being alone in the world. It is often a woman's lot to wish that she were let alone." Then she left him and retreated to the side of the grumpy gentleman's wife, feeling perhaps that it might be prudent to discontinue a conversation, which, seeing that Mr. Forrest was quite a stranger to her, was becoming particular.

" You're getting on famously, my dear," said the lady from Barbadoes.

" Pretty well, thank you, ma'am," said Miss Viner.

" Mr. Forrest seems to be making himself quite agreeable. I tell Amelia "—Amelia was the young lady to whom in their joint cabin Miss Viner could not reconcile herself—" I tell Amelia that she is wrong not to receive attentions from gentlemen on board ship. If it is not carried too far," and she put great emphasis on the " too far "—" I see no harm in it."

" Nor I, either," said Miss Viner.

" But then Amelia is so particular."

" The best way is to take such things as they come," said Miss Viner—perhaps meaning that such things never did come in the way of Amelia. " If a lady knows what she is about she need not fear a gentleman's attentions."

" That's just what I tell Amelia; but then, my dear, she has not had so much experience as you and I."

Such being the amenities which passed between Miss Viner and the prudent lady who had her in charge, it was not wonderful that the former should feel ill at ease with her own " party," as the family of the Grumpy Barbadian was generally considered to be by those on board.

" You're getting along like a house on fire with Miss Viner," said Matthew Morris, to his young friend.

" Not much fire, I can assure you," said Forrest.

" She ain't so ugly as you thought her? "

" Ugly!—no; she's not ugly. I don't think I ever said she was. But she is nothing particular as regards beauty."

" No; she won't be lovely for the next three days to come, I dare say. By the time you reach Panama, she'll be all that is perfect in woman. I know how these things go."

" Those sort of things don't go at all quickly with me,"

56

said Forrest, gravely. "Miss Viner is a very interesting young woman, and as it seems that her route and mine will be together for some time, it is well that we should be civil to each other. And the more so, seeing that the people she is with are not congenial to her."

"No; they are not. There is no young man with them. I generally observe that on board ship no one is congenial to unmarried ladies except unmarried men. It is a recognized nautical rule. Uncommon hot, isn't it? We are beginning to feel the tropical air. I shall go and cool myself with a cigar in the fiddle." The "fiddle" is a certain part of the ship devoted to smoking, and thither Mr. Morris betook himself. Forrest, however, did not accompany him, but going forward into the bow of the vessel, threw himself along upon the sail, and meditated on the loneliness of his life.

On board the *Serrapiqui*, the upper tier of cabins opened on to a long gallery, which ran round that part of the ship, immediately over the saloon, so that from thence a pleasant inspection could be made of the viands as they were being placed on the tables. The custom on board these ships is for two bells to ring preparatory to dinner, at an interval of half an hour. At the sound of the first, ladies would go to their cabins to adjust their toilets; but as dressing for dinner is not carried to an extreme at sea, these operations are generally over before the second bell, and the lady passengers would generally assemble in the balcony for some fifteen minutes before dinner. At first they would stand here alone, but by degrees they were joined by some of the more enterprising of the men, and so at last a kind of little drawing-room was formed. The cabins of Miss Viner's party opened to one side of this gallery, and that of Mr. Morris and Forrest on the other. Hitherto Forrest had been contented to remain on his own side, occasionally throw-

57

ing a word across to the ladies on the other; but on this day he boldly went over as soon as he had washed his hands and took his place between Amelia and Miss Viner.

"We are dreadfully crowded here, ma'am," said Amelia.

"Yes, my dear, we are," said her mother. "But what can one do?"

"There's plenty of room in the ladies' cabin," said Miss Viner. Now if there be one place on board a ship more distasteful to ladies than another, it is the ladies' cabin. Mr. Forrest stood his ground, but it may be doubted whether he would have done so had he fully understood all that Amelia had intended.

Then the last bell rang. Mr. Grumpy gave his arm to Miss Grumpy. The brother-in-law gave his arm to Amelia, and Forrest did the same to Miss Viner. She hesitated for a moment, and then took it, and by so doing transferred herself mentally and bodily from the charge of the prudent and married Mr. Grumpy to that of the perhaps imprudent, and certainly unmarried, Mr. Forrest. She was wrong. A kind-hearted, motherly old lady from Jamaica, who had seen it all, knew that she was wrong, and wished that she could tell her so.

But there are things of this sort which kind-hearted old ladies cannot find it in their hearts to say. After all, it was only for the voyage. Perhaps Miss Viner was imprudent, but who in Peru would be the wiser? Perhaps, indeed, it was the world that was wrong, and not Miss Viner. *Honi soit qui mal y pense*, she said to herself, as she took his arm, and leaning on it, felt that she was no longer so lonely as she had been. On that day she allowed him to give her a glass of wine out of his decanter. "Hadn't you better take mine, Miss

Viner?" asked Mr. Grumpy, in a loud voice, but before he could be answered, the deed had been done.

"Don't go too fast, old fellow," Morris said to our hero that night, as they were walking the deck together before they turned in. "One gets into a hobble in such matters before one knows where one is."

"I don't think I have anything particular to fear," said Forrest.

"I dare say not, only keep your eyes open. Such harridans as Mrs. Grumpy allow any latitude to their tongues out in these diggings. You'll find that unpleasant tidings will be put on board the ship going down to Panama, and everybody's eye will be upon you." So warned, Mr. Forrest did put himself on his guard, and the next day and a half his intimacy with Miss Viner progressed but little. These were, probably, the dullest hours that he had on the whole voyage.

Miss Viner saw this and drew back. On the afternoon of that second day she walked a turn or two on deck with the weak brother-in-law, and when Mr. Forrest came near her, she applied herself to her book. She meant no harm; but if she were not afraid of what people might say, why should he be so? So she turned her shoulder towards him at dinner, and would not drink of his cup.

"Have some of mine, Miss Viner," said Mr. Grumpy, very loudly. But on that day Miss Viner drank no wine.

The sun sets quickly as one draws near to the tropics, and the day was already gone, and the dusk had come on, when Mr. Forrest walked out upon the deck that evening a little after six. But the night was beautiful and mild, and there was a hum of many voices from the benches. He was already uncomfortable, and sore with a sense of being deserted. There was but one person on board the ship that he liked, and why should he avoid her and be avoided? He soon perceived where she was standing. The Grumpy family had a bench to themselves, and she was opposite to it, on her feet, leaning against the side of the vessel. "Will you walk this evening, Miss Viner?" he asked.

"I think not," she answered.

"Then I shall persevere in asking till you are sure. It will do you good, for I have not seen you walking all day."

"Have you not? Then I will take a turn. Oh, Mr. Forrest, if you knew what it was to have to live with such people as those." And then, out of that, on that evening, there grew up between them something like the confidence of real friendship. Things were told such as none but friends do tell to one another, and warm answering words were spoken such as the sympathy of friendship produces. Alas, they were both foolish; for friendship and sympathy should have deeper roots.

She told him all her story. She was going out to Peru to be married to a man who was nearly twenty years her senior. It was a long engagement, of ten years' standing. When first made, it was made as being contingent on certain circumstances. An option of escaping from it had then been given to her, but now there was no longer an option. He was rich, and she was penniless. He had even paid her passage-money and her outfit. She had not at last given way and taken these irrevocable steps till her only means of support in England had been taken from her. She had lived the last two years with a relative who was now dead. "And he also is my cousin—a distant cousin—you understand that."

"And do you love him?"

"Love him! What; as you loved her whom you have lost?—as she loved you when she clung to you before she went? No; certainly not. I shall never know anything of that love."

" And is he good? "

" He is a hard man. Men become hard when they deal in money as he has done. He was home five years since, and then I swore to myself that I would not marry him. But his letters to me are kind."

Forrest sat silent for a minute or two, for they were up in the bow again, seated on the sail that was bound round the bowsprit, and then he answered her, " A woman should never marry a man unless she loves him."

" Ah," says she, " of course you will condemn me. That is the way in which women are always treated. They have no choice given them, and are then scolded for choosing wrongly."

" But you might have refused him."

" No; I could not. I cannot make you understand the whole—how it first came about that the marriage was proposed, and agreed to by me under certain conditions. Those conditions have come about, and I am now bound to him. I have taken his money and have no escape. It is easy to say that a woman should not marry without love, as easy as it is to say that a man should not starve. But there are men who starve—starve although they work hard."

" I did not mean to judge you, Miss Viner."

" But I judge myself, and condemn myself so often. Where should I be in half an hour from this if I were to throw myself forward into the sea? I often long to do it. Don't you feel tempted sometimes to put an end to it all? "

" The waters look cool and sweet, but I own I am afraid of the bourne beyond."

" So am I, and that fear will keep me from it."

" We are bound to bear our burden of sorrow. Mine, I know, is heavy enough."

" Yours, Mr. Forrest! Have you not all the pleasures

of memory to fall back on, and every hope for the future? What can I remember, or what can I hope? But, however, it is near eight o'clock, and they have all been at tea this hour past. What will my Cerberus say to me? I do not mind the male mouth, if only the two feminine mouths could be stopped." Then she rose and went back to the stern of the vessel; but as she slid into a seat, she saw that Mrs. Grumpy was standing over her.

From thence to St. Thomas the voyage went on in the customary manner. The sun became very powerful, and the passengers in the lower part of the ship complained loudly of having their portholes closed. The Spaniards sat gambling in the cabin all day, and the ladies prepared for the general move which was to be made at St. Thomas. The alliance between Forrest and Miss Viner went on much the same as ever, and Mrs. Grumpy said very ill-natured things. On one occasion she ventured to lecture Miss Viner; but that lady knew how to take her own part, and Mrs. Grumpy did not get the best of it. The dangerous alliance, I have said, went on the same as ever; but it must not be supposed that either person in any way committed aught that was wrong. They sat together and talked together, each now knowing the other's circumstances; but had it not been for the prudish caution of some of the ladies there would have been nothing amiss. As it was there was not much amiss. Few of the passengers really cared whether or no Miss Viner had found an admirer. Those who were going down to Panama were mostly Spaniards, and as the great separation became nearer, people had somewhat else of which to think.

And then the separation came. They rode into that pretty harbour of St. Thomas early in the morning, and were ignorant, the most of them, that they were lying in the very worst centre of yellow fever among all those plague-spotted islands. St. Thomas is very pretty as seen from the ships; and when that has been said, all has been said that can be said in its favour. There was a busy, bustling time of it then. One vessel after another was brought up alongside of the big ship that had come from England, and each took its separate freight of passengers and luggage. First started the boat that ran down the Leeward Islands to Demerara, taking with her Mr. Grumpy and all his family.

"Good-bye, Miss Viner," said Mrs. Grumpy. "I hope you'll get quite safely to the end of your voyage; but do take care."

"I'm sure I hope everything will be right," said Amelia, as she absolutely kissed her enemy. It is astonishing how well young women can hate each other, and yet kiss at parting.

"As to everything being right," said Miss Viner, "that is too much to hope. But I do not know that anything is going especially wrong.—Good-bye, sir," and then she put out her hand to Mr. Grumpy. He was at the moment leaving the ship laden with umbrellas, sticks, and coats, and was forced to put them down in order to free his hand.

"Well, good-bye," he said. "I hope you'll do, till you meet your friends at the Isthmus."

"I hope I shall, sir," she replied; and so they parted. Then the Jamaica packet started.

"I dare say we shall never see each other again," said Morris, as he shook his friend's hand heartily. "One never does. Don't interfere with the rights of that gentleman in Peru, or he might run a knife into you."

"I feel no inclination to injure him on that point."

"That's well; and now good-bye." And thus they also were parted. On the following morning the branch ship was dispatched to Mexico; and then, on the afternoon of the third day that for Colon—as we Englishmen call the town on this side of the Isthmus of Panama. Into that vessel Miss Viner and Mr. Forrest moved themselves and their effects; and now that the three-headed Cerberus was gone, she had no longer hesitated in allowing him to do for her all those little things which it is well that men should do for women when they are travelling. A woman without assistance under such circumstances is very forlorn, very apt to go to the wall, very ill able to assert her rights as to accommodation; and I think that few can blame Miss Viner for putting herself and her belongings under the care of the only person who was disposed to be kind to her.

Late in the evening the vessel steamed out of St. Thomas' harbour, and as she went Ralph Forrest and Emily Viner were standing together at the stern of the boat looking at the retreating lights of the Danish town. If there be a place on the earth's surface odious to me, it is that little Danish isle to which so many of our young seamen are sent to die—there being no good cause whatever for such sending. But the question is one which cannot well be argued here.

" I have five more days of self and liberty left me," said Miss Viner. " That is my life's allowance."

" For heaven's sake do not say words that are so horrible."

" But am I to lie for heaven's sake, and say words that are false; or shall I be silent for heaven's sake, and say nothing during these last hours that are allowed to me for speaking? It is so. To you I can say that it is so, and why should you begrudge me the speech? "

" I would begrudge you nothing that I could do for you."

" No, you should not. Now that my incubus has gone to Barbadoes, let me be free for a day or two. What chance is there, I wonder, that the ship's machinery should all go wrong, and that we should be tossed about in the seas here for the next six months? I suppose it would be very wicked to wish it?"

"We should all be starved; that's all."

"What, with a cow on board, and a dozen live sheep, and thousands of cocks and hens! But we are to touch at Santa Martha and Cartagena. What would happen to me if I were to run away at Santa Martha?"

"I suppose I should be bound to run with you."

"Oh, of course. And therefore, as I would not wish to destroy you, I won't do it. But it would not hurt you much to be shipwrecked, and wait for the next packet."

"Miss Viner," he said after a pause—and in the meantime he had drawn nearer to her, too near to her considering all things—"in the name of all that is good, and true, and womanly, go back to England. With your feelings, if I may judge of them by words which are spoken half in jest——"

"Mr. Forrest, there is no jest."

"With your feelings a poorhouse in England would be better than a palace in Peru."

"An English workhouse would be better, but an English poorhouse is not open to me. You do not know what it is to have friends—no, not friends, but people belonging to you—just so near as to make your respectability a matter of interest to them, but not so near that they should care for your happiness. Emily Viner married to Mr. Gorloch in Peru is put out of the way respectably. She will cause no further trouble, but her name may be mentioned in family circles without annoyance. The fact is, Mr. Forrest, that there are people who have no business to live at all."

"I would go back to England," he added, after another pause. "When you talk to me with such bitterness of five more days of living liberty you scare my very soul. Return, Miss Viner, and brave the worst. He is to meet you at Panama. Remain on this side of the Isthmus, and send him word that you must return. I will be the bearer of the message."

"And shall I walk back to England?" said Miss Viner.

"I had not quite forgotten all that," he replied, very gently. "There are moments when a man may venture to propose that which under ordinary circumstances would be a liberty. Money, in a small moderate way, is not greatly an object to me. As a return for my valiant defence of you against your West Indian Cerberus, you shall allow me to arrange that with the agent at Colon."

"I do so love plain English, Mr. Forrest. You are proposing, I think, to give me something about fifty guineas."

"Well, call it so if you will," said he, "if you will have plain English that is what I mean."

"So that by my journey out here, I should rob and deceive the man I do know, and also rob the man I don't know. I am afraid of that bourne beyond the waters of which we spoke; but I would rather face that than act as you suggest."

"Of the feelings between him and you, I can of course be no judge."

"No, no; you cannot. But what a beast I am not to thank you! I do thank you. That which it would be mean in me to take, it is noble, very noble, in you to offer. It is a pleasure to me—I cannot tell why—but it is a pleasure to me to have had the offer. But think of me as a sister, and you will feel that it would not be accepted—could not be accepted, I mean, even if I could bring myself to betray that other man."

Thus they ran across the Caribbean Sea, renewing very often such conversations as that just given. They

66

touched at Santa Martha and Cartagena on the coast of the Spanish main, and at both places he went with her on shore. He found that she was fairly well educated, and anxious to see and to learn all that might be seen and learned in the course of her travels. On the last day, as they neared the Isthmus, she became more tranquil and quiet in the expression of her feelings than before, and spoke with less of gloom than she had done.

" After all ought I not to love him? " she said. " He is coming all the way up from Callao merely to meet me. What man would go from London to Moscow to pick up a wife? "

" I would—and thence round the world to Moscow again—if she were the wife I wanted."

" Yes; but a wife who has never said that she loved you! It is purely a matter of convenience. Well; I have locked my big box, and I shall give the key to him before it is ever again unlocked. He has a right to it, for he has paid for nearly all that it holds."

" You look at things from such a mundane point of view."

" A woman should, or she will always be getting into difficulty. Mind, I shall introduce you to him, and tell him all that you have done for me. How you braved Cerberus and the rest of it."

" I shall certainly be glad to meet him."

" But I shall not tell him of your offer—not yet at least. If he be good and gentle with me, I shall tell him that too after a time. I am very bad at keeping secrets —as no doubt you have perceived. We go across the Isthmus at once; do we not? "

" So the Captain says."

" Look! "—and she handed him back his own field-glass. " I can see the men on the wooden platform. Yes; and I can see the smoke of an engine." And then, in little more than an hour from that time the ship had swung round on her anchor.

Colon, or Aspinwall as it should be called, is a place in itself as detestable as St. Thomas. It is not so odious to an Englishman, for it is not used by Englishmen more than is necessary. We have no great depot of traffic there, which we might with advantage move elsewhere. Taken, however, on its own merits, Aspinwall is not a detestable place. Luckily, however, travellers across the Isthmus to the Pacific are never doomed to remain there long. If they arrive early in the day, the railway thence to Panama takes them on at once. If it be not so, they remain on board ship till the next morning. Of course it will be understood that the transit line chiefly affects Americans, as it is the highroad from New York to California.

In less than an hour from their landing, their baggage had been examined by the Custom House officers of New Grenada, and they were on the railway cars, crossing the Isthmus. The officials in those out-of-the-way places always seem like apes imitating the doings of men. The officers at Aspinwall open and look at the trunks just as monkeys might do, having clearly no idea of any duty to be performed, nor any conception that goods of this or that class should not be allowed to pass. It is the thing in Europe to examine luggage going into a new country; and why should not they be as good as Europeans?

" I wonder whether he will be at the station? " she said, when the three hours of the journey had nearly passed. Forrest could perceive that her voice trembled as she spoke, and that she was becoming nervous.

" If he has already reached Panama, he will be there. As far as I could learn the arrival up from Peru had not been telegraphed."

" Then I have another day—perhaps two. We cannot say how many. I wish he were there. Nothing is so intolerable as suspense."

" And the box must be opened again."

When they reached the station at Panama they found that the vessel from the South American coast was in the roads, but that the passengers were not yet on shore. Forrest, therefore, took Miss Viner down to the hotel, and there remained with her, sitting next to her in the common drawing-room of the house, when she had come back from her own bedroom. It would be necessary that they should remain there four or five days, and Forrest had been quick in securing a room for her. He had assisted in taking up her luggage, had helped her in placing her big box, and had thus been recognized by the crowd in the hotel as her friend. Then came the tidings that the passengers were landing, and he became nervous as she was. " I will go down and meet him," said he, " and tell him that you are here. I shall soon find him by his name." And so he went out.

Everybody knows the scrambling manner in which passengers arrive at an hotel out of a big ship. First came two or three energetic, heated men, who, by dint of screeching and bullying, have gotten themselves first disposed. They always get the worst rooms at the inns, the housekeepers having a notion that the richest people, those with the most luggage, must be more tardy in their movements. Four or five of this nature passed by Forrest in the hall, but he was not tempted to ask questions of them. One, from his age, might have been Mr. Gorloch, but he instantly declared himself to be Count Sapparello. Then came an elderly man alone, with a small bag in his hand. He was one of those who pride themselves on going from pole to pole without encumbrance, and who will be behoved to no one for the carriage of their luggage. To him, as he was alone in the street, Forrest addressed himself. "Gorloch," said he. "Gorloch: are you a friend of his?"

"A friend of mine is so," said Forrest.

"Ah, indeed; yes," said the other. And then he hesitated. "Sir," he then said, "Mr. Gorloch died at Callao, just seven days before the ship sailed. You had better see Mr. Cox." And then the elderly man passed in with his little bag.

Mr. Gorloch was dead. "Dead!" said Forrest, to himself, as he leaned back against the wall of the hotel still standing on the street pavement. "She has come out here; and now he is gone!" And then a thousand thoughts crowded on him. Who should tell her? And how would she bear it? Would it in truth be a relief to her to find that that liberty for which she had sighed had come to her? Or now that the testing of her feelings had come to her, would she regret the loss of home and wealth, and such position as life in Peru would give her? And above all would this sudden death of one who was to have been so near to her, strike her to the heart?

But what was he to do? How was he now to show his friendship? He was returning slowly in at the hotel door, where crowds of men and women were now thronging, when he was addressed by a middle-aged, good-looking gentleman, who asked him whether his name was Forrest. "I am told," said the gentleman, when Forrest had answered him, "that you are a friend of Miss Viner's. Have you heard the sad tidings from Callao?" It then appeared that this gentleman had been a stranger to Mr. Gorloch, but had undertaken to bring a letter up to Miss Viner. This letter was handed to Mr. Forrest, and he found himself burdened with the task of breaking the news to his poor friend. Whatever he did do, he must do at once, for all those who had come up by the

Pacific steamer knew the story, and it was incumbent on him that Miss Viner should not hear the tidings in a sudden manner and from a stranger's mouth.

He went up into the drawing-room, and found Miss Viner seated there in the midst of a crew of women. He went up to her, and taking her hand, asked her in a whisper whether she would come out with him for a moment.

" Where is he? " said she. " I know that something is the matter. What is it? "

" There is such a crowd here. Step out for a moment." And he led her away to her own room.

" Where is he? " said she. " What is the matter? He has sent to say that he no longer wants me. Tell me; am I free from him? "

" Miss Viner, you are free."

Though she had asked the question herself, she was astounded by the answer; but, nevertheless, no idea of the truth had yet come upon her. " It is so," she said. " Well, what else? Has he written? He has bought me, as he would a beast of burden, and has, I suppose, a right to treat me as he pleases."

" I have a letter; but, dear Miss Viner—— "

" Well, tell me all—out at once. Tell me everything."

" You are free, Miss Viner; but you will be cut to the heart when you learn the meaning of your freedom."

" He has lost everything in trade. He is ruined."

" Miss Viner, he is dead! "

She stood staring at him for a moment or two, as though she could not realize the information which he gave her. Then gradually she retreated to the bed, and sat upon it. " Dead, Mr. Forrest! " she said. He did not answer her, but handed her the letter, which she took and read as though it were mechanically. The letter was from Mr. Gorloch's partner, and told her

71

everything which it was necessary that she should know.

"Shall I leave you now?" he said, when he saw that she had finished reading it.

"Leave me; yes—no. But you had better leave me, and let me think about it. Alas me, that I should have so spoken of him!"

"But you have said nothing unkind."

"Yes; much that was unkind. But spoken words cannot be recalled. Let me be alone now, but come to me soon. There is no one else here that I can speak to."

He went out, and finding that the hotel dinner was ready, he went in and dined. Then he strolled into the town, among the hot, narrow, dilapidated streets; and then, after two hours' absence, returned to Miss Viner's room. When he knocked, she came and opened the door, and he found that the floor was strewed with clothes. "I am preparing, you see, for my return. The vessel starts back for St. Thomas the day after to-morrow."

"You are quite right to go—to go at once. Oh, Miss Viner! Emily, now at least you must let me help you."

He had been thinking of her most during those last two hours, and her voice had become pleasant to his ears, and her eyes very bright to his sight.

"You shall help me," she said. "Are you not helping me when at such a time you come to speak to me?"

"And you will let me think that I have a right to act as your protector?"

"My protector! I do know that I want such aid as that. During the days that we are here together you shall be my friend."

"You shall not return alone. My journeyings are nothing to me. Emily, I will return with you to England."

Then she rose up from her seat and spoke to him.

"Not for the world," she said. "Putting out of question the folly of your forgetting your own objects, do you think it possible that I should go with you, now that he is dead? To you I have spoken of him harshly; and now that it is my duty to mourn for him, could I do so heartily if you were with me? While he lived, it seemed to me that in those last days I had a right to speak my thoughts plainly. You and I were to part and meet no more, and I regarded us both as people apart, who for a while might drop the common usages of the world. It is so no longer. Instead of going with you farther, I must ask you to forget that we were ever together."

" Emily, I shall never forget you."

" Let your tongue forget me. I have given you no cause to speak good of me, and you will be too kind to speak evil."

After that she explained to him all that the letter had contained. The arrangements for her journey had all been made; money also had been sent to her; and Mr. Gorloch in his will had provided for her, not liberally, seeing that he was rich, but still sufficiently.

And so they parted at Panama. She would not allow him even to cross the Isthmus with her, but pressed his hand warmly as he left her at the station. " God bless you! " he said. " And may God bless you, my friend! " she answered.

Thus alone she took her departure for England, and he went on his way to California.

ANTHONY TROLLOPE—*Lotta Schmidt and Other Stories.*

BROTHER MORGAN'S STORY OF
THE DEAD HAND

WHEN this present nineteenth century was younger by a good many years than it is now, a certain friend of mine, named Arthur Holliday, happened to arrive in the town of Doncaster exactly in the middle of race-week, or, in other words, in the middle of the month of September.

He was one of those reckless, rattlepated, open-hearted and open-mouthed young gentlemen who possess the gift of familiarity in its highest perfection, and who scramble carelessly along the journey of life, making friends, as the phrase is, wherever they go. His father was a rich manufacturer, and had bought landed property enough in one of the midland counties to make all the born squires in his neighbourhood thoroughly envious of him.

Arthur was his only son, possessor in prospect of the great estate and the great business after his father's death; well supplied with money, and not too rigidly looked after, during his father's lifetime. Report, or scandal, which ever you please, said that the old gentleman had been rather wild in his youthful days, and that, unlike most parents, he was not disposed to be violently indignant when he found that his son took after him. This may be true or not. I myself only knew the elder Mr. Holliday when he was getting on in years, and then he was as quiet and as respectable a gentleman as ever I met with.

Well, one September, as I told you, young Arthur

comes to Doncaster, having suddenly decided in his hare-brained way, that he would go to the races. He did not reach the town till towards the close of evening, and he went at once to see about his dinner and bed at the principal hotel. Dinner they were ready enough to give him; but as for a bed, they laughed when he mentioned it. In the race-week at Doncaster, it is no uncommon thing for visitors who have not bespoken apartments, to pass the night in their carriages at the inn doors. As for the lower sort of strangers, I myself have often seen them, at that full time, sleeping out on the doorsteps for want of a covered place to creep under. Rich as he was, Arthur's chance of getting a night's lodging (seeing that he had not written beforehand to secure one) was more than doubtful. He tried the second hotel, and the third hotel, and two of the inferior inns after that; and was met everywhere with the same form of answer. No accommodation for the night of any sort was left. All the bright golden sovereigns in his pocket would not buy him a bed at Doncaster in the race-week.

To a young fellow of Arthur's temperament, the novelty of being turned away into the street like a penniless vagabond, at every house where he asked for a lodging, presented itself in the light of a new and highly amusing experience. He went on with his carpet-bag in his hand, applying for a bed at every place of entertainment for travellers that he could find in Doncaster until he wandered into the outskirts of the town.

By this time the last glimmer of twilight had faded out, the moon was rising dimly in a mist, the wind was getting cold, the clouds were gathering heavily, and there was every prospect that it was soon going to rain.

The look of the night had rather a lowering effect on young Holliday's good spirits. He began to contemplate the houseless situation in which he was placed, from the serious rather than the humorous point of view; and he looked about him for another public-house to inquire at, with something very like downright anxiety in his mind on the subject of a lodging for the night.

The suburban part of the town towards which he had now strayed was hardly lighted at all, and he could see nothing of the houses as he passed them, except that they got progressively smaller and dirtier the farther he went. Down the winding road before him shone the dull gleam of an oil lamp, the one faint lonely light that struggled ineffectually with the foggy darkness all round him. He resolved to go on as far as this lamp; then, if it showed him nothing in the shape of an inn, to return to the central part of the town, and to try if he could not at least secure a chair to sit down on, through the night, at one of the principal hotels.

As he got near the lamp, he heard voices; and, walking close under it, found that it lighted the entrance to a narrow court, on the wall of which was painted a long hand in faded flesh colour, pointing with a lean fore-finger to this inscription:

"THE TWO ROBINS."

Arthur turned into the court without hesitation, to see what the Two Robins could do for him. Four or five men were standing together round the door of the house, which was at the bottom of the court, facing the entrance from the street. The men were all listening to one other man, better dressed than the rest, who was telling his audience something, in a low voice, in which they were apparently much interested.

On entering the passage, Arthur was passed by a stranger with a knapsack in his hand, who was evidently leaving the house.

" No," said the traveller with the knapsack, turning round and addressing himself cheerfully to a fat, sly-looking, bald-headed man, with a dirty white apron on, who had followed him down the passage. " No, Mr. Landlord, I am not easily scared by trifles; but I don't mind confessing that I can't quite stand *that*."

It occurred to young Holliday, the moment he heard these words, that the stranger had been asked an exorbitant price for a bed at the Two Robins; and that he was unable or unwilling to pay it. The moment his back was turned, Arthur, comfortably conscious of his own well-filled pockets, addressed himself in a great hurry, for fear any other benighted traveller should slip in and forestall him, to the sly-looking landlord with the dirty apron and the bald head.

" If you have got a bed to let," he said, " and if that gentleman who has just gone out won't pay your price for it, I will."

The sly landlord looked hard at Arthur.

" Will you, sir? " he asked in a meditative, doubtful way.

" Name your price," said young Holliday; thinking that the landlord's hesitation sprang from some boorish distrust of him. " Name your price, and I'll give you the money at once, if you like."

" Are you game for five shillings? " inquired the landlord, rubbing his stubby double chin, and looking up thoughtfully at the ceiling above him.

Arthur nearly laughed in the man's face; but thinking it prudent to control himself, offered the five shillings as seriously as he could. The sly landlord held out his hand, then suddenly drew it back again.

" You're acting all fair and above-board by me," he said; " and, before I take your money, I'll do the same by you. Look here, this is how it stands. You can have a bed all to yourself for five shillings; but you can't have more than a half share of the room it stands in. Do you see what I mean, young gentleman?"

"Of course I do," returned Arthur, a little irritably. "You mean that it is a double-bedded room, and that one of the beds is occupied?"

The landlord nodded his head, and rubbed his double chin harder than ever. Arthur hesitated, and mechanically moved back a step or two towards the door. The idea of sleeping in the same room with a total stranger did not present an attractive prospect to him. He felt more than half inclined to drop his five shillings into his pocket, and to go out into the street once more.

"Is it yes, or no?" asked the landlord. "Settle it as quick as you can, because there's lots of people wanting a bed at Doncaster, to-night, besides you."

Arthur looked towards the court, and heard the rain falling heavily in the street outside. He thought he would ask a question or two before he rashly decided on leaving the shelter of the Two Robins.

"What sort of man is it who has got the other bed?" he inquired. "Is he a gentleman? I mean is he a quiet, well-behaved person?"

"The quietest man I ever came across," said the landlord, rubbing his fat hands stealthily one over the other. "As sober as a judge, and as regular as clockwork in his habits. It hasn't struck nine, not ten minutes ago, and he's in his bed already. I don't know whether that comes up to your notion of a quiet man: it goes a long way ahead of mine, I can tell you."

"Is he asleep, do you think?" asked Arthur.

"I know he's asleep," returned the landlord. "And what is more, he's gone off so fast, that I'll warrant you don't wake him. This way, sir," said the landlord, speaking over young Holliday's shoulder, as if he was addressing some new guest who was approaching the house.

"Here you are," said Arthur, determined to be beforehand with the stranger whoever he might be. "I'll take the bed." And he handed the five shillings to the landlord, who nodded, dropped the money carelessly into his waistcoat pocket, and lighted a candle.

"Come up and see the room," said the host of the Two Robins, leading the way to the staircase quite briskly, considering how fat he was.

They mounted to the second floor of the house. The landlord half opened a door, fronting the landing, then stopped, and turned round to Arthur.

"It's a fair bargain, mind you, on my side as well as on yours," he said. "You give me five shillings; I will give you in return a clean, comfortable bed; and I warrant, beforehand, that you won't be interfered with, or annoyed in any way, by the man who sleeps in the same room with you." Saying those words, he looked hard for a moment in young Holliday's face, and then led the way into the room.

It was larger and cleaner than Arthur expected it would be. The two beds stood parallel with each other —a space of about six feet intervening between them. They were both of the same medium size and both had the same plain white curtains, made to draw, if necessary, all round them.

The occupied bed was the bed nearest the window. The curtains were all drawn round it, except the half curtain at the bottom, on the side of the bed farthest from the window. Arthur saw the feet of the sleeping man raising the scanty clothes into a sharp little eminence, as if he were lying flat on his back. He took the candle, and advanced softly to draw the curtain—

stopped half-way, and listened for a moment—then turned to the landlord.

"He is a very quiet sleeper," said Arthur.

"Yes," returned the landlord, "very quiet."

Young Holliday advanced with the candle, and looked in at the man cautiously.

"How pale he is," said Arthur.

"Yes," said the landlord, "pale enough, isn't he?"

Arthur looked closer at the man. The bedclothes were drawn up to his chin, and they lay perfectly still over the region of his chest. Surprised and vaguely startled, as he noticed this, Arthur stooped down closer over the stranger; looked at his ashy parted lips; listened breathlessly for an instant; looked again at the still face, and the motionless lips and chest; and turned round suddenly on the landlord, with his own cheeks as pale, for the moment, as the hollow cheeks of the man on the bed.

"Come here," he whispered, under his breath. "Come here, for God's sake! The man's not asleep—he is dead."

"You have found that out sooner than I thought you would," said the landlord composedly. "Yes, he's dead, sure enough. He died at five o'clock to-day."

"How did he die? Who is he?" asked Arthur, staggered for the moment by the audacious coolness of the answer.

"As to who he is," rejoined the landlord, "I know no more about him than you do. There are his books and letters and things, all sealed up in that brown-paper parcel, for the Coroner's inquest to open to-morrow or next day. He's been here a week, paying his way fairly enough, and stopping indoors, for the most part, as if he was ailing. My girl brought up his tea at five to-day and as he was pouring of it out, he fell down in a faint, or a fit, or a compound of both for anything I know. We couldn't bring him to—and the doctor said he was dead.

And there he is. And the Coroner's inquest coming as soon as it can. And that's as much as I know about it."

Arthur held the candle close to the man's lips. The flame still burnt straight up, as steadily as ever. There was a moment of silence; and the rain pattered drearily through it against the panes of the window.

"If you haven't got nothing more to say to me," continued the landlord, "I suppose I may go. You don't expect your five shillings back, do you? There's the bed I promised you, clean and comfortable. There's the man I warranted not to disturb you, quiet in this world for ever. If you're frightened to stop alone with him, that's not my look-out. I've kept my part of the bargain, and I mean to keep the money. I'm not Yorkshire myself, young gentleman; but I've lived long enough in these parts to have my wits sharpened; and I shouldn't wonder if you found out the way to brighten up yours, next time you come among us."

With those words, the landlord turned towards the door, and laughed to himself softly, in high satisfaction at his own sharpness.

Startled and shocked as he was, Arthur had by this time sufficiently recovered himself to feel indignant at the trick that had been played on him, and at the insolent manner in which the landlord exulted in it.

"Don't laugh, till you are quite sure you have got the laugh against me," he said sharply. "You shan't have the five shillings for nothing, my man. I'll keep the bed."

"Will you?" said the landlord. "Then I wish you a good night's rest." With that brief farewell, he went out, and shut the door after him.

A good night's rest! The words had hardly been spoken, the door had hardly been closed, before Arthur half repented the hasty words that had just escaped him.

Though not naturally over-sensitive, and not wanting in courage of the moral as well as the physical sort, the presence of the dead man had an instantaneously chilling effect on his mind when he found himself alone in the room—alone, and bound by his own rash words to stay there till the next morning. An older man would have thought nothing of those words, and would have acted without reference to them, as his calmer sense suggested. But Arthur was too young to treat the ridicule, even of his inferiors, with contempt—too young not to fear the momentary humiliation of falsifying his own foolish boast, more than he feared the trial of watching out the long night in the same chamber with the dead.

"It is but a few hours," he thought to himself, "and I can get away the first thing in the morning."

He was looking towards the occupied bed, as that idea passed through his mind, and the sharp angular eminence made in the clothes by the dead man's upturned feet, again caught his eye. He advanced and drew the curtains, purposely abstaining, as he did so, from looking at the face of the corpse, lest he might unnerve himself at the outset by fastening some ghastly impression of it on his mind. He drew the curtain very gently, and sighed involuntarily as he closed it.

"Poor fellow!" he said almost as sadly as if he had known the man. "Ah, poor fellow!"

He went next to the window. The night was black, and he could see nothing from it. The rain still pattered heavily against the glass. He inferred, from hearing it, that the window was at the back of the house; remembering that the front was sheltered from the weather by the court and the buildings over it.

While he was still standing at the window—for even the dreary rain was a relief, because of the sound it

made; a relief, also, because it moved, and had some
faint suggestion, in consequence, of life and companionship in it—while he was standing at the window, and
looking vacantly into the black darkness outside, he
heard a distant church-clock strike ten. Only ten! How
was he to pass the time till the house was astir the next
morning?

Under any other circumstances, he would have gone
down to the public-house parlour, would have called for
his grog, and would have laughed and talked with the
company assembled as familiarly as if he had known
them all his life. But the very thought of whiling away
the time in this manner was now distasteful to him. The
new situation in which he was placed seemed to have
altered him to himself already. Thus far, his life had
been the common, trifling, prosaic surface-life of a prosperous young man, with no troubles to conquer, and no
trials to face. He had lost no relation whom he loved,
no friend whom he treasured. Till this night, what
share he had of the immortal inheritance that is divided
amongst us all, had lain dormant with him. Till
this night Death and he had not once met, even in
thought.

He took a few turns up and down the room—then
stopped. The noise made by his boots on the poorly
carpeted floor jarred on his ear. He hesitated a little,
and ended by taking the boots off, and walking back-
wards and forwards noiselessly.

All desire to sleep or to rest had left him. The bare
thought of lying down on the unoccupied bed, instantly
drew the picture on his mind of a dreadful mimicry of
the position of the dead man. Who was he? What was
the story of his past life? Poor he must have been or he
would not have stopped at such a place as the Two
Robins Inn—and weakened, probably, by long illness, or

83

he could hardly have died in the manner which the landlord had described. Poor, ill, lonely—dead in a strange place; dead, with nobody but a stranger to pity him. A sad story; truly, on the mere face of it, a very sad story.

While these thoughts were passing through his mind, he had stopped insensibly at the window, close to which stood the foot of the bed with the closed curtains. At first he looked at it absently; then he became conscious that his eyes were fixed on it; and then, a perverse desire took possession of him to do the very thing which he had resolved not to do, up to this time—to look at the dead man.

He stretched out his hand towards the curtains; but checked himself in the very act of undrawing them, turned his back sharply on the bed, and walked towards the chimney-piece, to see what things were placed on it, and to try if he could keep the dead man out of his mind that way.

There was a pewter ink-stand on the chimney-piece, with some mildewed remains of ink in the bottle. There were two coarse china ornaments of the commonest kind; and there was a square of embossed card, dirty and fly-blown, with a collection of wretched riddles printed on it, in all sorts of zig-zag directions and in variously coloured inks. He took the card and went away to read it at the table on which the candle was placed; sitting down, with his back resolutely turned to the curtained bed.

He read the first riddle, the second, the third, all in one corner of the card—then turned it round impatiently to look at another. Before he could begin reading the riddles printed here, the sound of the church clock stopped him.

Eleven.

He had got through an hour of the time, in the room with the dead man.

Once more he looked at the card. It was not easy to make out the letters printed on it, in consequence of the dimness of the light which the landlord had left him—a common tallow candle, furnished with a pair of heavy old-fashioned steel snuffers. Up to this time, his mind had been too much occupied to think of the light. He had left the wick of the candle unsnuffed, till it had risen higher than the flame, and had burnt into an odd pent-house shape at the top, from which morsels of the charred cotton fell off, from time to time, in little flakes. He took up the snuffers now, and trimmed the wick. The light brightened directly and the room became less dismal.

Again he turned to the riddles; reading them doggedly and resolutely now in one corner of the card, now in another. All his efforts, however, could not fix his attention on them. He pursued his occupation mechanically, deriving no sort of impression from what he was reading. It was as if a shadow from the curtained bed had got between his mind and the gaily printed letters— a shadow that nothing could dispel. At last he gave up the struggle, threw the card from him impatiently, and took to walking softly up and down the room again.

The dead man, the dead man, the hidden man on the bed!

There was the one persistent idea still haunting him. Hidden! Was it only the body being there—or was it the body being there, concealed, that was preying on his mind? He stopped at the window with that doubt in him; once more listening to the pattering rain, once more looking out into the black darkness.

Still the dead man!

The darkness forced his mind back upon itself, and set

his memory at work, reviving, with a painfully vivid distinctness, the momentary impression it had received from his first sight of the corpse. Before long, the face seemed to be hovering out in the middle of the rain and darkness, confronting him through the window, with the paleness whiter, with the dreadful dull line of light between the imperfectly closed eyelids broader than he had seen it—with the parted lips slowly dropping farther and farther away from each other—with the features growing larger and moving closer, till they seemed to fill the window, and silence the rain and shut out the night.

The sound of a voice shouting below stairs woke him suddenly from the dream of his own distempered fancy. He recognized it as the voice of the landlord.

"Shut up at twelve, Ben," he heard it say. "I'm off to bed."

He wiped away the damp that had gathered on his forehead, reasoned with himself for a little while, and resolved to shake his mind free of the ghastly counterfeit which still clung to it, by forcing himself to confront, if it was only for a moment, the solemn reality. Without allowing himself an instant to hesitate he parted the curtains at the foot of the bed, and looked through.

There was the sad, peaceful, white face, with the awful mystery of stillness on it, laid back upon the pillow. No stir, no change there! He only looked at it for a moment before he closed the curtains again; but that moment steadied him, calmed him, restored him—mind and body to himself.

He returned to his old occupation of walking up and down the room; persevering in it, this time, till the clock struck again.

Twelve.

As the sound of the clock bell died away, it was succeeded by the confused noise, down stairs, of the drinkers in the taproom leaving the house. The next sound, after an interval of silence, was caused by the barring of the door, and the closing of the shutters at the back of the inn. Then the silence followed again and was disturbed no more.

He was alone now—absolutely, hopelessly alone with the dead man, till the next morning.

The wick of the candle wanted trimming again. He took up the snuffers—but paused suddenly on the very point of using them and looked attentively at the candle then back, over his shoulder, at the curtained bed—then again at the candle. It had been lighted for the first time, to show him the way upstairs, and three parts of it, at least, were already consumed. In another hour it would be burnt out. In another hour—unless he called at once to the man who had shut up the inn for a fresh candle—he would be left in the dark.

Strongly as his mind had been affected since he had entered the room, his unreasonable dread of encountering ridicule, and of exposing his courage to suspicion, had not altogether lost its influence over him yet.

He lingered irresolutely by the table, waiting till he could prevail on himself to open the door, and call from the landing to the man who had shut up the inn. In his present hesitating frame of mind, it was a kind of relief to gain a few moments only by engaging in the trifling occupation of snuffing the candle. His hand trembled a little, and the snuffers were heavy and awkward to use. When he closed them on the wick he closed them a hair's-breadth too low. In an instant the candle was out, and the room was plunged in pitch darkness.

The one impression which the absence of light immediately produced on his mind was distrust of the curtained bed—distrust which shaped itself into no distinct idea, but which was powerful enough, in its very vagueness, to bind him down to his chair, to make his heart beat fast, and to set him listening intently. No sound stirred in the room but the familiar sound of the rain against the window, louder and sharper now than he had heard it yet.

Still the vague distrust, the inexpressible dread, possessed him, and kept him in his chair. He had put his carpet-bag on the table when he first entered the room; and he now took the key from his pocket, reached out his hand softly, opened the bag, and groped in it for his travelling writing-case, in which he knew that there was a small store of matches. When he had got one of the matches he waited before he struck it on the coarse wooden table, and listened intently again without knowing why. Still there was no sound in the room but the steady, ceaseless rattling sound of the rain.

He lighted the candle again, without another moment of delay; and, on the instant of its burning up, the first object in the room that his eyes sought for was the curtained bed.

Just before the light had been put out, he had looked in that direction, and had seen no change, no disarrangement of any sort, in the folds of the closely drawn curtains.

When he looked at the bed now he saw, hanging over the side of it, a long white hand.

It lay perfectly motionless, midway on the side of the bed, where the curtain at the head and the curtain at the foot met. Nothing more was visible. The clinging curtains hid everything but the long white hand.

He stood looking at it, unable to stir, unable to call out; feeling nothing, knowing nothing; every faculty he possessed gathered up and lost in the one seeing faculty. How long that first panic held him, he never could tell afterwards. It might have been only for a moment; it

88

might have been for many minutes together. How he got to the bed—whether he ran to it headlong, or whether he approached it slowly—how he wrought himself up to unclose the curtains and look in, he never has remembered, and never will remember, to his dying day. It is enough that he did go to the bed, and that he did look inside the curtains.

The man had moved. One of his arms was outside the clothes; his face was turned a little on the pillow; his eyelids were wide open. Changed as to position, and as to one of the features, the face was otherwise fearfully and wonderfully unaltered. The dead paleness and the dead quiet were on it still.

One glance showed Arthur this—one glance before he flew breathlessly to the door, and alarmed the house.

The man whom the landlord called "Ben" was the first to appear on the stairs. In three words, Arthur told him what had happened, and sent him for the nearest doctor.

I, who tell you this story, was then staying with a medical friend of mine in practice at Doncaster, taking care of his patients for him during his absence in London; and I, for the time being, was the nearest doctor. They had sent for me from the inn when the stranger was taken ill in the afternoon; but I was not at home, and medical assistance was sought for elsewhere. When the man from the Two Robins rang the night-bell, I was just thinking of going to bed. Naturally enough, I did not believe a word of his story about "a dead man who had come to life again." However, I put on my hat, armed myself with one or two bottles of restorative medicine, and ran to the Inn, expecting to find nothing more remarkable when I got there than a patient in a fit.

My surprise at finding that the man had spoken the literal truth was almost, if not quite, equalled by my astonishment at finding myself face to face with Arthur Holliday as soon as I entered the bedroom. It was no time then for giving or seeking explanations. We just shook hands amazedly; and then I ordered everybody but Arthur out of the room, and hurried to the man on the bed.

The kitchen fire had not been long out. There was plenty of hot water in the boiler, and plenty of flannel to be had. With these, with my medicines, and with such help as Arthur could render under my direction, I dragged the man, literally, out of the jaws of death. In less than an hour from the time when I had been called in, he was alive and talking, in the bed on which he had been laid out to wait for the coroner's inquest.

You will naturally ask me what had been the matter with him; I might treat you, in reply, to a long theory, plentifully sprinkled with what the children call hard words. I prefer telling you that, in this case, cause and effect could not be satisfactorily joined together by any theory whatever. There are mysteries in life, and in the conditions of it, which human science has not fathomed yet; and I candidly confess to you that, in bringing that man back to existence, I was, morally speaking, groping haphazard in the dark. I know (from the testimony of the doctor who attended him in the afternoon) that the vital machinery, so far as its action is appreciable by our senses, had, in this case, unquestionably stopped; and I am equally certain (seeing that I recovered him) that the vital principle was not extinct. When I add that he had suffered from a long and complicated illness, and that his whole nervous system was utterly deranged, I have told you all I really know of the physical condition of my dead-alive patient at the Two Robins Inn.

When he " came to," as the phrase goes, he was a startling object to look at, with his colourless face, his sunken cheeks, his wild black eyes, and his long black hair. The first question he asked me about himself, when he could speak, made me suspect that I had been called in to a man in my own profession. I mentioned to him my surmise, and he told me that I was right.

He said he had come last from Paris, where he had been attached to a hospital. That he had lately returned to England, on his way to Edinburgh, to continue his studies; that he had been taken ill on the journey; and that he had stopped to rest and recover himself at Doncaster. He did not add a word about his name, or who he was, and of course I did not question him on the subject. All I enquired, when he ceased speaking, was what branch of the profession he intended to follow.

"Any branch," he said, bitterly, "which will put bread into the mouth of a poor man."

At this, Arthur, who had been hitherto watching him in silent curiosity, burst out impetuously in his usual good-humoured way:

"My dear fellow!" (everybody was "my dear fellow" with Arthur) "now you have come to life again, don't begin by being down-hearted about your prospects. I'll answer for it, I can help you to some capital thing in the medical line—or if I can't, I know my father can."

The medical student looked at him steadily.

"Thank you," he said coldly; then added, "May I ask who your father is?"

"He's well enough known all about this part of the country," replied Arthur. "He is a great manufacturer, and his name is Holliday."

My hand was on the man's wrist during this brief conversation. The instant the name of Holliday was pronounced, I felt the pulse under my fingers flutter, stop, go on suddenly with a bound, and beat afterwards for a minute or two at the fever rate.

"How did you come here?" asked the stranger quickly, excitably, passionately.

Arthur related briefly what had happened from the time of his first taking the bed at the inn.

"I am indebted to Mr. Holliday's son, then, for the help that has saved my life," said the medical student, speaking to himself, with a singular sarcasm in his voice. "Come here!"

He held out, as he spoke, his long, white, bony right hand.

"With all my heart," said Arthur, taking his hand cordially. "I may confess it now," he continued, laughing; "upon my honour you almost frightened me out of my wits."

The stranger did not seem to listen. His wild black eyes were fixed with a look of eager interest on Arthur's face, and his long bony fingers kept tight hold of Arthur's hand. Young Holliday, on his side, returned the gaze, amazed and puzzled by the medical student's odd language and manners. The two faces were close together; I looked at them; and, to my amazement, I was suddenly impressed by the sense of a likeness between them—not in features or complexion but solely in expression. It must have been a strong likeness, or I should certainly not have found it out, for I am naturally slow at detecting resemblances between faces.

"You have saved my life," said the strange man, still looking hard in Arthur's face, still holding tightly by his hand. "If you had been my own brother, you could not have done more for me than that."

He laid a singularly strong emphasis on those three words, "my own brother," and a change passed over his face as he pronounced them—a change that no language of mine is competent to describe.

"I hope I have not done being of service to you yet,"

said Arthur. "I'll speak to my father as soon as I get home."

"You seem to be fond and proud of your father," said the medical student. "I suppose, in return, he is fond and proud of you?"

"Of course he is," answered Arthur, laughing. "Is there anything wonderful in that? Isn't *your* father fond——"

The stranger suddenly dropped young Holliday's hand, and turned his face away.

"I beg your pardon," said Arthur. "I hope I have not unintentionally pained you. I hope you have not lost your father?"

"I can't well lose what I have never had," retorted the medical student, with a harsh mocking laugh.

"What you have never had!"

The strange man suddenly caught Arthur's hand again, suddenly looked once more hard in his face.

"Yes," he said, with a repetition of the bitter laugh. "You have brought a poor devil back into the world, who has no business there. Do I astonish you? Well! I have a fancy of my own for telling you what men in my situation generally keep a secret. I have no name and no father. The merciful law of Society tells me I am Nobody's son! Ask your father if he will be my father too, and help me on in life with the family name."

Arthur looked at me more puzzled than ever.

I signed to him to say nothing, and then laid my fingers on the man's wrist. No! In spite of the extraordinary speech that he had just made, he was not, as I had been disposed to suspect, beginning to get light-headed. His pulse by this time had fallen back to a quiet, slow beat, and his skin was moist and cool. Not a symptom of fever or agitation about him.

Finding that neither of us answered him, he turned to

me and began talking of the extraordinary nature of his case, and asking my advice about the future course of medical treatment to which he ought to subject himself. I said the matter required careful thinking over, and suggested that I should send him a prescription a little later. He told me to write it at once, as he would most likely be leaving Doncaster in the morning, before I was up. It was quite useless to represent to him the folly and danger of such a proceeding as this. He heard me politely and patiently, but held to his resolution, without offering any reasons or explanations, and repeated to me, that if I wished to give him a chance of seeing my prescription, I must write it at once.

Hearing this, Arthur volunteered the loan of a travelling writing-case, which, he said, he had with him, and, bringing it to the bed, shook the notepaper out of the pocket of the case forthwith in his usual careless way. With the paper there fell out, on the counterpane of the bed, a small packet of sticking-plaster and a little water-colour drawing of a landscape.

The medical student took up the drawing and looked at it. His eye fell on some initials, neatly written in cipher, in one corner. He started, and trembled; his pale face grew whiter than ever; his wild black eyes turned on Arthur, and looked through and through him.

"A pretty drawing," he said in a remarkably quiet tone of voice.

"Ah, and done by such a pretty girl," said Arthur. "Oh, such a pretty girl! I wish it was not a landscape—I wish it was a portrait of her!"

"You admire her very much?"

Arthur, half in jest, half in earnest, kissed his hand for answer.

"Love at first sight," said young Holliday, putting the drawing away again. "But the course of it doesn't run smooth. It's the old story. She's monopolized, as usual. Trammelled by a rash engagement to some poor man who is never likely to get money enough to marry her. I was lucky I heard of it in time, or I should certainly have risked a declaration when she gave me that drawing. Here, doctor! Here is pen, ink, and paper, all ready for you."

"When she gave you that drawing! Gave it. Gave it."

He repeated the words slowly to himself, and suddenly closed his eyes. A momentary distortion passed across his face, and I saw one of his hands clutch up the bed-clothes and squeeze them hard. I thought he was going to be ill again, and begged that there might be no more talking. He opened his eyes when I spoke, fixed them once more, searchingly, on Arthur, and said, slowly and distinctly:

"You like her, and she likes you. The poor man may die out of your way. Who can tell that she may not give you herself as well as her drawing after all?"

Before young Holliday could answer, he turned to me, and said in a whisper, "Now for the prescription." From that time, though he spoke to Arthur again, he never looked at him more.

When I had written the prescription, he examined it, approved of it, and then astonished us both by abruptly wishing us good night. I offered to sit up with him, and he shook his head. Arthur offered to sit up with him, and he said, shortly, with his face turned away, "No." I insisted on having somebody left to watch him. He gave way when he found I was determined, and said he would accept the services of the waiter at the inn.

"Thank you both," he said, as we rose to go. "I have one last favour to ask—not of you, doctor, for I leave you to exercise your professional discretion, but of Mr. Holliday." His eyes, while he spoke, still rested steadily on me, and never once turned towards Arthur. " I beg that Mr. Holliday will not mention to any one—least of all to his father—the events that have occurred, and the words that have passed, in this room. I entreat him to bury me in his memory, as but for him, I might have been buried in my grave. I cannot give my reasons for making this strange request. I can only implore him to grant it."

His voice faltered for the first time, and he hid his face on the pillow. Arthur, completely bewildered, gave the required pledge. I took young Holliday away with me, immediately afterwards, to the house of my friend; determining to go back to the inn and to see the medical student again before he had left in the morning.

I returned to the inn at eight o'clock, purposely abstaining from waking Arthur, who was sleeping off the past night's excitement on one of my friend's sofas. A suspicion had occurred to me, as soon as I was alone in my bedroom, which made me resolve that Holliday and the stranger whose life he had saved should not meet again, if I could prevent it.

I have already alluded to certain reports, or scandals, which I knew of, relating to the early life of Arthur's father. While I was thinking, in my bed, of what had passed at the inn—of the change in the student's pulse when he heard the name of Holliday; of the resemblance of expression that I had discovered between his face and Arthur's; of the emphasis he had laid on those three words, " my own brother "; and of his incomprehensible acknowledgement of his own illegitimacy—while I was thinking of these things, the reports I have mentioned suddenly flew into my mind, and linked themselves fast to the chain of my previous reflections. Something within me whispered, " It is best that those two young men should not meet again." I felt it before I slept; I felt it when I woke; and I went, as I told you, alone to the inn the next morning.

I had missed my only opportunity of seeing my nameless patient again. He had been gone nearly an hour when I inquired for him.

I have now told you everything that I know for certain, in relation to the man whom I brought back to life in the double-bedded room of the inn at Doncaster. What I have next to add is matter for inference and surmise, and is not, strictly speaking, matter of fact.

I have to tell you first, that the medical student turned out to be strangely and unaccountably right in assuming it as more than probable that Arthur Holliday would marry the young lady who had given him the water-colour drawing of the landscape. That marriage took place a little more than a year after the events occurred which I have just been relating.

The young couple came to live in the neighbourhood in which I was then established in practice. I was present at the wedding, and was rather surprised to find that Arthur was singularly reserved with me, both before and after his marriage, on the subject of the young lady's prior engagement. He only referred to it once, when we were alone, merely telling me, on that occasion, that his wife had done all that honour and duty required of her in the matter, and that the engagement had been broken off with the full approval of her parents. I never heard more from him than this. For three years he and his wife lived together happily. At the expiration of that time, the symptoms of a serious illness first declared themselves in Mrs. Arthur Holliday. It turned out to be a long, lingering, hopeless malady. I attended her throughout. We had been great friends when she was well, and we became more attached to each other than ever when she was ill. I had many long and interesting conversations with her in the intervals when she suffered least. The result of one of those conversations I may briefly relate, leaving you to draw any inferences from it that you please.

The interview to which I refer, occurred shortly before her death.

I called one evening as usual, and found her alone, with a look in her eyes which told me she had been crying. She only informed me, at first, that she had been depressed in spirits; but, by little and little, she became more communicative, and confessed to me that she had been looking over some old letters, which had been addressed to her, before she had seen Arthur, by a man to whom she had been engaged to be married. I asked her how the engagement came to be broken off. She replied that it had not been broken off, but that it had died out in a very mysterious manner. The person to whom she was engaged—her first love, she called him —was poor, and there was no immediate prospect of their being married. He followed my profession, and went abroad to study. They had corresponded regularly, until the time when, as she believed, he returned to England. From that period she heard no more of him. However that might be, he had never written to her again; and after waiting a year, she had married Arthur. I asked when the first estrangement had begun, and found that the time at which she ceased to hear anything of her first lover, exactly corresponded with the time at which I had been called in to my mysterious patient at the Two Robins Inn.

A fortnight after that conversation, she died. In course of time Arthur married again. Of late years he has lived principally in London, and I have seen little or nothing of him.

I have some years to pass over before I can approach

to anything like a conclusion of this fragmentary narra-
tive. And even when that later period is reached, the
little that I have to say will not occupy your attention
for more than a few minutes.

One rainy autumn evening, while I was still practising
as a country doctor, I was sitting alone, thinking over a
case then under my charge, when I heard a low knock
at the door of my room.

"Come in," I cried, looking up curiously to see who
wanted me.

After a momentary delay, the lock moved, and a long
white bony hand stole round the door as it opened,
gently pushing it over a fold in the carpet which hin-
dered it from working freely on the hinges. The hand
was followed by a man whose face instantly struck me
with a very strange sensation. There was something
familiar to me in the look of him; and yet it was also
something that suggested the idea of change.

He quietly introduced himself as "Mr. Lorn"; presented to me some excellent professional recommenda-
tions; and proposed to fill the place, then vacant, of my
assistant. While he was speaking, I noticed it as singular
that we did not appear to be meeting each other like
strangers; and that, while I was certainly startled at
seeing him, he did not appear to be at all startled at
seeing me.

It was on the tip of my tongue to say that I thought
I had met him before. But there was something in his
face, and something in my recollections—I can hardly say
what—which unaccountably restrained me from speaking, and which, as unaccountably, attracted me to him
at once, and made me feel ready and glad to accept his
proposal.

He took his assistant's place on that very day. We got
on together as if we had been old friends from the first;

but throughout the whole time of his residence in my house, he never volunteered any confidences on the subject of his past life; and I never approached the forbidden topic except by hints, which he resolutely refused to understand.

I had long had a notion that my patient at the inn might have been a natural son of the elder Mr. Holliday's, and that he might also have been the man who was engaged to Arthur's first wife. And, now, another idea occurred to me, that Mr. Lorn was the only person in existence who could, if he chose, enlighten me on both those doubtful points. But he never did choose— and I was never enlightened. He remained with me till I removed to London to try my fortune there, as a physician, for the second time; and then he went his way, and I went mine, and we have never seen one another since.

I can add no more. I may have been right in my suspicion or I may have been wrong. All I know is, that, in those days of my country practice, when I came home late and found my assistant asleep and woke him, he used to look in coming to, wonderfully like the stranger at Doncaster as he raised himself in the bed on that memorable night.

WILKIE COLLINS—*Queen of Hearts.*

TENNESSEE'S PARTNER

I DO not think that we ever knew his real name. Our ignorance of it certainly never gave us any social inconvenience, for at Sandy Bar in 1854 most men were christened anew. Sometimes these appellatives were derived from some distinctiveness of dress, as in the case of "Dungaree Jack"; or from some peculiarity of habit, as shown in "Saleratus Bill," so called from an undue proportion of that chemical in his daily bread; or from some unlucky slip, as exhibited in "The Iron Pirate," a mild, inoffensive man, who earned that baleful title by his unfortunate mispronunciation of the term "iron pyrites." Perhaps this may have been the beginning of a rude heraldry; but I am constrained to think that it was because a man's real name in that day rested solely upon his own unsupported statement. "Call yourself Clifford, do you?" said Boston, addressing a timid newcomer with infinite scorn; "hell is full of such Cliffords!" He then introduced the unfortunate man, whose name happened to be really Clifford, as "Jay-bird Charley"—an unhallowed inspiration of the moment that clung to him ever after.

But to return to Tennessee's Partner, whom we never knew by any other than this relative title; that he had ever existed as a separate and distinct individuality we only learned later. It seems that in 1853 he left Poker Flat to go to San Francisco, ostensibly to procure a wife. He never got any farther than Stockton. At that place he was attracted by a young person who waited upon the table at the hotel where he took his meals. One morning he said something to her which caused her to smile not unkindly, to somewhat coquettishly break a plate of toast over his upturned, serious simple face, and to retreat to the kitchen. He followed her, and emerged a few moments later, covered with more toast and victory. That day week they were married by a Justice of the Peace, and returned to Poker Flat. I am aware that something more might be made of this episode, but I prefer to tell it as it was current at Sandy Bar—in the gulches and bar-rooms—where all sentiment was modified by a strong sense of humour.

Of their married felicity but little is known, perhaps for the reason that Tennessee, then living with his partner, one day took occasion to say something to the bride on his own account, at which, it is said, she smiled not unkindly and chastely retreated—this time as far as Marysville, where Tennessee followed her, and where they went to housekeeping without the aid of a Justice of the Peace. Tennessee's Partner took the loss of his wife simply and seriously, as was his fashion. But to everybody's surprise, when Tennessee one day returned from Marysville, without his partner's wife—she having smiled and retreated with somebody else—Tennessee's Partner was the first man to shake his hand and greet him with affection. The boys who had gathered in the cañon to see the shooting were naturally indignant. Their indignation might have found vent in sarcasm, but for a certain look in Tennessee's Partner's eye that indicated a lack of humorous appreciation. In fact, he was a grave man, with a steady application to practical detail which was unpleasant in a difficulty.

Meanwhile a popular feeling against Tennessee had grown up on the Bar. He was known to be a gambler; he was suspected to be a thief. In these suspicions

Tennessee's Partner was equally compromised; his continued intimacy with Tennessee after the affair above quoted could only be accounted for on the hypothesis of a co-partnership of crime. At last Tennessee's guilt became flagrant. One day he overtook a stranger on his way to Red Dog. The stranger afterwards related that Tennessee beguiled the time with interesting anecdote and reminiscence, but illogically concluded the interview in the following words:

"And now, young man, I'll trouble you for your knife, your pistols, and your money. You see, your weppings might get you into trouble at Red Dog, and your money's a temptation to the evilly disposed. I think you said your address was San Francisco. I shall endeavour to call." It may be stated here that Tennessee had a fine flow of humour, which no business preoccupation could wholly subdue.

This exploit was his last. Red Dog and Sandy Bar made common cause against the highwayman. Tennessee was hunted in very much the same fashion as his prototype, the grizzly. As the toils closed around him he made a desperate dash through the Bar, emptying his revolver at the crowd before the Arcade Saloon, and so on up Grizzly Cañon; but at its farther extremity he was stopped by a small man on a grey horse. The men looked at each other a moment in silence. Both were fearless, both self-possessed and independent; and both types of a civilization that in the seventeenth century would have been called heroic, but in the nineteenth simply "reckless."

"What have you got there? I call," said Tennessee, quietly.

"Two bowers and an ace," said the stranger, as quietly, showing two revolvers and a bowie-knife. "That takes me," returned Tennessee; and with this gambler's epigram he threw away his useless pistol, and rode back with his captor.

.   .   .   .

It was a warm night. The cool breeze which usually sprang up with the going down of the sun behind the *chaparral*-crested mountain was that evening withheld from Sandy Bar. The little cañon was stifling with heated resinous odours, and the decaying driftwood on the Bar sent forth faint, sickening exhalations. The feverishness of day, and its fierce passions, still filled the camp. Lights moved restlessly along the bank of the river, striking no answering reflection from its tawny current. Against the blackness of the pines the windows of the old loft above the express-office stood out staringly bright; and through their curtainless panes the loungers below could see the forms of those who were even then deciding the fate of Tennessee, and above all this, etched on the dark firmament, rose the Sierra, remote and passionless, crowned with remoter passionless stars.

The trial of Tennessee was conducted as fairly as was consistent with a judge and jury who felt themselves to some extent obliged to justify in their verdict the previous irregularities of arrest and indictment. The law of Sandy Bar was implacable, but not vengeful. The excitement and personal feeling of the chase were over; with Tennessee safe in their hands, they were ready to listen patiently to any defence, which they were already satisfied was insufficient. There being no doubt in their own minds, they were willing to give the prisoner the benefit of any that might exist. Secure in the hypothesis that he ought to be hanged, on general principles they indulged him with more latitude of defence than his reckless hardihood seemed to ask. The Judge appeared to be more anxious than the prisoner, who, otherwise unconcerned, evidently took a grim pleasure in the responsibility he had created. "I don't take any hand in this yer game," had been his invariable but good-humoured reply to all questions. The Judge—who was also his captor—for a moment vaguely regretted that he had not shot him "on sight" that morning but presently dismissed this human weakness as unworthy of the judicial mind. Nevertheless, when there was a tap at the door, and it was said that Tennessee's Partner was there on behalf of the prisoner, he was admitted at once without question. Perhaps the younger members of the jury, to whom the proceedings were becoming irksomely thoughtful, hailed him as a relief.

For he was not, certainly, an imposing figure. Short and stout, with a square face, sunburned into a preter-natural redness, clad in a loose duck "jumper," and trousers streaked and splashed with red soil, his aspect under any circumstances would have been quaint, and was now even ridiculous. As he stooped to deposit at his feet a heavy carpet-bag he was carrying, it became obvious, from partially developed legends and inscriptions, that the material with which his trousers had been patched had been originally intended for a less ambitious covering. Yet he advanced with great gravity, and after having shaken the hand of each person in the room with laboured cordiality, he wiped his serious, perplexed face on a red bandanna handkerchief, a shade lighter than his complexion, laid his powerful hand upon the table to steady himself, and thus addressed the Judge:

"I was passin' by," he began, by way of apology, "and I thought I'd just step in and see how things was git-tin' on with Tennessee thar—my pardner. It's a hot night. I disremember any sich weather before on the Bar."

He paused a moment, but nobody volunteering any other meteorological recollection, he again had recourse to his pocket-handkerchief, and for some moments mopped his face diligently.

"Have you anything to say in behalf of the prisoner?" said the Judge, finally.

"Thet's it," said Tennessee's Partner, in a tone of relief. "I come yar as Tennessee's pardner—knowing him nigh on four year, off and on, wet and dry, in luck and out o' luck. His ways ain't allers my ways, but thar ain't any p'ints in that young man, thar ain't any live- liness as he's been up to, as I don't know. And you sez to me, sez you—confidential-like, and between man and man—sez you, 'Do you know anything in his behalf?' and I sez to you, sez I—confidential-like, as between man and man—'What should a man know of his pardner?'"

"Is this all you have to say?" asked the Judge, impa- tiently, feeling, perhaps, that a dangerous sympathy of humour was beginning to humanize the Court.

"Thet's so," continued Tennessee's Partner. "It ain't for me to say anything agin him. And now, what's the case? Here's Tennessee wants money, wants it bad, and doesn't like to ask it of his old pardner. Well, what does Tennessee do? He lays for a stranger, and he fetches that stranger. And you lays for *him*, and you fetches *him*—and the honours is easy. And I put it to you, bein' a far-minded man, and to you, gentlemen, all, as far- minded men, ef this isn't so."

"Prisoner," said the Judge, interrupting, "have you any questions to ask this man?"

"No! no!" continued Tennessee's Partner, hastily. "I play this yer hand alone. To come down to the bed- rock, it's just this: Tennessee, thar, has played it pretty rough and expensive-like on a stranger, and on this yer camp. And now, what's the fair thing? Some would say more; some would say less. Here's seventeen hun- dred dollars in coarse gold and a watch—it's about all my pile—and call it square!" And before a hand could be raised to prevent him, he had emptied the contents of the carpet-bag upon the table.

For a moment his life was in jeopardy. One or two men sprang to their feet, several hands groped for hidden weapons, and a suggestion to "throw him from the window" was only overridden by a gesture from the Judge. Tennessee laughed. And apparently oblivious of the excitement, Tennessee's Partner improved the opportunity to mop his face again with his handkerchief.

When order was restored, and the man was made to understand, by the use of forcible figures and rhetoric, that Tennessee's offence could not be condoned by money, his face took a more serious and sanguinary hue, and those who were nearest to him noticed that his rough hand trembled slightly on the table. He hesitated a moment as he slowly returned the gold to the carpet-bag, as if he had not yet entirely caught the elevated sense of justice which swayed the tribunal, and was perplexed with the belief that he had not offered enough. Then he turned to the Judge, and saying, "This yer is a lone hand, played alone, and without my pardner," he bowed to the jury, and was about to withdraw, when the Judge called him back.

"If you have anything to say to Tennessee, you had better say it now."

For the first time that evening the eyes of the prisoner and his strange advocate met. Tennessee smiled, showed his white teeth, and, saying, "Euchred, old man!" held out his hand.

Tennessee's Partner took it in his own, and saying, "I just dropped in as I was passin' to see how things was gittin' on," let the hand passively fall, and adding that "it was a warm night," again mopped his face with his handkerchief, and without another word withdrew.

The two men never again met each other alive. For the unparalleled insult of a bribe offered to Judge Lynch —who, whether bigoted, weak, or narrow, was at least incorruptible—firmly fixed in the mind of that mythical personage any wavering determination of Tennessee's fate; and at the break of day he was marched, closely guarded, to meet it at the top of Marley's Hill.

How he met it, how cool he was, how he refused to say anything, how perfect were the arrangements of the committee, were all duly reported, with the addition of a warning moral and example to all future evil-doers, in the *Red Dog Clarion*, by its editor, who was present, and to whose vigorous English I cheerfully refer the reader. But the beauty of that midsummer morning, the blessed amity of earth and air and sky, the awakened life of the free woods and hills, the joyous renewal and promise of Nature, and above all, the infinite serenity that thrilled through each, was not reported, as not being a part of the social lesson. And yet, when the weak and foolish deed was done, and a life, with its possibilities and responsibilities, had passed out of the mis-shapen thing that dangled between earth and sky, the birds sang, the flowers bloomed, the sun shone as cheerily as before; and possibly the *Red Dog Clarion* was right.

Tennessee's Partner was not in the group that surrounded the ominous tree. But as they turned to disperse, attention was drawn to the singular appearance of a motionless donkey-cart halted at the side of the road. As they approached they at once recognized the venerable "Jenny" and the two-wheeled cart as the property of Tennessee's Partner—used by him in carrying dirt from his claim; and a few paces distant the owner of the equipage himself, sitting under a buckeye-tree, wiping the perspiration from his glowing face. In answer to an inquiry, he said he had come for the body of the

"diseased," "if it was all the same to the committee."
He didn't wish to "hurry anything"; he could "wait."
He was not working that day; and when the gentlemen
were done with the "diseased," he would take him. "Ef
thar is any present," he added, in his simple serious way,
"as would care to jine in the fun'l, they kin come."
Perhaps it was from a sense of humour, which I have
already intimated was a feature of Sandy Bar—perhaps
it was from something even better than that; but two-
thirds of the loungers accepted the invitation at once.

It was noon when the body of Tennessee was delivered into the hands of his partner. As the cart drew
up to the fatal tree, we noticed that it contained a rough
oblong box—apparently made from a section of sluicing
—and half filled with bark and the tassels of pine. The
cart was further decorated with slips of willow, and made
fragrant with buckeye-blossoms. When the body was
deposited in the box, Tennessee's Partner drew over it a
piece of tarred canvas, and gravely mounting the narrow
seat in front, with his feet upon the shafts, urged the
little donkey forward. The equipage moved slowly on,
at that decorous pace which was habitual with "Jenny"
even under less solemn circumstances. The men—half
curiously, half jestingly, but all good-humouredly—
strolled along beside the cart: some in advance, some a
little in the rear of the homely catafalque. But, whether
from the narrowing of the road, or some present sense
of decorum, as the cart passed on the company fell to the
rear in couples, keeping step, and otherwise assuming
the external show of a formal procession. Jack Folins-
bee, who had at the outset played a funeral march in
dumb-show upon an imaginary trombone, desisted, from
a lack of sympathy and appreciation—not having, perhaps, your true humorist's capacity to be content with
the enjoyment of his own fun.

The way led through Grizzly Cañon—by this time clothed in funeral drapery and shadows. The redwoods, burying their moccasined feet in the red soil, stood in Indian file along the track, trailing an uncouth benediction from their bending boughs upon the passing bier. A hare, surprised into helpless inactivity, sat upright and pulsating in the ferns by the roadside as the *cortège* went by. Squirrels hastened to gain a secure outlook from higher boughs; and the blue-jays, spreading their wings, fluttered before them like outriders, until the outskirts of Sandy Bar were reached, and the solitary cabin of Tennessee's Partner.

Viewed under more favourable circumstances, it would not have been a cheerful place. The unpicturesque site, the rude and unlovely outlines, the unsavoury details, which distinguish the nest-building of the California miner, were all here, with the dreariness of decay super-added. A few paces from the cabin there was a rough enclosure, which, in the brief days of Tennessee's Part-ner's matrimonial felicity, had been used as a garden, but was now overgrown with fern. As we approached it we were surprised to find that what we had taken for a recent attempt at cultivation was the broken soil about an open grave.

The cart was halted before the enclosure; and rejecting the offers of assistance with the same air of simple self-reliance he had displayed throughout, Tennessee's Part-ner lifted the rough coffin on his back, and deposited it, unaided, within the shallow grave. He then nailed down the board which served as a lid; and mounting the little mound of earth beside it, took off his hat, and slowly mopped his face with his handkerchief. This the crowd felt was a preliminary to speech; and they disposed themselves variously on stumps and boulders, and sat expectant.

"When a man," began Tennessee's Partner slowly, "has been running free all day, what's the natural thing for him to do? Why, to come home! And if he ain't in a condition to go home, what can his best friend do? Why, bring him home! And here's Tennessee has been running free, and we brings him home from his wandering." He paused, and picked up a fragment of quartz, rubbed it thoughtfully on his sleeve, and went on: "It ain't the first time that I've packed him on my back, as you see'd me now. It ain't the first time that I brought him to this yer cabin when he couldn't help himself; it ain't the first time that I and 'Jinny' have waited for him on yon hill, and picked him up and so fetched him home, when he couldn't speak and didn't know me. And now that it's the last time, why"—he paused, and rubbed the quartz gently on his sleeve—"you see, it's sort of rough on his pardner. And now, gentlemen," he added, abruptly, picking up his long-handled shovel, "the fun'l's over; and my thanks, and Tennessee's thanks, to you for your trouble."

Resisting any proffers of assistance, he began to fill in the grave, turning his back upon the crowd, that after a few moments' hesitation gradually withdrew. As they crossed the little ridge that hid Sandy Bar from view, some, looking back, thought they could see Tennessee's Partner, his work done, sitting upon the grave, his shovel between his knees, and his face buried in his red bandanna handkerchief. But it was argued by others that you couldn't tell his face from his handkerchief at that distance; and this point remained undecided.

.   .   .   .

In the reaction that followed the feverish excitement of that day, Tennessee's Partner was not forgotten. A secret investigation had cleared him of any complicity in Tennessee's guilt, and left only a suspicion of his general sanity. Sandy Bar made a point of calling on him, and proffering various uncouth but well-meant kindnesses. But from that day his rude health and great strength seemed visibly to decline; and when the rainy season fairly set in, and the tiny grass-blades were beginning to peep from the rocky mound above Tennessee's grave, he took to his bed.

One night, when the pines beside the cabin were swaying in the storm, and trailing their slender fingers over the roof, and the roar and rush of the swollen river were heard below, Tennessee's Partner lifted his head from the pillow, saying, " It is time to go for Tennessee; I must put ' Jinny ' in the cart "; and would have risen from his bed but for the restraint of his attendant. Struggling, he still pursued his singular fancy: " There, now, steady, ' Jinny '—steady, old girl. How dark it is! Look out for the ruts—and look out for him, too, old gal! Sometimes, you know, when he's blind drunk, he drops down right in the trail. Keep on straight up to the pine on the top of the hill. Thar—I told you so!— thar he is!—coming this way, too—all by himself, sober, and his face a-shining. Tennessee! Pardner! "

And so they met.

BRET HARTE—*The Luck of Roaring Camp and other Sketches.*

A RESUMED IDENTITY

I. THE REVIEW AS A FORM OF WELCOME

ONE summer night a man stood on a low hill overlooking a wide expanse of forest and field. By the full moon hanging low in the west he knew what he might not have known otherwise: that it was near the hour of dawn. A light mist lay along the earth, partly veiling the lower features of the landscape, but above it the taller trees showed in well-defined masses against a clear sky. Two or three farmhouses were visible through the haze, but in none of them, naturally, was a light. Nowhere, indeed, was any sign or suggestion of life except the barking of a distant dog, which, repeated with mechanical iteration, served rather to accentuate than dispel the loneliness of the scene.

The man looked curiously about him on all sides, as one who among familiar surroundings is unable to determine his exact place and part in the scheme of things. It is so, perhaps, that we shall act when, risen from the dead, we await the call to judgment.

A hundred yards away was a straight road, showing white in the moonlight. Endeavouring to orient himself, as a surveyor or navigator might say, the man moved his eyes slowly along its visible length and at a distance of a quarter-mile to the south of his station saw, dim and grey in the haze, a group of horsemen riding to the north. Behind them were men afoot, marching in column, with dimly gleaming rifles aslant above their shoulders. They moved slowly and in silence. Another group of horsemen, another regiment of infantry, another and another—all in unceasing motion toward the man's point of view, past it, and beyond. A battery of artillery followed, the cannoneers riding with folded arms on limber and caisson. And still the interminable procession came out of the obscurity to south and passed into the obscurity to north, with never a sound of voice, nor hoof, nor wheel.

The man could not rightly understand: he thought himself deaf; said so, and heard his own voice, although it had an unfamiliar quality that almost alarmed him; it disappointed his ear's expectancy in the matter of timbre and resonance. But he was not deaf, and that for the moment sufficed.

Then he remembered that there are natural phenomena to which some one has given the name " acoustic shadows." If you stand in an acoustic shadow there is one direction from which you will hear nothing. At the battle of Gaines's Mill, one of the fiercest conflicts of the Civil War, with a hundred guns in play, spectators a mile and a half away on the opposite side of the Chickahominy valley heard nothing of what they clearly saw. The bombardment of Port Royal, heard and felt at St. Augustine, a hundred and fifty miles to the south, was inaudible two miles to the north in a still atmosphere. A few days before the surrender at Appomattox a thunderous engagement between the commands of Sheridan and Pickett was unknown to the latter commander, a mile in the rear of his own line.

These instances were not known to the man of whom we write, but less striking ones of the same character had not escaped his observation. He was profoundly disquieted, but for another reason than the uncanny silence of that moonlight march.

" Good Lord! " he said to himself—and again it was as if another had spoken his thought—" if those people are what I take them to be we have lost the battle and they are moving on Nashville! "

Then came a thought of self—an apprehension—a strong sense of personal peril, such as in another we call fear. He stepped quickly into the shadow of a tree. And still the silent battalions moved slowly forward in the haze.

The chill of a sudden breeze upon the back of his neck drew his attention to the quarter whence it came, and turning to the east he saw a faint grey light along the horizon—the first sign of returning day. This increased his apprehension.

" I must get away from here," he thought, " or I shall be discovered and taken."

He moved out of the shadow, walking rapidly towards the greying east. From the safer seclusion of a clump of cedars he looked back. The entire column had passed out of sight: the straight white road lay bare and desolate in the moonlight!

Puzzled before, he was now inexpressibly astonished. So swift a passing of so slow an army!—he could not comprehend it. Minute after minute passed unnoted; he had lost his sense of time. He sought with a terrible earnestness a solution of the mystery, but sought in vain. When at last he roused himself from his abstraction the sun's rim was visible above the hills, but in the new conditions he found no other light than that of day; his understanding was involved as darkly in doubt as before.

On every side lay cultivated fields showing no sign of war and war's ravages. From the chimneys of the farmhouses thin ascensions of blue smoke signalled preparations for a day's peaceful toil. Having stilled its immemorial allocution to the moon, the watch-dog was assisting a negro who, prefixing a team of mules to the plough, was flatting and sharping contentedly at his task. The hero of this tale stared stupidly at the pastoral picture as if he had never seen such a thing in all his life; then he put his hand to his head, passed it through his hair and, withdrawing it, attentively considered the palm—a singular thing to do. Apparently reassured by the act, he walked confidently toward the road.

II. WHEN YOU HAVE LOST YOUR LIFE CONSULT A PHYSICIAN

Dr. Stilling Malson, of Murfreesboro, having visited a patient six or seven miles away, on the Nashville road, had remained with him all night. At daybreak he set out for home on horseback, as was the custom of doctors of the time and region. He had passed into the neighbourhood of Stone's River battlefield when a man approached him from the roadside and saluted in the military fashion, with a movement of the right hand to the hat-brim. But the hat was not a military hat, the man was not in uniform and had not a martial bearing. The doctor nodded civilly, half thinking that the stranger's uncommon greeting was perhaps in deference to the historic surroundings. As the stranger evidently desired speech with him he courteously reined in his horse and waited.

"Sir," said the stranger, "although a civilian, you are perhaps an enemy."

"I am a physician," was the non-committal reply.

"Thank you," said the other. "I am a lieutenant, of the staff of General Hazen." He paused a moment and looked sharply at the person whom he was addressing, then added, "Of the Federal army."

The physician merely nodded.

"Kindly tell me," continued the other, "what has

happened here. Where are the armies? Which has won the battle?"

The physician regarded his questioner curiously with half-shut eyes. After a professional scrutiny, prolonged to the limit of politeness, "Pardon me," he said; "one asking information should be willing to impart it. Are you wounded?" he added, smiling.

"Not seriously—it seems."

The man removed the unmilitary hat, put his hand to his head, passed it through his hair and, withdrawing it, attentively considered the palm.

"I was struck by a bullet and have been unconscious. It must have been a light, glancing blow: I find no blood and feel no pain. I will not trouble you for treatment, but will you kindly direct me to my command—to any part of the Federal army—if you know?"

Again the doctor did not immediately reply: he was recalling much that is recorded in the books of his profession—something about lost identity and the effect of familiar scenes in restoring it. At length he looked the man in the face, smiled, and said:

"Lieutenant, you are not wearing the uniform of your rank and service."

At this the man glanced down at his civilian attire, lifted his eyes, and said with hesitation:

"That is true. I—I don't quite understand."

Still regarding him sharply but not unsympathetically, the man of science bluntly inquired:

"How old are you?"

"Twenty-three—if that has anything to do with it."

"You don't look it; I should hardly have guessed you to be just that."

The man was growing impatient. "We need not discuss that," he said: "I want to know about the army. Not two hours ago I saw a column of troops moving northward on this road. You must have met them. Be good enough to tell me the colour of their clothing, which I was unable to make out, and I'll trouble you no more."

"You are quite sure that you saw them?"

"Sure? My God, sir, I could have counted them!"

"Why, really," said the physician, with an amusing consciousness of his own resemblance to the loquacious barber of the *Arabian Nights*, "this is very interesting. I met no troops."

The man looked at him coldly, as if he had himself observed the likeness to the barber. "It is plain," he said, "that you do not care to assist me. Sir, you may go to the devil!"

He turned and strode away, very much at random, across the dewy fields, his half-penitent tormentor quietly watching him from his point of vantage in the saddle till he disappeared beyond an array of trees.

III. THE DANGER OF LOOKING INTO A POOL OF WATER

After leaving the road the man slackened his pace, and now went forward, rather deviously, with a distinct feeling of fatigue. He could not account for this, though truly the interminable loquacity of that country doctor offered itself in explanation. Seating himself upon a rock, he laid one hand upon his knee, back upward, and casually looked at it. It was lean and withered. He lifted both hands to his face. It was seamed and furrowed; he could trace the lines with the tips of his fingers. How strange!—a mere bullet-stroke and a brief unconsciousness should not make one a physical wreck.

"I must have been a long time in hospital," he said aloud. "Why, what a fool I am! The battle was in December, and it is now summer!" He laughed. "No wonder that fellow thought me an escaped lunatic. He was wrong: I am only an escaped patient."

At a little distance a small plot of ground enclosed by a stone wall caught his attention. With no very definite intent he rose and went to it. In the centre was a square, solid monument of hewn stone. It was brown with age, weather-worn at the angles, spotted with moss and lichen. Between the massive blocks were strips of grass the leverage of whose roots had pushed them apart. In answer to the challenge of this ambitious structure Time had laid his destroying hand upon it, and it would soon be "one with Nineveh and Tyre." In an inscription on one side his eye caught a familiar name. Shaking with excitement, he craned his body across the wall and read:

HAZEN'S BRIGADE
to
The Memory of Its Soldiers
who fell at
Stone River, Dec. 31, 1862.

The man fell back from the wall, faint and sick. Almost within an arm's length was a little depression in the earth; it had been filled by a recent rain—a pool of clear water. He crept to it to revive himself, lifted the upper part of his body on his trembling arms, thrust forward his head and saw the reflection of his face, as in a mirror. He uttered a terrible cry. His arms gave way; he fell, face downward, into the pool and yielded up the life that had spanned another life.

AMBROSE BIERCE—*Can Such Things Be.*

THE SIRE DE MALÉTROIT'S DOOR

DENIS DE BEAULIEU was not yet two-and-twenty, but he counted himself a grown man, and a very accomplished cavalier into the bargain. Lads were early formed in that rough, warfaring epoch; and when one has been in a pitched battle and a dozen raids, has killed one's man in an honourable fashion, and knows a thing or two of strategy and mankind, a certain swagger in the gait is surely to be pardoned. He had put up his horse with due care, and supped with due deliberation; and then, in a very agreeable frame of mind, went out to pay a visit in the grey of the evening. It was not a very wise proceeding on the young man's part. He would have done better to remain beside the fire or go decently to bed. For the town was full of the troops of Burgundy and England under a mixed command; and though Denis was there on safe-conduct, his safe-conduct was like to serve him little on a chance encounter.

It was September 1429; the weather had fallen sharp; a flighty piping wind, laden with showers, beat about the township; and the dead leaves ran riot along the streets. Here and there a window was already lighted up; and the noise of men-at-arms making merry over supper within came forth in fits and was swallowed up and carried away by the wind. The night fell swiftly; the flag of England, fluttering on the spire-top, grew ever fainter and fainter against the flying clouds—a black speck like a swallow in the tumultuous, leaden chaos of the sky. As the night fell the wind rose, and began to hoot under archways and roar amid the tree-tops in the valley below the town.

Denis de Beaulieu walked fast and was soon knocking at his friend's door; but though he promised himself to stay only a little while and make an early return, his welcome was so pleasant, and he found so much to delay him, that it was already long past midnight before he said good-bye upon the threshold. The wind had fallen again in the meanwhile; the night was as black as the grave; not a star, nor a glimmer of moonshine, slipped through the canopy of cloud. Denis was ill-acquainted with the intricate lanes of Château Landon; even by daylight he had found some trouble in picking his way; and in this absolute darkness he soon lost it altogether. He was certain of one thing only—to keep mounting the hill; for his friend's house lay at the lower end, or tail, of Château Landon, while the inn was up at the head, under the great church spire. With this clue to go upon he stumbled and groped forward, now breathing more freely in open places where there was a good slice of sky overhead, now feeling along the wall in stifling closes. It is an eerie and mysterious position to be thus submerged in opaque blackness in an almost unknown town. The silence is terrifying in its possibilities. The touch of cold window bars to the exploring hand startles the man like the touch of a toad; the inequalities of the pavement shake his heart into his mouth; a piece of denser darkness threatens an ambuscade or a chasm in the pathway; and where the air is brighter, the houses put on strange and bewildering appearances, as if to lead him farther from his way. For Denis, who had to regain his inn without attracting notice, there was real danger as well as mere discomfort in the walk; and he went warily and boldly at once, and at every corner paused to make an observation.

He had been for some time threading a lane so narrow that he could touch a wall with either hand, when it began to open out and go sharply downward. Plainly this lay no longer in the direction of his inn; but the hope of a little more light tempted him forward to reconnoitre. The lane ended in a terrace with a bartizan wall, which gave an outlook between high houses, as out of an embrasure, into the valley lying dark and formless several hundred feet below. Denis looked down, and could discern a few tree-tops waving and a single speck of brightness where the river ran across a weir. The weather was clearing up, and the sky had lightened, so as to show the outline of the heavier clouds and the dark margin of the hills. By the uncertain glimmer, the house on his left hand should be a place of some pretensions; it was surmounted by several pinnacles and turret-tops; the round stern of a chapel, with a fringe of flying buttresses, projected boldly from the main block; and the door was sheltered under a deep porch carved with figures and overhung by two long gargoyles. The windows of the chapel gleamed through their intricate tracery with a light as of many tapers, and threw out the buttresses and the peaked roof in a more intense blackness against the sky. It was plainly the hôtel of some great family of the neighbourhood; and as it reminded Denis of a town house of his own at Bourges, he stood for some time gazing up at it and mentally gauging the skill of the architects and the consideration of the two families.

There seemed to be no issue to the terrace but the lane by which he had reached it; he could only retrace his steps, but he had gained some notion of his whereabouts, and hoped by this means to hit the main thoroughfare and speedily regain the inn. He was reckoning without that chapter of accidents which was to make this night

memorable above all others in his career; for he had not
gone back above a hundred yards before he saw a light
coming to meet him, and heard loud voices speaking
together in the echoing narrows of the lane. It was a
party of men-at-arms going the night round with torches.
Denis assured himself that they had all been making free
with the wine-bowl, and were in no mood to be particular
about safe-conducts or the niceties of chivalrous war. It
was as like as not that they would kill him like a dog
and leave him where he fell. The situation was inspirit-
ing but nervous. Their own torches would conceal him
from sight, he reflected; and he hoped that they would
drown the noise of his footsteps with their own empty
voices. If he were but fleet and silent, he might evade
their notice altogether.

Unfortunately, as he turned to beat a retreat, his foot
rolled upon a pebble; he fell against the wall with an
ejaculation, and his sword rang loudly on the stones.
Two or three voices demanded who went there—some
in French, some in English; but Denis made no reply,
and ran the faster down the lane. Once upon the
terrace, he paused to look back. They still kept calling
after him, and just then began to double the pace in
pursuit, with a considerable clank of armour, and great
tossing of the torchlight to and fro in the narrow jaws
of the passage.

Denis cast a look around and darted into the porch.
There he might escape observation, or—if that were too
much to expect—was in a capital posture whether for
parley or defence. So thinking, he drew his sword and
tried to set his back against the door. To his surprise,
it yielded behind his weight; and though he turned in
a moment, continued to swing back on oiled and noiseless hinges, until it stood wide open on a black interior.
When things fall out opportunely for the person con-

cerned, he is not apt to be critical about the how or why, his own immediate personal convenience seeming a sufficient reason for the strangest oddities and revolutions in our sublunary things; and so Denis, without a moment's hesitation, stepped within and partly closed the door behind him to conceal his place of refuge. Nothing was further from his thoughts than to close it altogether; but for some inexplicable reason—perhaps by a spring or a weight—the ponderous mass of oak whipped itself out of his fingers and clanked to, with a formidable rumble and a noise like the falling of an automatic bar.

The round, at that very moment, debouched upon the terrace and proceeded to summon him with shouts and curses. He heard them ferreting in the dark corners; and the stock of a lance even rattled along the outer surface of the door behind which he stood; but these gentlemen were in too high a humour to be long delayed, and soon made off down a corkscrew pathway which had escaped Denis's observation, and passed out of sight and hearing along the battlements of the town.

Denis breathed again. He gave them a few minutes' grace for fear of accidents, and then groped about for some means of opening the door and slipping forth again. The inner surface was quite smooth, not a handle, not a moulding, not a projection of any sort. He got his finger-nails round the edges and pulled, but the mass was immovable. He shook it, it was as firm as a rock. Denis de Beaulieu frowned and gave vent to a little noiseless whistle. What ailed the door? he wondered. Why was it open? How came it to shut so easily and so effectually after him? There was something obscure and underhand about all this that was little to the young man's fancy. It looked like a snare; and yet who could suppose a snare in such a quiet by-street and in a house of so prosperous and even noble an exterior? And yet—snare or no snare, intentionally or unintentionally—here he was, prettily trapped; and for the life of him he could see no way out of it again. The darkness began to weigh upon him. He gave ear; all was silent without, but within and close by he seemed to catch a faint sighing, a faint sobbing rustle, a little stealthy creak —as though many persons were at his side, holding themselves quite still, and governing even their respiration with the extreme of slyness. The idea went to his vitals with a shock, and he faced about suddenly as if to defend his life. Then, for the first time, he became aware of a light about the level of his eyes and at some distance in the interior of the house—a vertical thread of light, widening towards the bottom, such as might escape between two wings of arras over a doorway. To see anything was a relief to Denis; it was like a piece of solid ground to a man labouring in a morass; his mind seized upon it with avidity; and he stood staring at it and trying to piece together some logical conception of his surroundings. Plainly there was a flight of steps ascending from his own level to that of this illuminated doorway; and indeed he thought he could make out another thread of light, as fine as a needle and as faint as phosphorescence, which might very well be reflected along the polished wood of a handrail. Since he had begun to suspect that he was not alone, his heart had continued to beat with smothering violence, and an intolerable desire for action of any sort had possessed itself of his spirit. He was in deadly peril, he believed. What could be more natural than to mount the staircase, lift the curtain, and confront his difficulty at once? At least he would be dealing with something tangible; at least he would be no longer in the dark. He stepped slowly forward with outstretched hands, until his foot struck the bottom step; then he rapidly scaled the stairs, stood for a moment to compose his expression, lifted the arras and went in.

He found himself in a large apartment of polished stone. There were three doors; one on each of three sides; all similarly curtained with tapestry. The fourth side was occupied by two large windows and a great stone chimney-piece, carved with the arms of the Malétroits. Denis recognized the bearings, and was gratified to find himself in such good hands. The room was strongly illuminated; but it contained little furniture except a heavy table and a chair or two, the hearth was innocent of fire, and the pavement was but sparsely strewn with rushes clearly many days old.

On a high chair beside the chimney, and directly facing Denis as he entered, sat a little old gentleman in a fur tippet. He sat with his legs crossed and his hands folded, and a cup of spiced wine stood by his elbow on a bracket on the wall. His countenance had a strongly masculine cast; not properly human, but such as we see in the bull, the goat, or the domestic boar; something equivocal and wheedling, something greedy, brutal, and dangerous. The upper lip was inordinately full, as though swollen by a blow or a toothache; and the smile, the peaked eyebrows, and the small, strong eyes were quaintly and almost comically evil in expression. Beautiful white hair hung straight all round his head, like a saint's, and fell in a single curl upon the tippet. His beard and moustache were the pink of venerable sweetness. Age, probably in consequence of inordinate precautions, had left no mark upon his hands; and the Malétroit hand was famous. It would be difficult to imagine anything at once so fleshy and so delicate in design; the taper, sensual fingers were like those of one of Leonardo's women; the fork of the thumb made a dimpled protuberance when closed; the nails were perfectly shaped, and of a dead, surprising whiteness. It rendered his aspect tenfold more redoubtable, that a man with hands like these should keep them devoutly folded in his lap like a virgin martyr—that a man with so intense and startling an expression of face should sit patiently on his seat and contemplate people with an unwinking stare, like a god, or a god's statue. His quiescence seemed ironical and treacherous, it fitted so poorly with his looks.

Such was Alain, Sire de Malétroit.

Denis and he looked silently at each other for a second or two.

"Pray step in," said the Sire de Malétroit. "I have been expecting you all the evening."

He had not risen, but he accompanied his words with a smile, and a slight but courteous inclination of the head. Partly from the smile, partly from the strange musical murmur with which the Sire prefaced his observation, Denis felt a strong shudder of disgust go through his marrow. And what with disgust and honest confusion of mind, he could scarcely get words together in reply.

"I fear," he said, "that this is a double accident. I am not the person you suppose me. It seems you were looking for a visit; but for my part, nothing was further from my thoughts—nothing could be more contrary to my wishes—than this intrusion."

"Well, well," replied the old gentleman indulgently, "here you are, which is the main point. Seat yourself, my friend, and put yourself entirely at your ease. We shall arrange our little affairs presently."

Denis perceived that the matter was still complicated with some misconception, and he hastened to continue his explanations.

"Your door . . ." he began.

"About my door?" asked the other, raising his peaked eyebrows. "A little piece of ingenuity." And he shrugged his shoulders. "A hospitable fancy! By your own account, you were not desirous of making my acquaintance. We old people look for such reluctance now and then; and when it touches our honour, we cast about until we find some way of overcoming it. You arrive uninvited, but believe me, very welcome."

"You persist in error, sir," said Denis. "There can be no question between you and me. I am a stranger in this countryside. My name is Denis, damoiseau de Beaulieu. If you see me in your house, it is only——"

"My young friend," interrupted the other, "you will permit me to have my own ideas on that subject. They probably differ from yours at the present moment," he added with a leer, "but time will show which of us is in the right."

Denis was convinced he had to do with a lunatic. He seated himself with a shrug, content to wait the upshot; and a pause ensued, during which he thought he could distinguish a hurried gabbling as of prayer from behind the arras immediately opposite him. Sometimes there seemed to be but one person engaged, sometimes two; and the vehemence of the voice, low as it was, seemed to indicate either great haste or an agony of spirit. It occurred to him that this piece of tapestry covered the entrance to the chapel he had noticed from without.

The old gentleman meanwhile surveyed Denis from head to foot with a smile, and from time to time emitted little noises like a bird or a mouse, which seemed to indicate a high degree of satisfaction. This state of matters became rapidly insupportable; and Denis, to put an end to it, remarked politely that the wind had gone down.

The old gentleman fell into a fit of silent laughter, so prolonged and violent that he became quite red in the face. Denis got upon his feet at once, and put on his hat with a flourish.

"Sir," he said, "if you are in your wits, you have affronted me grossly. If you are out of them, I flatter myself I can find better employment for my brains than to talk with lunatics. My conscience is clear; you have made a fool of me from the first moment; you have refused to hear my explanations; and now there is no power under God will make me stay here any longer; and if I cannot make my way out in a more decent fashion, I will hack your door in pieces with my sword."

The Sire de Malétroit raised his right hand and wagged it at Denis with the fore and little fingers extended.

"My dear nephew," he said, "sit down."

"Nephew!" retorted Denis, "you lie in your throat"; and he snapped his fingers in his face.

"Sit down, you rogue!" cried the old gentleman, in a sudden, harsh voice, like the barking of a dog. "Do you fancy," he went on, "that when I made my little contrivance for the door I had stopped short with that? If you prefer to be bound hand and foot till your bones ache, rise and try to go away. If you choose to remain a free young buck, agreeably conversing with an old gentleman—why, sit where you are in peace, and God be with you."

"Do you mean I am a prisoner?" demanded Denis.

"I state the facts," replied the other. "I would rather leave the conclusion to yourself."

Denis sat down again. Externally he managed to keep pretty calm; but within, he was now boiling with anger, now chilled with apprehension. He no longer felt convinced that he was dealing with a madman. And if the old gentleman was sane, what, in God's name, had he to look for? What absurd or tragical adventure had befallen him? What countenance was he to assume?

While he was thus unpleasantly reflecting, the arras that overhung the chapel door was raised, and a tall priest in his robes came forth and, giving a long, keen stare at Denis, said something in an undertone to Sire de Malétroit.

"She is in a better frame of spirit?" asked the latter.

"She is more resigned, messire," replied the priest.

"Now the Lord help her, she is hard to please!" sneered the old gentleman. "A likely stripling—not ill-born—and of her own choosing, too? Why, what more would the jade have?"

"The situation is not usual for a young damsel," said the other, "and somewhat trying to her blushes."

"She should have thought of that before she began the dance? It was none of my choosing, God knows that: but since she is in it, by our Lady, she shall carry it to the end." And then addressing Denis, "Monsieur de Beaulieu," he asked, "may I present you to my niece? She has been waiting your arrival, I may say, with even greater impatience than myself."

Denis had resigned himself with a good grace—all he desired was to know the worst of it as speedily as possible; so he rose at once, and bowed in acquiescence. The Sire de Malétroit followed his example and limped, with the assistance of the chaplain's arm, towards the chapel door. The priest pulled aside the arras, and all three entered. The building had considerable architectural pretensions. A light groining sprang from six stout columns, and hung down in two rich pendants from the centre of the vault. The place terminated behind the altar in a round end, embossed and honey-combed with a superfluity of ornament in relief, and pierced by many little windows shaped like stars, trefoils, or wheels. These windows were imperfectly glazed, so that the night air circulated freely in the chapel. The tapers, of which there must have been half a hundred burning on the altar, were unmercifully blown about; and the light went through many different phases of brilliancy and semi-eclipse. On the steps in front of the altar knelt a young girl richly attired as a bride. A chill settled over Denis as he observed her costume; he fought with desperate energy against the conclusion that was being thrust upon his mind; it could not—it should not—be as he feared.

" Blanche," said the Sire, in his most flute-like tones, " I have brought a friend to see you, my little girl; turn round and give him your pretty hand. It is good to be devout; but it is necessary to be polite, my niece."

The girl rose to her feet and turned towards the new-comers. She moved all of a piece; and shame and exhaustion were expressed in every line of her fresh young body; and she held her head down and kept her eyes upon the pavement, as she came slowly forward. In the course of her advance, her eyes fell upon Denis de Beaulieu's feet—feet of which he was justly vain, be it remarked, and wore in the most elegant accoutrement even while travelling. She paused—started, as if his yellow boots had conveyed some shocking meaning—and glanced suddenly up into the wearer's countenance. Their eyes met; shame gave place to horror and terror in her looks; the blood left her lips; with a piercing scream she covered her face with her hands and sank upon the chapel floor.

"That is not the man!" she cried. "My uncle; that is not the man!"

The Sire de Malétroit chirped agreeably. "Of course not," he said, "I expected as much. It was so unfortunate you could not remember his name."

"Indeed," she cried, "indeed, I have never seen this person till this moment—I have never so much as set eyes upon him—I never wish to see him again. Sir," she said, turning to Denis, "if you are a gentleman, you will bear me out. Have I ever seen you—have you ever seen me—before this accursed hour?"

"To speak for myself, I have never had that pleasure," answered the young man. "This is the first time, messire, that I have met with your engaging niece."

The old gentleman shrugged his shoulders.

"I am distressed to hear it," he said. "But it is never too late to begin. I had little more acquaintance with my own lady ere I married her; which proves," he added with a grimace, "that these impromptu marriages may often produce an excellent understanding in the long-run. As the bridegroom is to have a voice in the matter, I will give him two hours to make up for lost time before we proceed with the ceremony." And he turned towards the door, followed by the clergyman.

The girl was on her feet in a moment. "My uncle, you cannot be in earnest," she said. "I declare before God I will stab myself rather than be forced on that young man. The heart rises at it; God forbids such marriages; you dishonour your white hair. Oh, my uncle, pity me! There is not a woman in all the world but would prefer death to such a nuptial. Is it possible," she added, faltering—"is it possible that you do not believe me—that you still think this"—and she pointed at Denis with a tremor of anger and contempt—"that you still think *this* to be the man?"

"Frankly," said the old gentleman, pausing on the threshold, "I do. But let me explain to you once for all, Blanche de Malétroit, my way of thinking about this affair. When you took it into your head to dishonour my family and the name that I have borne, in peace and war, for more than threescore years, you forfeited, not only the right to question my designs, but that of looking me in the face. If your father had been alive, he would have spat on you and turned you out of doors. His was the hand of iron. You may bless your God you have only to deal with the hand of velvet, mademoiselle. It was my duty to get you married without delay. Out of pure goodwill, I have tried to find your own gallant for you. And I believe I have succeeded. But before God and all the holy angels, Blanche de Malétroit, if I have not, I care not one jack-straw. So let me recommend you to be polite to our young friend; for upon my word, your next groom may be less appetizing."

And with that he went out, with the chaplain at his heels; and the arras fell behind the pair.

The girl turned upon Denis with flashing eyes.

"And what, sir," she demanded, "may be the meaning of all this?"

"God knows," returned Denis gloomily. "I am a prisoner in this house, which seems full of mad people. More I know not; and nothing do I understand."

"And pray how came you here?" she asked.

He told her as briefly as he could. "For the rest," he added, "perhaps you will follow my example, and tell me the answer to all these riddles, and what, in God's name, is like to be the end of it."

She stood silent for a little, and he could see her lips tremble and her tearless eyes burn with a feverish lustre. Then she pressed her forehead in both hands.

" Alas, how my head aches! " she said wearily—" to
say nothing of my poor heart! But it is due to you
to know my story, unmaidenly as it must seem. I am
called Blanche de Malétroit: I have been without father
or mother for—oh! for as long as I can recollect, and
indeed I have been most unhappy all my life. Three
months ago a young captain began to stand near me
every day in church. I could see that I pleased him; I
am much to blame, but I was so glad that anyone should
love me; and when he passed me a letter, I took it home
with me and read it with great pleasure. Since that time
he has written many. He was so anxious to speak with
me, poor fellow! and kept asking me to leave the door
open some evening that we might have two words upon
the stair. For he knew how much my uncle trusted me."
She gave something like a sob at that, and it was a
moment before she could go on. " My uncle is a hard
man, but he is very shrewd," she said at last. " He has
performed many feats in war, and was a great person at
court, and much trusted by Queen Isabeau in old days.
How he came to suspect me I cannot tell; but it is hard
to keep anything from his knowledge; and this morning,
as we came from mass, he took my hand in his, forced
it open, and read my little billet, walking by my side
all the while. When he had finished, he gave it back
to me with great politeness. It contained another request
to have the door left open; and this has been the ruin
of us all. My uncle kept me strictly in my room until
evening, and then ordered me to dress myself as you see
me—a hard mockery for a young girl; do you not think
so? I suppose, when he could not prevail with me to
tell him the young captain's name, he must have laid a
trap for him: into which, alas! you have fallen in the
anger of God. I looked for much confusion; for how
could I tell whether he was willing to take me for his

wife on these sharp terms? He might have been trifling with me from the first; or I might have made myself too cheap in his eyes. But truly I had not looked for such a shameful punishment as this! I could not think that God would let a girl be so disgraced before a young man. And now I have told you all; and I can scarcely hope that you will not despise me."

Denis made her a respectful inclination.

"Madam," he said, "you have honoured me by your confidence. It remains for me to prove that I am not unworthy of the honour. Is Messire de Malétroit at hand?"

"I believe he is writing in the salle without," she answered.

"May I lead you thither, madam?" asked Denis, offering his hand with his most courtly bearing.

She accepted it; and the pair passed out of the chapel, Blanche in a very drooping and shamefast condition, but Denis strutting and ruffling in the consciousness of a mission, and the boyish certainty of accomplishing it with honour.

The Sire de Malétroit rose to meet them with an ironical obeisance.

"Sir," said Denis, with the grandest possible air, "I believe I am to have some say in the matter of this marriage; and let me tell you at once, I will be no party to forcing the inclination of this young lady. Had it been freely offered to me, I should have been proud to accept her hand, for I perceive she is as good as she is beautiful; but as things are, I have now the honour, messire, of refusing."

Blanche looked at him with gratitude in her eyes; but the old gentleman only smiled and smiled, until his smile grew positively sickening to Denis.

"I am afraid," he said, "Monsieur de Beaulieu, that

you do not perfectly understand the choice I have to offer you. Follow me, I beseech you, to this window." And he led the way to one of the large windows which stood open on the night. "You observe," he went on, "there is an iron ring in the upper masonry, and reeved through that a very efficacious rope. Now, mark my words: if you should find your disinclination to my niece's person insurmountable, I shall have you hanged out of this window before sunrise. I shall only proceed to such an extremity with the greatest regret, you may believe me. For it is not at all your death that I desire, but my niece's establishment in life. At the same time, it must come to that if you prove obstinate. Your family, Monsieur de Beaulieu, is very well in its way; but if you sprang from Charlemagne, you should not refuse the hand of a Malétroit with impunity—not if she had been as common as the Paris road—not if she were as hideous as the gargoyle over my door. Neither my niece nor you, nor my own private feelings, move me at all in this matter. The honour of my house has been compromised; I believe you to be the guilty person; at least you are now in the secret; and you can hardly wonder if I request you to wipe out the stain. If you will not, your blood be on your own head! It will be no great satisfaction to me to have your interesting relics kicking their heels in the breeze below my windows; but half a loaf is better than no bread, and if I cannot cure the dishonour, I shall at least stop the scandal."

There was a pause.

"I believe there are other ways of settling such imbroglios among gentlemen," said Denis. "You wear a sword, and I hear you have used it with distinction."

The Sire de Malétroit made a signal to the chaplain, who crossed the room with long silent strides and raised the arras over the third of the three doors. It was only a moment before he let it fall again; but Denis had time to see a dusky passage full of armed men.

"When I was a little younger, I should have been delighted to honour you, Monsieur de Beaulieu," said Sire Alain; "but I am now too old. Faithful retainers are the sinews of age, and I must employ the strength I have. This is one of the hardest things to swallow as a man grows up in years; but with a little patience, even this becomes habitual. You and the lady seem to prefer the salle for what remains of your two hours; and as I have no desire to cross your preference, I shall resign it to your use with all the pleasure in the world. No haste!" he added, holding up his hand, as he saw a dangerous look come into Denis de Beaulieu's face. "If your mind revolts against hanging, it will be time enough two hours hence to throw yourself out of the window or upon the pikes of my retainers. Two hours of life are always two hours. A great many things may turn up in even as little a while as that. And, besides, if I understand her appearance, my niece has still something to say to you. You will not disfigure your last hours by want of politeness to a lady?"

Denis looked at Blanche, and she made him an imploring gesture.

It is likely that the old gentleman was hugely pleased at this symptom of an understanding; for he smiled on both, and added sweetly: "If you will give me your word of honour, Monsieur de Beaulieu, to await my return at the end of the two hours before attempting anything desperate, I shall withdraw my retainers, and let you speak in greater privacy with mademoiselle."

Denis again glanced at the girl, who seemed to beseech him to agree.

"I give you my word of honour," he said.

Messire de Malétroit bowed, and proceeded to limp about the apartment, clearing his throat the while with that odd musical chirp which had already grown so irritating in the ears of Denis de Beaulieu. He first possessed himself of some papers which lay upon the table; then he went to the mouth of the passage and appeared to give an order to the men behind the arras; and lastly, he hobbled out through the door by which Denis had come in, turning upon the threshold to address a last smiling bow to the young couple, and followed by the chaplain with a hand-lamp.

No sooner were they alone than Blanche advanced towards Denis with her hands extended. Her face was flushed and excited, and her eyes shone with tears.

" You shall not die! " she cried, " you shall marry me after all."

" You seem to think, madam," replied Denis, " that I stand much in fear of death."

" Oh no, no," she said, " I see you are no poltroon. It is for my own sake—I could not bear to have you slain for such a scruple."

" I am afraid," returned Denis, " that you underrate the difficulty, madam. What you may be too generous to refuse, I may be too proud to accept. In a moment of noble feeling towards me, you forgot what you perhaps owe to others."

He had the decency to keep his eyes upon the floor as he said this, and after he had finished, so as not to spy upon her confusion. She stood silent for a moment, then walked suddenly away, and falling on her uncle's chair, fairly burst out sobbing. Denis was in the acme of embarrassment. He looked round, as if to seek for inspiration, and seeing a stool, plumped down upon it for something to do. There he sat, playing with the guard of his rapier, and wishing himself dead a thousand times over, and buried in the nastiest kitchen-heap in France. His eyes wandered round the apartment, but found nothing to arrest them. There were such wide spaces between the furniture, the light fell so baldly and cheerlessly over all, the dark outside air looked in so coldly through the windows, that he thought he had never seen a church so vast, nor a tomb so melancholy. The regular sobs of Blanche de Malétroit measured out the time like the ticking of a clock. He read the device upon the shield over and over again, until his eyes became obscured; he stared into shadowy corners until he imagined they were swarming with horrible animals; and every now and again he awoke with a start, to remember that his last two hours were running, and death was on the march.

Oftener and oftener, as the time went on, did his glance settle on the girl herself. Her face was bowed forward and covered with her hands, and she was shaken at intervals by the convulsive hiccup of grief. Even thus she was not an unpleasant object to dwell upon, so plump and yet so fine, with a warm brown skin, and the most beautiful hair, Denis thought, in the whole world of womankind. Her hands were like her uncle's; but they were more in place at the end of her young arms, and looked infinitely soft and caressing. He remembered how her blue eyes had shone upon him, full of anger, pity, and innocence. And the more he dwelt on her perfections, the uglier death looked, and the more deeply was he smitten with penitence at her continued tears. Now he felt that no man could have the courage to leave a world which contained so beautiful a creature; and now he would have given forty minutes of his last hour to unsay this cruel speech.

Suddenly a hoarse and ragged peal of cockcrow rose to their ears from the dark valley below the windows.

And this shattering noise in the silence of all around was like a light in a dark place, and shook them both out of their reflections.

"Alas, can I do nothing to help you?" she said, looking up.

"Madam," replied Denis, with a fine irrelevancy, "if I have said anything to wound you, believe me, it was for your own sake and not for mine."

She thanked him with a tearful look.

"I feel your position cruelly," he went on. "The world has been bitter hard on you. Your uncle is a disgrace to mankind. Believe me, madam, there is no young gentleman in all France but would be glad of my opportunity, to die in doing you a momentary service."

"I know already that you can be very brave and generous," she answered. "What I *want* to know is whether I can serve you—now or afterwards," she added, with a quaver.

"Most certainly," he answered with a smile. "Let me sit beside you as if I were a friend, instead of a foolish intruder; try to forget how awkwardly we are placed to one another; make my last moments go pleasantly; and you will do me the chief service possible."

"You are very gallant," she added, with a yet deeper sadness . . . "very gallant . . . and it somehow pains me. But draw nearer, if you please; and if you find anything to say to me, you will at least make certain of a very friendly listener. Ah! Monsieur de Beaulieu," she broke forth—"ah! Monsieur de Beaulieu, how can I look you in the face?" And she fell to weeping again with a renewed effusion.

"Madam," said Denis, taking her hand in both of his, "reflect on the little time I have before me, and the great bitterness into which I am cast by the sight of your distress. Spare me, in my last moments, the spectacle of what I cannot cure even with the sacrifice of my life."

"I am very selfish," answered Blanche. "I will be braver, Monsieur de Beaulieu, for your sake. But think if I can do you no kindness in the future—if you have no friends to whom I could carry your adieux. Charge me as heavily as you can; every burden will lighten, by so little, the invaluable gratitude I owe you. Put it in my power to do something more for you than weep."

"My mother is married again, and has a young family to care for. My brother Guichard will inherit my fiefs; and if I am not in error, that will content him amply for my death. Life is a little vapour that passeth away, as we are told by those in holy orders. When a man is in a fair way and sees all life open in front of him, he seems to himself to make a very important figure in the world. His horse whinnies to him; the trumpets blow and the girls look out of window as he rides into town before his company; he receives many assurances of trust and regard—sometimes by express in a letter—sometimes face to face, with persons of great consequence falling on his neck. It is not wonderful if his head is turned for a time. But once he is dead, were he as brave as Hercules or as wise as Solomon, he is soon forgotten. It is not ten years since my father fell, with many other knights around him, in a very fierce encounter, and I do not think that any one of them, nor so much as the name of the fight, is now remembered. No, no, madam, the nearer you come to it, you see that death is a dark and dusty corner, where a man gets into his tomb and has the door shut after him till the Judgment Day. I have few friends just now, and once I am dead I shall have none."

"Ah, Monsieur de Beaulieu!" she exclaimed, "you forget Blanche de Malétroit."

"You have a sweet nature, madam, and you are pleased to estimate a little service far beyond its worth."

"It is not that," she answered. "You mistake me if you think I am so easily touched by my own concerns. I say so, because you are the noblest man I have ever met; because I recognize in you a spirit that would have made even a common person famous in the land."

"And yet here I die in a mousetrap—with no more noise about it than my own squeaking," answered he.

A look of pain crossed her face, and she was silent for a little while. Then a light came into her eyes, and with a smile she spoke again.

"I cannot have my champion think meanly of himself. Anyone who gives his life for another will be met in Paradise by all the heralds and angels of the Lord God. And you have no such cause to hang your head. For . . . Pray, do you think me beautiful?" she asked, with a deep flush.

"Indeed, madam, I do," he said.

"I am glad of that," she answered heartily. "Do you think there are many men in France who have been asked in marriage by a beautiful maiden—with her own lips—and who have refused her to her face? I know you men would half despise such a triumph; but believe me, we women know more of what is precious in love. There is nothing that should set a person higher in his own esteem; and we women would prize nothing more dearly."

"You are very good," he said; "but you cannot make me forget that I was asked in pity and not for love."

"I am not so sure of that," she replied, holding down her head. "Hear me to an end, Monsieur de Beaulieu. I know how you must despise me; I feel you are right to do so; I am too poor a creature to occupy one thought of your mind, although, alas! you must die for me this morning. But when I asked you to marry me, indeed, and indeed, it was because I respected and admired you, and loved you with my whole soul, from the very moment that you took my part against my uncle. If you had seen yourself, and how noble you looked, you would pity rather than despise me. And now," she went on, hurriedly checking him with her hand, "although I have laid aside all reserve and told you so much, remember that I know your sentiments towards me already. I would not, believe me, being nobly born, weary you with importunities into consent. I too have a pride of my own: and I declare before the holy mother of God, if you should now go back from your word already given, I would no more marry you than I would marry my uncle's groom."

Denis smiled a little bitterly.

"It is a small love," he said, "that shies at a little pride."

She made no answer, although she probably had her own thoughts.

"Come hither to the window," he said, with a sigh. "Here is the dawn."

And indeed the dawn was already beginning. The hollow of the sky was full of essential daylight, colourless and clean; and the valley underneath was flooded with a grey reflection. A few thin vapours clung in the coves of the forest or lay along the winding course of the river. The scene disengaged a surprising effect of stillness, which was hardly interrupted when the cocks began once more to crow among the steadings. Perhaps the same fellow who had made so horrid a clangour in the darkness not half an hour before, now sent up the merriest cheer to greet the coming day. A little wind went bustling and eddying among the tree-tops underneath the windows. And still the daylight kept flooding insensibly out of the east, which was soon to grow incandescent and cast up that red-hot cannonball, the rising sun.

Denis looked out over all this with a bit of a shiver. He had taken her hand and retained it in his almost unconsciously.

"Has the day begun already?" she said; and then, illogically enough: "the night has been so long! Alas! what shall we say to my uncle when he returns?"

"What you will," said Denis, and he pressed her fingers in his.

She was silent.

"Blanche," he said, with a swift, uncertain, passionate utterance, "you have seen whether I fear death. You must know well enough that I would as gladly leap out of that window into the empty air as lay a finger on you without your free and full consent. But if you care for me at all, do not let me lose my life in a misapprehension; for I love you better than the whole world; and though I will die for you blithely, it would be like all the joys of Paradise to live on and spend my life in your service."

As he stopped speaking, a bell began to ring loudly in the interior of the house; and a clatter of armour in the corridor showed that the retainers were returning to their post, and the two hours were at an end.

"After all that you have heard?" she whispered, leaning towards him with her lips and eyes.

"I have heard nothing," he replied.

"The captain's name was Florimond de Champ-divers," she said in his ear.

"I did not hear it," he answered, taking her supple body in his arms, and covered her wet face with kisses.

A melodious chirping was audible behind, followed by a beautiful chuckle, and the voice of Messire de Malé-troit wished his new nephew a good morning.

R. L. STEVENSON—the magazine *Temple Bar*.

THE THREE STRANGERS

AMONG the few features of agricultural England which retain an appearance but little modified by the lapse of centuries, may be reckoned the high, grassy and furzy downs, coombs, or ewe-leases, as they are indifferently called, that fill a large area of certain counties in the south and south-west. If any mark of human occupation is met with hereon, it usually takes the form of the solitary cottage of some shepherd.

Fifty years ago such a lonely cottage stood on such a down, and may possibly be standing there now. In spite of its loneliness, however, the spot, by actual measurement, was not more than five miles from a county-town. Yet that affected it little. Five miles of irregular upland, during the long inimical seasons, with their sleets, snows, rains, and mists, afford withdrawing space enough to isolate a Timon or a Nebuchadnezzar; much less, in fair weather, to please that less repellent tribe, the poets, philosophers, artists, and others who " conceive and meditate of pleasant things."

Some old earthen camp or barrow, some clump of trees, at least some starved fragment of ancient hedge is usually taken advantage of in the erection of these forlorn dwellings. But, in the present case, such a kind of shelter had been disregarded. Higher Crowstairs, as the house was called, stood quite detached and undefended. The only reason for its precise situation seemed to be the crossing of two footpaths at right-angles hard by, which may have crossed there and thus for a good five hundred years. Hence the house was exposed to the elements on all sides. But, though the wind up here blew unmistakably when it did blow, and the rain hit hard whenever it fell, the various weathers of the winter season were not quite so formidable on the coomb as they were imagined to be by dwellers on low ground. The raw rimes were not so pernicious as in the hollows, and the frosts were scarcely so severe. When the shepherd and his family who tenanted the house were pitied for their sufferings from the exposure, they said that upon the whole they were less inconvenienced by " wuzzes and flames " (hoarses and phlegms) than when they had lived by the stream of a snug neighbouring valley.

The night of March 28, 182–, was precisely one of the nights that were wont to call forth these expressions of commiseration. The level rainstorm smote walls, slopes, and hedges like the clothyard shafts of Senlac and Crecy. Such sheep and outdoor animals as had no shelter stood with their buttocks to the winds; while the tails of little birds trying to roost on some scraggy thorn were blown inside-out like umbrellas. The gable-end of the cottage was stained with wet, and the eavesdroppings flapped against the wall. Yet never was commiseration for the shepherd more misplaced. For that cheerful rustic was entertaining a large party in glorification of the christening of his second girl.

The guests had arrived before the rain began to fall, and they were all now assembled in the chief or living-room of the dwelling. A glance into the apartment at eight o'clock on this eventful evening would have resulted in the opinion that it was as cosy and comfortable a nook as could be wished for in boisterous weather. The calling of its inhabitant was proclaimed by a number of highly polished sheep-crooks without stems that were hung ornamentally over the fireplace, the curl of each shining crook varying from the antiquated type engraved in the patriarchal pictures of old family Bibles to the most approved fashion of the last local sheep-fair. The room was lighted by half a dozen candles, having wicks only a trifle smaller than the grease which enveloped them, in candlesticks that were never used but at high-days, holy-days, and family feasts. The lights were scattered about the room, two of them standing on the chimney-piece. This position of candles was in itself significant. Candles on the chimney-piece always meant a party.

On the hearth, in front of a back-brand to give substance, blazed a fire of thorns, that crackled "like the laughter of the fool."

Nineteen persons were gathered here. Of these, five women, wearing gowns of various bright hues, sat in chairs along the wall; girls shy and not shy filled the window-bench; four men, including Charley Jake the hedge-carpenter, Elijah New the parish-clerk, and John Pitcher, a neighbouring dairyman, the shepherd's father-in-law, lolled in the settle; a young man and maid, who were blushing over tentative *pourparlers* on a life-companionship, sat beneath the corner-cupboard; and an elderly engaged man of fifty or upward moved restlessly about from spots where his betrothed was not to the spot where she was. Enjoyment was pretty general, and so much the more prevailed in being unhampered by conventional restrictions. Absolute confidence in each other's good opinion begat perfect ease, while the finishing stroke of manner, amounting to a truly princely serenity, was lent to the majority by the absence of any expression or trait denoting that they wished to get on in the world, enlarge their minds, or do any eclipsing thing whatever—which nowadays so generally nips the bloom and *bonhomie* of all except the two extremes of the social scale.

Shepherd Fennel had married well, his wife being a dairyman's daughter from a vale at a distance, who brought fifty guineas in her pocket—and kept them there, till they should be required for ministering to the needs of a coming family. This frugal woman had been somewhat exercised as to the character that should be given to the gathering. A sit-still party had its advantages; but an undisturbed position of ease in chairs and settles was apt to lead on the men to such an unconscionable deal of toping that they would sometimes fairly drink the house dry. A dancing-party was the alternative; but this, while avoiding the foregoing objection on the score of good drink, had a counterbalancing disadvantage in the matter of good victuals, the ravenous appetites engendered by the exercise causing immense havoc in the buttery. Shepherdess Fennel fell back upon the intermediate plan of mingling short dances with short periods of talk and singing, so as to hinder any ungovernable rage in either. But this scheme was entirely confined to her own gentle mind: the shepherd himself was in the mood to exhibit the most reckless phases of hospitality.

The fiddler was a boy of those parts, about twelve years of age, who had a wonderful dexterity in jigs and reels, though his fingers were so small and short as to necessitate a constant shifting for the high notes, from which he scrambled back to the first position with sounds not of unmixed purity of tone. At seven the shrill tweedle-dee of this youngster had begun, accompanied by a booming ground-bass from Elijah New, the parish-clerk, who had thoughtfully brought with him his favourite musical instrument, the serpent. Dancing was instantaneous, Mrs. Fennel privately enjoining the players on no account to let the dance exceed the length of a quarter of an hour.

But Elijah and the boy, in the excitement of their position, quite forgot the injunction. Moreover, Oliver Giles, a man of seventeen, one of the dancers, who was enamoured of his partner, a fair girl of thirty-three rolling years, had recklessly handed a new crown-piece to the musicians, as a bribe to keep going as long as they had muscle and wind. Mrs. Fennel, seeing the steam begin to generate on the countenances of her guests, crossed over and touched the fiddler's elbow and put her hand on the serpent's mouth. But they took no notice, and fearing she might lose her character of genial hostess if she were to interfere too markedly, she retired and sat down helpless. And so the dance whizzed on with cumulative fury, the performers moving in their planet-like courses, direct and retrograde, from apogee to perigee, till the hand of the well-kicked clock at the bottom of the room had travelled over the circumference of an hour.

While these cheerful events were in course of enactment within Fennel's pastoral dwelling, an incident having considerable bearing on the party had occurred in the gloomy night without. Mrs. Fennel's concern about the growing fierceness of the dance corresponded in point of time with the ascent of a human figure to the solitary hill of Higher Crowstairs from the direction of the distant town. This personage strode on through the rain without a pause, following the little-worn path which, farther on in its course, skirted the shepherd's cottage.

It was nearly the time of full moon, and on this account, though the sky was lined with a uniform sheet of dripping cloud, ordinary objects out of doors were readily visible. The sad wan light revealed the lonely pedestrian to be a man of supple frame; his gait suggested that he had somewhat passed the period of perfect and instinctive agility, though not so far as to be otherwise than rapid of motion when occasion required. At a rough guess, he might have been about forty years of age. He appeared tall, but a recruiting sergeant, or other person accustomed to the judging of men's heights by the eye, would have discerned that this was chiefly owing to his gauntness, and that he was not more than five feet eight or nine.

Notwithstanding the regularity of his tread, there was caution in it, as in that of one who mentally feels his way; and despite the fact that it was not a black coat nor a dark garment of any sort that he wore, there was something about him which suggested that he naturally belonged to the black-coated tribes of men. His clothes were of fustian, and his boots hobnailed, yet in his progress he showed not the mud-accustomed bearing of hobnailed and fustianed peasantry.

By the time that he had arrived abreast of the shepherd's premises the rain came down, or rather came along, with yet more determined violence. The outskirts of the little settlement partially broke the force of wind and rain, and this induced him to stand still. The most salient of the shepherd's domestic erections was an empty sty at the forward corner of his hedgeless garden, for in these latitudes the principle of masking the homelier features of your establishment by a conventional frontage was unknown. The traveller's eye was attracted to this small building by the pallid shine of the wet slates that covered it. He turned aside, and, finding it empty, stood under the pent-roof for shelter.

While he stood, the boom of the serpent within the adjacent house, and the lesser strains of the fiddler, reached the spot as an accompaniment to the surging hiss of the flying rain on the sod, its louder beating on the cabbage-leaves of the garden, on the eight or ten beehives just discernible by the path, and its dripping from the eaves into a row of buckets and pans that had been placed under the walls of the cottage. For at Higher Crowstairs, as at all such elevated domiciles, the grand difficulty of housekeeping was an insufficiency of water; and a casual rainfall was utilized by turning out, as catchers, every utensil that the house contained. Some queer stories might be told of the contrivances for economy in suds and dish-waters that are absolutely necessitated in upland habitations during the droughts of summer. But at this season there were no such exigencies; a mere acceptance of what the skies bestowed was sufficient for an abundant store.

At last the notes of the serpent ceased and the house was silent. This cessation of activity aroused the solitary pedestrian from the reverie into which he had lapsed, and, emerging from the shed, with an apparently new intention, he walked up the path to the house-door. Arrived here, his first act was to kneel down on a large stone beside the row of vessels, and to drink a copious draught from one of them. Having quenched his thirst he rose and lifted his hand to knock, but paused with his eye upon the panel. Since the dark surface of the wood revealed absolutely nothing, it was evident that he must be mentally looking through the door, as if he wished to measure thereby all the possibilities that a house of this sort might include, and how they might bear upon the question of his entry.

In his indecision he turned and surveyed the scene around. Not a soul was anywhere visible. The garden-path stretched downward from his feet, gleaming like the track of a snail; the roof of the little well (mostly dry), the well-cover, the top rail of the garden-gate, were varnished with the same dull liquid glaze; while, far away in the vale, a faint whiteness of more than usual extent showed that the rivers were high in the meads. Beyond all this winked a few bleared lamplights through the beating drops—lights that denoted the situation of the county-town from which he had appeared to come. The absence of all notes of life in that direction seemed to clinch his intentions, and he knocked at the door.

Within, a desultory chat had taken the place of movement and musical sound. The hedge-carpenter was suggesting a song to the company, which nobody just then was inclined to undertake, so that the knock afforded a not unwelcome diversion.

" Walk in! " said the shepherd promptly.

The latch clicked upward, and out of the night our pedestrian appeared upon the door-mat. The shepherd arose, snuffed two of the nearest candles, and turned to look at him.

Their light disclosed that the stranger was dark in complexion and not unprepossessing as to feature. His hat, which for a moment he did not remove, hung low over his eyes, without concealing that they were large, open, and determined, moving with a flash rather than a glance round the room. He seemed pleased with his survey, and, baring his shaggy head, said, in a rich deep voice, " The rain is so heavy, friends, that I ask leave to come in and rest awhile."

" To be sure, stranger," said the shepherd. " And faith, you've been lucky in choosing your time, for we are having a bit of a fling for a glad cause—though, to be sure, a man could hardly wish that glad cause to happen more than once a year."

" Nor less," spoke up a woman. " For 'tis best to get your family over and done with, as soon as you can, so as to be all the earlier out of the fag o't."

"And what may be this glad cause?" asked the stranger.

"A birth and christening," said the shepherd.

The stranger hoped his host might not be made unhappy either by too many or too few of such episodes, and being invited by a gesture to pull at the mug, he readily acquiesced. His manner, which, before entering, had been so dubious, was now altogether that of a careless and candid man.

"Late to be traipsing athwart this coomb—hey?" said the engaged man of fifty.

"Late it is, master, as you say.—I'll take a seat in the chimney-corner, if you have nothing to urge against it, ma'am; for I am a little moist on the side that was next the rain."

Mrs. Shepherd Fennel assented, and made room for the self-invited comer, who, having got completely inside the chimney-corner, stretched out his legs and his arms with the expansiveness of a person quite at home.

"Yes, I am rather cracked in the vamp," he said freely, seeing that the eyes of the shepherd's wife fell upon his boots, "and I am not well fitted either. I have had some rough times lately, and have been forced to pick up what I can get in the way of wearing, but I must find a suit better fit for working-days when I reach home."

"One of hereabouts?" she inquired.

"Not quite that—farther up the country."

"I thought so. And so be I; and by your tongue you come from my neighbourhood."

"But you would hardly have heard of me," he said quickly. "My time would be long before yours, ma'am, you see."

This testimony to the youthfulness of his hostess had the effect of stopping her cross-examination.

"There is only one thing more wanted to make me happy," continued the new-comer. "And that is a little baccy, which I am sorry to say I am out of."

"I'll fill your pipe," said the shepherd.

"I must ask you to lend me a pipe likewise."

"A smoker, and no pipe about 'ee?"

"I have dropped it somewhere on the road."

The shepherd filled and handed him a new clay pipe, saying, as he did so, "Hand me your baccy-box—I'll fill that too, now I am about it."

The man went through the movement of searching his pockets.

"Lost that too?" said his entertainer, with some surprise.

"I am afraid so," said the man with some confusion. "Give it to me in a screw of paper." Lighting his pipe at the candle with a suction that drew the whole flame into the bowl, he resettled himself in the corner and bent his looks upon the faint steam from his damp legs, as if he wished to say no more.

Meanwhile the general body of guests had been taking little notice of this visitor by reason of an absorbing discussion in which they were engaged with the band about a tune for the next dance. The matter being settled, they were about to stand up when an interruption came in the shape of another knock at the door.

At the sound of the same the man in the chimney-corner took up the poker and began stirring the brands as if doing it thoroughly were the one aim of his existence; and a second time the shepherd said, "Walk in!" In a moment another man stood upon the straw-woven door-mat. He too was a stranger.

This individual was one of a type radically different from the first. There was more of the commonplace in his manner, and a certain jovial cosmopolitanism sat upon his features. He was several years older than the first arrival, his hair being slightly frosted, his eyebrows bristly, and his whiskers cut back from his cheeks. His face was rather full and flabby, and yet it was not altogether a face without power. A few grog-blossoms marked the neighbourhood of his nose. He flung back his long drab greatcoat, revealing that beneath it he wore a suit of cinder-grey shade throughout, large heavy seals, of some metal or other that would take a polish, dangling from his fob as his only personal ornament. Shaking the water-drops from his low-crowned glazed hat, he said, "I must ask for a few minutes' shelter, comrades, or I shall be wetted to my skin before I get to Casterbridge."

"Make yourself at home, master," said the shepherd, perhaps a trifle less heartily than on the first occasion. Not that Fennel had the least tinge of niggardliness in his composition; but the room was far from large, spare chairs were not numerous, and damp companions were not altogether desirable at close quarters for the women and girls in their bright-coloured gowns.

However, the second comer, after taking off his great-coat, and hanging his hat on a nail in one of the ceiling-beams as if he had been specially invited to put it there, advanced and sat down at the table. This had been pushed so closely into the chimney-corner, to give all available room to the dancers, that its inner edge grazed the elbow of the man who had ensconced himself by the fire; and thus the two strangers were brought into close companionship. They nodded to each other by way of breaking the ice of unacquaintance, and the first stranger handed his neighbour the family mug—a huge vessel of brown ware, having its upper edge worn away like a threshold by the rub of whole generations of thirsty lips that had gone the way of all flesh, and bearing the following inscription burnt upon its rotund side in yellow letters:

THERE IS NO FUN .
UNTILL i CUM

The other man, nothing loth, raised the mug to his lips, and drank on, and on, and on, and on—till a curious blueness overspread the countenance of the shepherd's wife, who had regarded with no little surprise the first stranger's free offer to the second of what did not belong to him to dispense.

"I knew it!" said the toper to the shepherd with much satisfaction. "When I walked up your garden before coming in, and saw the hives all of a row, I said to myself, 'Where there's bees there's honey, and where there's honey there's mead.' But mead of such a truly comfortable sort as this I really didn't expect to meet in my older days." He took yet another pull at the mug, till it assumed an ominous elevation.

"Glad you enjoy it!" said the shepherd warmly.

"It is goodish mead," assented Mrs. Fennel, with an absence of enthusiasm which seemed to say that it was possible to buy praise for one's cellar at too heavy a price. "It is trouble enough to make—and really I hardly think we shall make any more. For honey sells well, and we ourselves can make shift with a drop o' small mead and metheglin for common use from the comb-washings."

"Oh, but you'll never have the heart!" reproachfully cried the stranger in cinder-grey, after taking up the mug a third time and setting it down empty. "I love mead, when 'tis old like this, as I love to go to church o' Sundays, or to relieve the needy any day of the week."

"Ha, ha, ha!" said the man in the chimney-corner, who, in spite of the taciturnity induced by the pipe of

F*

tobacco, could not or would not refrain from this slight testimony to his comrade's humour.

Now the old mead of those days, brewed of the purest first-year or maiden honey, four pounds to the gallon— with its due complement of white of eggs, cinnamon, ginger, cloves, mace, rosemary, yeast, and processes of working, bottling, and cellaring—tasted remarkably strong; but it did not taste so strong as it actually was. Hence, presently, the stranger in cinder-grey at the table, moved by its creeping influence, unbuttoned his waist-coat, threw himself back in his chair, spread his legs, and made his presence felt in various ways.

"Well, well, as I say," he resumed, "I am going to Casterbridge, and to Casterbridge I must go. I should have been almost there by this time; but the rain drove me into your dwelling, and I'm not sorry for it."

"You don't live in Casterbridge?" said the shepherd.

"Not as yet; though I shortly mean to move there."

"Going to set up in trade, perhaps?"

"No, no," said the shepherd's wife. "It is easy to see that the gentleman is rich, and don't want to work at anything."

The cinder-grey stranger paused, as if to consider whether he would accept that definition of himself. He presently rejected it by answering, "Rich is not quite the word for me, dame. I do work, and I must work. And even if I only get to Casterbridge by midnight I must begin work there at eight to-morrow morning. Yes, het or wet, blow or snow, famine or sword, my day's work to-morrow must be done."

"Poor man! Then, in spite o' seeming, you be worse off than we?" replied the shepherd's wife.

"'Tis the nature of my trade, men and maidens. 'Tis the nature of my trade more than my poverty. . . . But really and truly I must up and off, or I shan't get a lodging in the town." However, the speaker did not move, and directly added, "There's time for one more draught of friendship before I go; and I'd perform it at once if the mug were not dry."

"Here's a mug o' small," said Mrs. Fennel. "Small, we call it, though to be sure 'tis only the first wash o' the combs."

"No," said the stranger disdainfully. "I won't spoil your first kindness by partaking o' your second."

"Certainly not," broke in Fennel. "We don't increase and multiply every day, and I'll fill the mug again." He went away to the dark place under the stairs where the barrel stood. The shepherdess followed him.

"Why should you do this?" she said reproachfully, as soon as they were alone. "He's emptied it once, though it held enough for ten people; and now he's not contented wi' the small, but must needs call for more o' the strong! And a stranger unbeknown to any of us. For my part, I don't like the look o' the man at all."

"But he's in the house, my honey; and 'tis a wet night and a christening. Daze it, what's a cup of mead more or less? There'll be plenty more next bee-burning."

"Very well—this time, then," she answered, looking wistfully at the barrel. "But what is the man's calling, and where is he one of, that he should come in and join us like this?"

"I don't know. I'll ask him again."

The catastrophe of having the mug drained dry at one pull by the stranger in cinder-grey was effectually guarded against this time by Mrs. Fennel. She poured out his allowance in a small cup, keeping the large one at a discreet distance from him. When he had tossed off his portion the shepherd renewed his inquiry about the stranger's occupation.

The latter did not immediately reply, and the man in the chimney-corner, with sudden demonstrativeness, said, "Anybody may know my trade—I'm a wheel-wright."

"A very good trade for these parts," said the shepherd.

"And anybody may know mine—if they've the sense to find it out," said the stranger in cinder-grey.

"You may generally tell what a man is by his claws," observed the hedge-carpenter, looking at his own hands. "My fingers be as full of thorns as an old pin-cushion is of pins."

The hands of the man in the chimney-corner instinctively sought the shade, and he gazed into the fire as he resumed his pipe. The man at the table took up the hedge-carpenter's remark, and added smartly, "True; but the oddity of my trade is that, instead of setting a mark upon me, it sets a mark upon my customers."

No observation being offered by anybody in elucidation of this enigma, the shepherd's wife once more called for a song. The same obstacles presented themselves as at the former time—one had no voice, another had forgotten the first verse. The stranger at the table, whose soul had now risen to a good working temperature, relieved the difficulty by exclaiming that, to start the company, he would sing himself. Thrusting one thumb into the arm-hole of his waistcoat, he waved the other hand in the air, and, with an extemporizing gaze at the shining sheep-crooks above the mantelpiece, began:

"O my trade it is the rarest one,
　　　　　　　Simple shepherds all—
　　My trade is a sight to see;
For my customers I tie, and take them up on high,
　　And waft 'em to a far countree!"

The room was silent when he had finished the verse—
with one exception, that of the man in the chimney-
corner, who, at the singer's word, "Chorus!" joined
him in a deep bass voice of musical relish—

"And waft 'em to a far countree!"

Oliver Giles, John Pitcher the dairyman, the parish-
clerk, the engaged man of fifty, the row of young
women against the wall, seemed lost in thought not of
the gayest kind. The shepherd looked meditatively on
the ground, the shepherdess gazed keenly at the singer,
and with some suspicion; she was doubting whether
this stranger were merely singing an old song from
recollection, or was composing one there and then for
the occasion. All were as perplexed at the obscure reve-
lation as the guests at Belshazzar's Feast, except the man
in the chimney-corner, who quietly said, "Second verse,
stranger," and smoked on.

The singer thoroughly moistened himself from his
lips inwards, and went on with the next stanza as
requested:

"My tools are but common ones,
        Simple shepherds all—
  My tools are no sight to see:
A little hempen string, and a post whereon to swing,
  Are implements enough for me!"

Shepherd Fennel glanced round. There was no longer
any doubt that the stranger was answering his question
rhythmically. The guests one and all started back with
suppressed exclamations. The young woman engaged
to the man of fifty fainted half-way, and would have
proceeded, but finding him wanting in alacrity for catch-
ing her she sat down trembling.

"Oh, he's the ——! " whispered the people in the background, mentioning the name of an ominous public officer. "He's come to do it! 'Tis to be at Casterbridge jail to-morrow—the man for sheep-stealing—the poor clock-maker we heard of, who used to live away at Shottsford and had no work to do—Timothy Summers, whose family were a-starving, and so he went out of Shottsford by the high-road, and took a sheep in open daylight, defying the farmer and the farmer's wife and the farmer's lad, and every man jack among 'em. He " (and they nodded towards the stranger of the deadly trade) " is come from up the country to do it because there's not enough to do in his own county-town, and he's got the place here now our own county man's dead; he's going to live in the same cottage under the prison wall."

The stranger in cinder-grey took no notice of this whispered string of observations, but again wetted his lips. Seeing that his friend in the chimney-corner was the only one who reciprocated his joviality in any way, he held out his cup towards that appreciative comrade, who also held out his own. They clinked together, the eyes of the rest of the room hanging upon the singer's actions. He parted his lips for the third verse; but at that moment another knock was audible upon the door. This time the knock was faint and hesitating.

The company seemed scared; the shepherd looked with consternation towards the entrance, and it was with some effort that he resisted his alarmed wife's deprecatory glance, and uttered for the third time the welcoming words, " Walk in! "

The door was gently opened, and another man stood upon the mat. He, like those who had preceded him, was a stranger. This time it was a short, small personage, of fair complexion, and dressed in a decent suit of dark clothes.

" Can you tell me the way to ——? " he began : when, gazing round the room to observe the nature of the company amongst whom he had fallen, his eyes lighted on the stranger in cinder-grey. It was just at the instant when the latter, who had thrown his mind into his song with such a will that he scarcely heeded the interruption, silenced all whispers and inquiries by bursting into his third verse:

> " To-morrow is my working day,
> > > Simple shepherds all—
> To-morrow is a working day for me:
> For the farmer's sheep is slain, and the lad who did it ta'en,
> > And on his soul may God ha' merc-y! "

The stranger in the chimney-corner, waving cups with the singer so heartily that his mead splashed over on the hearth, repeated in his bass voice as before:

> " And on his soul may God ha' merc-y! "

All this time the third stranger had been standing in the doorway. Finding now that he did not come forward or go on speaking, the guests particularly regarded him. They noticed to their surprise that he stood before them the picture of abject terror—his knees trembling, his hand shaking so violently that the door-latch by which he supported himself rattled audibly : his white lips were parted, and his eyes fixed on the merry officer of justice in the middle of the room. A moment more and he had turned, closed the door, and fled.

" What a man can it be? " said the shepherd.

The rest, between the awfulness of their late discovery and the odd conduct of this third visitor, looked as if they knew not what to think, and said nothing. Instinctively they withdrew farther and farther from the grim gentleman in their midst, whom some of them seemed to take for the Prince of Darkness himself, till they formed a remote circle, an empty space of floor being left between them and him—

"... circulus, cujus centrum diabolus."

The room was so silent—though there were more than twenty people in it—that nothing could be heard but the patter of the rain against the window-shutters, accompanied by the occasional hiss of a stray drop that fell down the chimney into the fire, and the steady puffing of the man in the corner, who had now resumed his pipe of long clay.

The stillness was unexpectedly broken. The distant sound of a gun reverberated through the air—apparently from the direction of the county-town.

"Be jiggered!" cried the stranger who had sung the song, jumping up.

"What does that mean?" asked several.

"A prisoner escaped from the jail—that's what it means."

All listened. The sound was repeated, and none of them spoke but the man in the chimney-corner, who said quietly, "I've often been told that in this county they fire a gun at such times; but I never heard it till now."

"I wonder if it is *my* man?" murmured the personage in cinder-grey.

"Surely it is!" said the shepherd involuntarily. "And surely we've zeed him! That little man who looked in at the door by now, and quivered like a leaf when he zeed ye and heard your song!"

164

"His teeth chattered, and the breath went out of his body," said the dairyman.

"And his heart seemed to sink within him like a stone," said Oliver Giles.

"And he bolted as if he'd been shot at," said the hedge-carpenter.

"True—his teeth chattered, and his heart seemed to sink; and he bolted as if he'd been shot at," summed up the man in the chimney-corner.

"I didn't notice it," remarked the hangman.

"We were all a-wondering what made him run off in such a fright," faltered one of the women against the wall, "and now 'tis explained!"

The firing of the alarm-gun went on at intervals, low and sullenly, and their suspicions became a certainty. The sinister gentleman in cinder-grey roused himself. "Is there a constable here?" he asked, in thick tones. "If so, let him step forward."

The engaged man of fifty stepped quavering out from the wall, his betrothed beginning to sob on the back of the chair.

"You are a sworn constable?"

"I be, sir."

"Then pursue the criminal at once, with assistance, and bring him back here. He can't have gone far."

"I will, sir, I will—when I've got my staff. I'll go home and get it, and come sharp here, and start in a body."

"Staff!—never mind your staff; the man'll be gone!"

"But I can't do nothing without my staff—can I, William, and John, and Charles Jake? No; for there's the king's royal crown a painted on en in yaller and gold, and the lion and the unicorn, so as when I raise en up and hit my prisoner, 'tis made a lawful blow thereby. I wouldn't 'tempt to take up a man without my staff—

no, not I. If I hadn't the law to gie me courage, why, instead o' my taking up him he might take up me! "

"Now, I'm a king's man myself, and can give you authority enough for this," said the formidable officer in grey. "Now then, all of ye, be ready. Have ye any lanterns? "

"Yes—have ye any lanterns?—I demand it! " said the constable.

"And the rest of you able-bodied——"

"Able-bodied men—yes—the rest of ye! " said the constable.

"Have you some good stout staves and pitch-forks——"

"Staves and pitchforks—in the name o' the law! And take 'em in yer hands and go in quest, and do as we in authority tell ye! "

Thus aroused, the men prepared to give chase. The evidence was, indeed, though circumstantial, so convincing, that but little argument was needed to show the shepherd's guests that after what they had seen it would look very much like connivance if they did not instantly pursue the unhappy third stranger, who could not as yet have gone more than a few hundred yards over such uneven country.

The shepherd is always well provided with lanterns; and, lighting these hastily, and with hurdle-staves in their hands, they poured out of the door, taking a direction along the crest of the hill, away from the town, the rain having fortunately a little abated.

Disturbed by the noise, or possibly by unpleasant dreams of her baptism, the child who had been christened began to cry heart-brokenly in the room overhead. These notes of grief came down through the chinks of the floor to the ears of the women below, who jumped up one by one, and seemed glad of the excuse to ascend and comfort the baby, for the incidents of the last half-hour greatly oppressed them. Thus in the space of two or three minutes the room on the ground floor was deserted quite.

But it was not for long. Hardly had the sound of footsteps died away when a man returned round the corner of the house from the direction the pursuers had taken. Peeping in at the door, and seeing nobody there, he entered leisurely. It was the stranger of the chimney-corner, who had gone out with the rest. The motive of his return was shown by his helping himself to a cut piece of skimmer-cake that lay on a ledge beside where he had sat, and which he had apparently forgotten to take with him. He also poured out half a cup more mead from the quantity that remained, ravenously eating and drinking these as he stood. He had not finished when another figure came in just as quietly—his friend in cinder-grey.

"Oh—you here?" said the latter, smiling. "I thought you had gone to help in the capture." And this speaker also revealed the object of his return by looking solicitously round for the fascinating mug of old mead.

"And I thought you had gone," said the other, continuing his skimmer-cake with some effort.

"Well, on second thoughts, I felt there were enough without me," said the first confidentially, "and such a night as it is, too. Besides, 'tis the business o' the Government to take care of its criminals—not mine."

"True; so it is. And I felt as you did, that there were enough without me."

"I don't want to break my limbs running over the humps and hollows of this wild country."

"Nor I neither, between you and me."

"These shepherd-people are used to it—simple-minded souls, you know, stirred up to anything in a moment.

They'll have him ready for me before the morning, and
no trouble to me at all."

"They'll have him, and we shall have saved ourselves
all labour in the matter."

"True, true. Well, my way is to Casterbridge; and
'tis as much as my legs will do to take me that far.
Going the same way?"

"No, I am sorry to say! I have to get home over
there" (he nodded indefinitely to the right), "and I feel
as you do, that it is quite enough for my legs to do
before bedtime."

The other had by this time finished the mead in the
mug, after which, shaking hands heartily at the door,
and wishing each other well, they went their several
ways.

In the meantime the company of pursuers had reached
the end of the hog's-back elevation which dominated
this part of the down. They had decided on no particular plan of action; and, finding that the man of the
baleful trade was no longer in their company, they
seemed quite unable to form any such plan now. They
descended in all directions down the hill, and straight-
way several of the party fell into the snare set by Nature
for all misguided midnight ramblers over this part of
the cretaceous formation. The "lanchets," or flint
slopes, which belted the escarpment at intervals of a
dozen yards, took the less cautious ones unawares, and
losing their footing on the rubbly steep they slid sharply
downwards, the lanterns rolling from their hands to the
bottom, and there lying on their sides till the horn was
scorched through.

When they had again gathered themselves together,
the shepherd, as the man who knew the country best,
took the lead, and guided them round these treacherous
inclines. The lanterns, which seemed rather to dazzle

their eyes and warn the fugitive than to assist them in their exploration, were extinguished, due silence was observed; and in this more rational order they plunged into the vale. It was a grassy, briery, moist defile, affording some shelter to any person who had sought it; but the party perambulated it in vain, and ascended on the other side. Here they wandered apart, and after an interval closed together again to report progress. At the second time of closing in they found themselves near a lonely ash, the single tree on this part of the coomb, probably sown there by a passing bird some fifty years before. And here, standing a little to one side of the trunk, as motionless as the trunk itself, appeared the man they were in quest of, his outline being well defined against the sky beyond. The band noiselessly drew up and faced him.

" Your money or your life! " said the constable sternly to the still figure.

" No, no," whispered John Pitcher. " 'Tisn't our side ought to say that. That's the doctrine of vagabonds like him, and we be on the side of the law."

" Well, well," replied the constable impatiently; " I must say something, mustn't I? and if you had all the weight o' this undertaking upon your mind, perhaps you'd say the wrong thing too!—Prisoner at the bar, surrender, in the name of the Father—the Crown, I mane! "

The man under the tree seemed now to notice them for the first time, and, giving them no opportunity whatever for exhibiting their courage, he strolled slowly towards them. He was, indeed, the little man, the third stranger; but his trepidation had in a great measure gone.

" Well, travellers," he said, " did I hear ye speak to me? "

"You did: you've got to come and be our prisoner at once!" said the constable. "We arrest 'ee on the charge of not biding in Casterbridge jail in a decent proper manner to be hung to-morrow morning. Neighbours, do your duty, and seize the culpet!"

On hearing the charge, the man seemed enlightened, and, saying not another word, resigned himself with preternatural civility to the search-party, who, with their staves in their hands, surrounded him on all sides, and marched him back towards the shepherd's cottage.

It was eleven o'clock by the time they arrived. The light shining from the open door, a sound of men's voices within, proclaimed to them as they approached the house that some new events had arisen in their absence. On entering they discovered the shepherd's living-room to be invaded by two officers from Casterbridge jail, and a well-known magistrate who lived at the nearest country-seat, intelligence of the escape having become generally circulated.

"Gentlemen," said the constable, "I have brought back your man—not without risk and danger; but every-one must do his duty! He is inside this circle of able-bodied persons, who have lent me useful aid, considering their ignorance of Crown work. Men, bring forward your prisoner!" And the third stranger was led to the light.

"Who is this?" said one of the officials.

"The man," said the constable.

"Certainly not," said the turnkey; and the first corroborated his statement.

"But how can it be otherwise?" asked the constable. "Or why was he so terrified at sight o' the singing instrument of the law who sat there?" Here he related the strange behaviour of the third stranger on entering the house during the hangman's song.

"Can't understand it," said the officer coolly. "All I know is that it is not the condemned man. He's quite a different character from this one; a gauntish fellow, with dark hair and eyes, rather good-looking, and with a musical bass voice that if you heard it once you'd never mistake as long as you lived."

"Why, souls—'twas the man in the chimney-corner!"

"Hey—what?" said the magistrate, coming forward after inquiring particulars from the shepherd in the background. "Haven't you got the man after all?"

"Well, sir," said the constable, "he's the man we were in search of, that's true; and yet he's not the man we were in search of. For the man we were in search of was not the man we wanted, sir, if you understand my every-day way; for 'twas the man in the chimney-corner!"

"A pretty kettle of fish altogether!" said the magistrate. "You had better start for the other man at once."

The prisoner now spoke for the first time. The mention of the man in the chimney-corner seemed to have moved him as nothing else could do. "Sir," he said, stepping forward to the magistrate, "take no more trouble about me. The time is come when I may as well speak. I have done nothing; my crime is that the condemned man is my brother. Early this afternoon I left home at Shottsford to tramp it all the way to Casterbridge jail to bid him farewell. I was benighted, and called here to rest and ask the way. When I opened the door I saw before me the very man, my brother, that I thought to see in the condemned cell at Casterbridge. He was in this chimney-corner; and jammed close to him, so that he could not have got out if he had tried, was the executioner who'd come to take his life, singing a song about it and not knowing that it was his victim who was close by, joining in to save appearances. My brother looked a glance of agony at me, and I knew he meant, 'Don't reveal what you see; my life depends on it.' I was so terror-struck that I could hardly stand, and, not knowing what I did, I turned and hurried away."

The narrator's manner and tone had the stamp of truth, and his story made a great impression on all around. "And do you know where your brother is at the present time?" asked the magistrate.

"I do not. I have never seen him since I closed this door."

"I can testify to that, for we've been between ye ever since," said the constable.

"Where does he think to fly to?—what is his occupation?"

"He's a watch-and-clock-maker, sir."

"'A said 'a was a wheelwright—a wicked rogue," said the constable.

"The wheels of clocks and watches he meant, no doubt," said Shepherd Fennel. "I thought his hands were palish for's trade."

"Well, it appears to me that nothing can be gained by retaining this poor man in custody," said the magistrate; "your business lies with the other, unquestionably."

And so the little man was released off-hand; but he looked nothing the less sad on that account, it being beyond the power of magistrate or constable to raze out the written troubles in his brain, for they concerned another whom he regarded with more solicitude than himself. When this was done, and the man had gone his way, the night was found to be so far advanced that it was deemed useless to renew the search before the next morning.

Next day, accordingly, the quest for the clever sheep-stealer became general and keen, to all appearance at least. But the intended punishment was cruelly disproportioned to the transgression, and the sympathy of a great many country-folk in that district was strongly on the side of the fugitive. Moreover, his marvellous coolness and daring in hob-and-nobbing with the hangman, under the unprecedented circumstances of the shepherd's party, won their admiration. So that it may be questioned if all those who ostensibly made themselves so busy in exploring woods and fields and lanes were quite so thorough when it came to the private examination of their own lofts and outhouses. Stories were afloat of a mysterious figure being occasionally seen in some old overgrown trackway or other, remote from turnpike roads; but when a search was instituted in any of these suspected quarters nobody was found. Thus the days and weeks passed without tidings.

In brief, the bass-voiced man of the chimney-corner was never recaptured. Some said that he went across the sea, others that he did not, but buried himself in the depths of a populous city. At any rate, the gentleman in cinder-grey never did his morning's work at Casterbridge, nor met anywhere at all, for business purposes, the genial comrade with whom he had passed an hour of relaxation in the lonely house on the coomb.

The grass has long been green on the graves of Shepherd Fennel and his frugal wife; the guests who made up the christening party have mainly followed their entertainers to the tomb; the baby in whose honour they all had met is a matron in the sere and yellow leaf. But the arrival of the three strangers at the shepherd's that night, and the details connected therewith, is a story as well known as ever in the country about Higher Crowstairs.

THOMAS HARDY—*Wessex Tales.*

THE HOUSE OF EULALIE

IT was a pretty little house, in very charming country—
in an untravelled corner of Normandy, near the sea;
a country of orchards and colza-fields, of soft green
meadows where cattle browsed, and of deep elm-shaded
lanes.

One was rather surprised to see this little house just
here, for all the other houses in the neighbourhood were
rude farm-houses or labourers' cottages; and this was a
coquettish little chalet, white-walled, with slim French
windows, and balconies of twisted ironwork, and Vene-
tian blinds: a gay little pleasure-house, standing in a
bright little garden, among rose-bushes, and parterres
of geraniums, and smooth stretches of greensward.
Beyond the garden there was an orchard—rows and
couples of old gnarled apple-trees, bending towards one
another like fantastic figures arrested in the middle
of a dance. Then, turning round, you looked over
feathery colza-fields and yellow corn-fields, a mile
away, to the sea, and to a winding perspective of
white cliffs, and the sea bathed in transparent greens
and purples, luminous shadows of its own nameless
hues.

A board attached to the wall confirmed, in roughly-
painted characters, the information I had had from an
agent in Dieppe. The house was to let; and I had driven
out—a drive of two long hours—to inspect it. Now I
stood on the doorstep and rang the bell. It was a big
bell, hung in the porch, with a pendent handle of bronze,

wrought in the semblance of a rope and tassel. Its voice would carry far on that still country air.

It carried, at any rate, as far as a low thatched farm-house, a hundred yards down the road. Presently a man and a woman came out of the farm-house, gazed for an instant in my direction, and then moved towards me: an old brown man, an old grey woman, the man in corduroys, the woman wearing a neat white cotton cap and a blue apron, both moving with the burdened gait of peasants.

"You are Monsieur and Madame Leroux?" I asked, when we had accomplished our preliminary good-days; and I explained that I had come from the agent in Dieppe to look over their house. For the rest, they must have been expecting me; the agent had said that he would let them know.

But, to my perplexity, this business-like announcement seemed somehow to embarrass them; even, I might have thought, to agitate, to distress them. They lifted up their worn old faces, and eyed me anxiously. They exchanged anxious glances with each other. The woman clasped her hands, nervously working her fingers. The man hesitated and stammered a little, before he was able to repeat vaguely, "You have come to look over the house, Monsieur?"

"Surely," I said, "the agent has written to you? I understood from him that you would expect me at this hour to-day."

"Oh yes," the man admitted, "we were expecting you." But he made no motion to advance matters. He exchanged another anxious glance with his wife. She gave her head a sort of helpless nod, and looked down.

"You see, Monsieur," the man began, as if he were about to elucidate the situation, "you see——" But then he faltered, frowning at the air, as one at a loss for words.

" The house is already let, perhaps? " suggested I.

" No, the house is not let," said he.

" You had better go and fetch the key," his wife said at last, in a dreary way, still looking down.

He trudged heavily back to the farm-house. While he was gone we stood by the door in silence, the woman always nervously working the fingers of her clasped hands. I tried, indeed, to make a little conversation : I ventured something about the excellence of the site, the beauty of the view. She replied with a murmur of assent, civilly but wearily; and I did not feel encouraged to persist.

By-and-by her husband rejoined us, with the key; and they began silently to lead me through the house.

There were two pretty drawing-rooms on the ground floor, a pretty dining-room, and a delightful kitchen, with a broad hearth of polished red bricks, a tiled chimney, and shining copper pots and pans. The drawing-rooms and the dining-room were pleasantly furnished in a light French fashion, and their windows opened to the sun and to the fragrance and greenery of the garden. I expressed a good deal of admiration; whereupon, little by little, the manner of my conductors changed. From constrained, depressed, it became responsive; even, in the end, effusive. They met my exclamations with smiles, my inquiries with voluble eager answers. But it remained an agitated manner, the manner of people who were shaken by an emotion. Their old hands trembled as they opened the doors for me or drew up the blinds; their voices trembled. There was something painful in their very smiles, as if these were but momentary ripples on the surface of a trouble.

" Ah," I said to myself, " they are hard-pressed for

money. They have put their whole capital into this house, very likely. They are excited by the prospect of securing a tenant."

"Now, if you please, Monsieur, we will go upstairs, and see the bedrooms," the old man said.

The bedrooms were airy, cheerful rooms, gaily papered, with chintz curtains and the usual French bedroom furniture. One of them exhibited signs of being actually lived in; there were things about it, personal things, a woman's things. It was the last room we visited, a front room, looking off to the sea. There were combs and brushes on the toilet-table; there were pens, an inkstand, and a portfolio on the writing-desk; there were books in the bookcase. Framed photographs stood on the mantelpiece. In the closet dresses were suspended, and shoes and slippers were primly ranged on the floor. The bed was covered with a counterpane of blue silk; a crucifix hung on the wall above it; beside it there was a *priedieu*, with a little porcelain holy-water vase.

"Oh," I exclaimed, turning to Monsieur and Madame Leroux, "this room is occupied?"

Madame Leroux did not appear to hear me. Her eyes were fixed in a dull stare before her, her lips were parted slightly. She looked tired, as if she would be glad when our tour through the house was finished. Monsieur Leroux threw his hand up towards the ceiling in an odd gesture, and said, "No, the room is not occupied at present."

We went back downstairs, and concluded an agreement. I was to take the house for the summer. Madame Leroux would cook for me. Monsieur Leroux would drive to Dieppe on Wednesday to fetch me and my luggage out.

.   .   .   .

On Wednesday we had been driving for something

like half an hour without speaking, when all at once Leroux said to me, "That room, Monsieur, the room you thought was occupied——"

"Yes?" I questioned, as he paused.

"I have a proposition to make," said he. He spoke, as it seemed to me, half shyly, half doggedly, gazing the while at the ears of his horse.

"What is it?" I asked.

"If you will leave that room as it is, with the things in it, we will make a reduction in the rent. If you will let us keep it as it is?" he repeated, with a curious pleading intensity. "You are alone. The house will be big enough for you without that room, will it not, Monsieur?"

Of course, I consented at once. If they wished to keep the room as it was, they were to do so, by all means.

"Thank you, thank you very much. My wife will be grateful to you," he said.

For a little while longer we drove on without speaking. Presently, "You are our first tenant. We have never let the house before," he volunteered.

"Ah? Have you had it long?" I asked.

"I built it. I built it, five, six, years ago," said he. Then, after a pause, he added, "I built it for my daughter."

His voice sank, as he said this. But one felt that it was only the beginning of something he wished to say. I invited him to continue by an interested "Oh?"

"You see what we are, my wife and I," he broke out suddenly. "We are rough people, we are peasants. But my daughter, sir"—he put his hand on my knee, and looked earnestly into my face—"my daughter was as fine as satin, as fine as lace."

He turned back to his horse, and again drove for a minute or two in silence. At last, always with his eyes on the horse's ears, " There was not a lady in this country finer than my daughter," he went on, speaking rapidly, in a thick voice, almost as if to himself. " She was beautiful, she had the sweetest character, she had the best education. She was educated at the convent, in Rouen, at the Sacré Cœur. Six years—from twelve to eighteen—she studied at the convent. She knew English, sir—your language. She took prizes for history. And the piano! Nobody living can touch the piano as my daughter could. Well," he demanded abruptly, with a kind of fierceness, " was a rough farm-house good enough for her? " He answered his own question. " No, Monsieur. You would not soil fine lace by putting it in a dirty box. My daughter was finer than lace. Her hands were softer than Lyons velvet. And oh," he cried, " the sweet smell they had, her hands! It was good to smell her hands. I used to kiss them and smell them, as you would smell a rose." His voice died away at the reminiscence, and there was another interval of silence. By-and-by he began again, " I had plenty of money. I was the richest farmer of this neighbourhood. I sent to Rouen for the best architect they have there. Monsieur Clermont, the best architect of Rouen, laureate of the Fine Arts School of Paris, he built that house for my daughter; he built it and furnished it, to make it fit for a countess, so that when she came home for good from the convent she should have a home worthy of her. Look at this, Monsieur. Would the grandest palace in the world be too good for her? "

He had drawn a worn red leather case from his pocket, and taken out a small photograph, which he handed to me. It was the portrait of a girl, a delicate-looking girl, of about seventeen. Her face was pretty, with the irregular prettiness not uncommon in France, and very sweet and gentle. The old man almost held his breath while

I was examining the photograph. "Est-elle gentille? Est-elle belle, Monsieur?" he besought me, with a very hunger for sympathy, as I returned it. One answered, of course, what one could, as best one could. He, with shaking fingers, replaced the photograph in its case. "Here, Monsieur," he said, extracting from an opposite compartment a little white card. It was the usual French memorial of mourning: an engraving of the Cross and Dove, under which was printed: "Eulalie-Joséphine-Marie Leroux. Born the 16th May, 1874. Died the 12th August, 1892. Pray for her."

"The good God knows what He does. I built that house for my daughter, and when it was built the good God took her away. We were mad with grief, my wife and I; but that could not save her. Perhaps we are still mad with grief," the poor old man said simply. "We can think of nothing else. We never wish to speak of anything else. We could not live in the house—her house, without her. We never thought to let it. I built that house for my daughter, I furnished it for her, and when it was ready for her—she died. Was it not hard, Monsieur? How could I let the house to strangers? But lately I have had losses. I am compelled to let it, to pay my debts. I would not let it to everybody. You are an Englishman. Well, if I did not like you, I would not let it to you for a million English pounds. But I am glad I have let it to you. You will respect her memory. And you will allow us to keep that room—her room. We shall be able to keep it as it was, with her things in it. Yes, that room which you thought was occupied—that was my daughter's room."

Madame Leroux was waiting for us in the garden of the chalet. She looked anxiously up at her husband as we arrived. He nodded his head, and called out, "It's all right. Monsieur agrees."

The old woman took my hands, wringing them hysterically almost. "Ah, Monsieur, you are very good," she said. She raised her eyes to mine. But I could not look into her eyes. There was a sorrow in them, an awfulness, a sacredness of sorrow, which, I felt, it would be like sacrilege for me to look at.

.   .   .   .

We became good friends, the Leroux and I, during the three months I passed as their tenant. Madame, indeed, did for me and looked after me with a zeal that was almost maternal. Both of them, as the old man had said, loved above all things to talk of their daughter, and I hope I was never loath to listen. Their passion, their grief, their constant thought of her, appealed to me as very beautiful, as well as very touching. And something like a pale spirit of the girl seemed gently, sweetly, always to be present in the house, the house that Love had built for her, not guessing that Death would come, as soon as it was finished, and call her away. "Oh, but it is a joy, Monsieur, that you have left us her room," the old couple were never tired of repeating. One day Madame took me up into the room, and showed me Eulalie's pretty dresses, her trinkets, her books, the handsomely bound books that she had won as prizes at the convent. And on another day she showed me some of Eulalie's letters, asking me if she hadn't a beautiful handwriting, if the letters were not beautifully expressed. She showed me photographs of the girl at all ages; a lock of her hair; her baby clothes; the priest's certificate of her first communion; the bishop's certificate of her confirmation. And she showed me letters from the good sisters of the Sacred Heart, at Rouen, telling of Eulalie's progress in her studies, praising her conduct and her character. "Oh, to think that she is gone, that she is gone!" the old woman wailed, in a kind of helpless incomprehension, incredulity, of loss. Then, in a moment, she murmured, with what submissiveness she could. " Le bon Dieu sait ce qu'il fait," crossing herself.

On the 12th of August, the anniversary of her death, I went with them to the parish church, where a mass was said for the repose of Eulalie's soul. And the kind old curé afterwards came round, and pressed their hands, and spoke words of comfort to them.

.   .   .   .

In September I left them, returning to Dieppe. One afternoon I chanced to meet that same old curé in the high street there. We stopped and spoke together— naturally, of the Leroux, of what excellent people they were, of how they grieved for their daughter. " Their love was more than love. They adored the child, they idolized her. I have never witnessed such affection," the curé told me. " When she died, I seriously feared they would lose their reason. They were dazed, they were beside themselves; for a long while they were quite as if mad. But God is merciful. They have learnt to live with their affliction."

" It is very beautiful," said I, " the way they have sanctified her memory, the way they worship it. You know, of course, they keep her room, with her things in it, exactly as she left it. That seems to me very beautiful."

" Her room? " questioned the curé, looking vague. " What room? "

" Oh, didn't you know? " I wondered. " Her bedroom in the chalet. They keep it as she left it, with all her things about, her books, her dresses."

" I don't think I follow you," the curé said. " She never had a bedroom in the chalet."

" Oh, I beg your pardon. One of the front rooms on the first floor was her room," I informed him.

But he shook his head. "There is some mistake. She never lived in the chalet. She died in the old house. The chalet was only just finished when she died. The workmen were hardly out of it."

"No," I said, "it is you who must be mistaken; you must forget. I am quite sure. The Leroux have spoken of it to me times without number."

"But, my dear sir," the curé insisted, "I am not merely sure; I know. I attended the girl in her last agony. She died in the farm-house. They had not moved into the chalet. The chalet was being furnished. The last pieces of furniture were taken in the very day before her death. The chalet was never lived in. You are the only person who has ever lived in the chalet. I assure you of the fact."

"Well," I said, "that is very strange, that is very strange indeed." And for a minute I was bewildered, I did not know what to think. But only for a minute. Suddenly I cried out, "Oh, I see—I see. I understand."

I saw, I understood. Suddenly I saw the pious, the beautiful deception that these poor stricken souls had sought to practise on themselves; the beautiful, the fond illusion they had created for themselves. They had built the house for their daughter, and she had died just when it was ready for her. But they could not bear—they could not bear—to think that not for one little week even, not even for one poor little day or hour, had she lived in the house, enjoyed the house. That was the uttermost farthing of their sorrow, which they could not pay. They could not acknowledge it to their own stricken hearts. So, piously, reverently—with closed eyes, as it were, that they might not know what they were doing—they had carried the dead girl's things to the room they had meant for her, they had arranged them there, they had said, "This was her room; this *was* her room." They would not admit to themselves, they would not let themselves stop to think, that she had never, even for one poor night, slept in it, enjoyed it. They told a beautiful pious falsehood to themselves. It was a beautiful pious game of "make-believe," which, like children, they could play together. And—the curé had said it: God is merciful. In the end they had been enabled to confuse their beautiful falsehood with reality, and to find comfort in it; they had been enabled to forget that their "make-believe" was a "make-believe," and to mistake it for a beautiful comforting truth. The uttermost farthing of their sorrow, which they could not pay, was not exacted. They were suffered to keep it; and it became their treasure, precious to them as fine gold.

Falsehood—truth? Nay, I think there are illusions that are not falsehoods—that are Truth's own smiles of pity for us.

Henry Harland—*Comedies and Errors.*

THE HEADSWOMAN

I

It was a bland sunny morning of a medieval May—an old-style May of the most typical quality; and the Council of the little town of St. Radegonde were assembled, as was their wont at that hour, in the picturesque upper chamber of the Hôtel de Ville, for the despatch of the usual municipal business. Though the date was early sixteenth century, the members of this particular town-council possessed some resemblance to those of similar assemblies in the seventeenth, eighteenth, and even the nineteenth centuries, in a general absence of any characteristic at all—unless a pervading hopeless insignificance can be considered as such. All the character, indeed, in the room seemed to be concentrated in the girl who stood before the table, erect, yet at her ease, facing the members in general and Mr. Mayor in particular; a delicate-handed, handsome girl of some eighteen summers, whose tall, supple figure was well set off by the quiet, though tasteful mourning in which she was clad.

"Well, gentlemen," the Mayor was saying; "this little business appears to be—er—quite in order, and it only remains for me to—er—review the facts. You are aware that the town has lately had the misfortune to lose its executioner—a gentleman who, I may say, performed the duties of his office with neatness and despatch, and gave the fullest satisfaction to all with whom he—er—

came in contact. But the Council has already, in a vote
of condolence, expressed its sense of the—er—striking
qualities of the deceased. You are doubtless also aware
that the office is hereditary, being secured to a particular family in this town, so long as any one of its members is ready and willing to take it up. The deed lies
before me, and appears to be—er—quite in order. It is
true that on this occasion the Council might have been
called upon to consider and examine the title of the
claimant, the late lamented official having only left a
daughter—she who now stands before you; but I am
happy to say that Jeanne—the young lady in question—
with what I am bound to call great good-feeling on her
part, has saved us all trouble in that respect, by formally
applying for the family post, with all its—er—duties,
privileges, and emoluments; and her application appears
to be—er—quite in order. There is therefore, under the
circumstances, nothing left for us to do but to declare
the said applicant duly elected. I would wish, however,
before I—er—sit down, to make it quite clear to the—er
—fair petitioner, that if a laudable desire to save the
Council trouble in the matter has led her to a—er—
hasty conclusion, it is quite open to her to reconsider her
position. Should she determine not to press her claim,
the succession to the post would then apparently devolve
upon her cousin Enguerrand, well known to you all as
a practising advocate in the courts of this town. Though
the youth has not, I admit, up to now proved a conspicuous success in the profession he has chosen, still there is
no reason why a bad lawyer should not make an excellent executioner; and in view of the close friendship—
may I even say attachment?—existing between the
cousins, it is possible that this young lady may, in due
course, practically enjoy the solid emoluments of the
position without the necessity of discharging its (to some

girls uncongenial) duties. And so, though not the rose
herself, she would still be—er—near the rose!" And
the Mayor resumed his seat, chuckling over his little
pleasantry, which the keener wits of the Council proceeded to explain at length to the more obtuse.

"Permit me, Mr. Mayor," said the girl, quietly, "first
to thank you for what was evidently the outcome of a
kindly though misdirected feeling on your part; and
then to set you right as to the grounds of my application for the post to which you admit my hereditary
claim. As to my cousin, your conjecture as to the feeling
between us is greatly exaggerated; and I may further
say at once, from my knowledge of his character, that
he is little qualified either to adorn or to dignify an
important position such as this. A man who has
achieved such indifferent success in a minor and less
exacting walk of life, is hardly likely to shine in an
occupation demanding punctuality, concentration, judge-
ment—all the qualities, in fine, that go to make a good
business man. But this is beside the question. My
motives, gentlemen, in demanding what is my due, are
simple and (I trust) honest, and I desire that you should
know them. It is my wish to be dependent on no one.
I am both willing and able to work, and I only ask for
what is the common right of humanity—admission to
the labour market. How many poor toiling women
would simply jump at a chance like this which fortune
lays open to me! And shall I, from any false deference
to that conventional voice which proclaims this thing as
'nice,' and that thing as 'not nice,' reject a handicraft
which promises me both artistic satisfaction and a com-
petence? No, gentlemen; my claim is a small one—only
a fair day's wage for a fair day's work. But I can accept
nothing less, nor consent to forgo my rights, even for
any contingent remainder of possible cousinly favour!"

There was a touch of scorn in her fine contralto voice as she finished speaking; the Mayor himself beamed approval. He was not wealthy, and had a large family of daughters; so Jeanne's sentiments seemed to him entirely right and laudable.

"Well, gentlemen," he began, briskly, " then all we've got to do, is to——"

"Beg pardon, your worship," put in Master Robinet, the tanner, who had been sitting with a petrified, Bill-the-Lizard sort of expression during the speechifying; " but are we to understand as how this here young lady is going to be the public executioner? "

"Really, neighbour Robinet," said the Mayor somewhat pettishly, " you've got ears like the rest of us, I suppose; and you know the contents of the deed; and you've had my assurance that it's—er—quite in order; and as it's getting towards lunch-time——"

"But it's unheard-of," protested honest Robinet. "There hasn't ever been no such thing—leastways not as I've heard tell."

"Well, well, well," said the Mayor, " everything must have a beginning, I suppose. Times are different now, you know. There's the march of intellect, and—er—all that sort of the thing. We must advance with the times —don't you see, Robinet?—advance with the times! "

"Well I'm——" began the tanner.

But no one heard, on this occasion, the tanner's opinion as to his condition, physical or spiritual; for the clear contralto cut short his obtestations.

"If there's really nothing more to be said, Mr. Mayor," she remarked, " I need not trespass longer on your valuable time. I propose to take up the duties of my office to-morrow morning, at the usual hour. The salary will, I assume, be reckoned from the same date; and I shall make the customary quarterly application for such additional emoluments as may have accrued to me during that period. You see I am familiar with the routine. Good morning, gentlemen! " And as she passed from the Council chamber, her small head held erect, even the tanner felt that she took with her a large portion of the May sunshine which was condescending that morning to gild their deliberations.

II

One evening, a few weeks later, Jeanne was taking a stroll on the ramparts of the town, a favourite and customary walk of hers when business cares were over. The pleasant expanse of country that lay spread beneath her —the rich sunset, the gleaming sinuous river, and the noble old château that dominated both town and pasture from its adjacent height—all served to stir and bring out in her those poetic impulses which had lain dormant during the working day; while the cool evening breeze smoothed out and obliterated any little jars or worries which might have ensued during the practice of a profession in which she was still something of a novice. This evening she felt fairly happy and content. True, business was rather brisk, and her days had been fully occupied; but this mattered little so long as her modest efforts were appreciated, and she was now really beginning to feel that, with practice, her work was creditably and artistically done. In a satisfied, somewhat dreamy mood, she was drinking in the various sweet influences of the evening, when she perceived her cousin approaching.

" Good evening, Enguerrand," cried Jeanne pleasantly; she was thinking that since she had begun to work for her living, she had hardly seen him—and they used to be such good friends. Could anything have occurred to offend him?

Enguerrand drew near somewhat moodily, but could not help relaxing his expression at sight of her fair young face, set in its framework of rich brown hair, wherein the sunset seemed to have tangled itself and to cling, reluctant to leave it.

"Sit down, Enguerrand," continued Jeanne, "and tell me what you've been doing this long time. Been very busy, and winning forensic fame and gold?"

"Well, not exactly," said Enguerrand, moody once more. "The fact is, there's so much interest required nowadays at the courts, that unassisted talent never gets a chance. And you, Jeanne?"

"Oh, I don't complain," answered Jeanne, lightly. "Of course it's fair-time just now, you know, and we're always busy then. But work will be lighter soon, and then I'll get a day off, and we'll have a delightful ramble and picnic in the woods, as we used to do when we were children. What fun we had in those old days, Enguerrand! Do you remember when we were quite little tots, and used to play at executions in the back-garden, and you were a bandit and a buccaneer, and all sorts of dreadful things, and I used to chop off your head with a paper-knife? How pleased dear father used to be!"

"Jeanne," said Enguerrand, with some hesitation, "you've touched upon the very subject that I came to speak to you about. Do you know, dear, I can't help feeling—it may be unreasonable, but still the feeling is there—that the profession you have adopted is not quite —is just a little——"

"Now, Enguerrand!" said Jeanne, an angry flash sparkling in her eyes. She was a little touchy on this subject, the word she most affected to despise being also the one she most dreaded—the adjective "unladylike."

"Don't misunderstand me, Jeanne," went on Enguerrand, imploringly: "You may naturally think that, because I should have succeeded to the post, with its income and perquisites, had you relinquished your claim, there is therefore some personal feeling in my remonstrances. Believe me, it is not so. My own interests do not weigh with me for a moment. It is on your own account, Jeanne, and yours alone, that I ask you to consider whether the higher æsthetic qualities, which I know you possess, may not become cramped and thwarted by ' the trivial round, the common task,' which you have lightly undertaken. However laudable a professional life may be, one always feels that with a delicate organism such as woman, some of the bloom may possibly get rubbed off the peach."

"Well, Enguerrand," said Jeanne, composing herself with an effort, though her lips were set hard, "I will do you the justice to believe that personal advantage does not influence you, and I will try to reason calmly with you, and convince you that you are simply hide-bound by old-world prejudice. Now, take yourself, for instance, who come here to instruct me: what does *your* profession amount to, when all's said and done? A mass of lies, quibbles, dodges, and tricks, that would make any self-respecting executioner blush! And even with the dirty weapons at your command, you make but a poor show of it. There was that wretched fellow you defended only two days ago. (I was in court during the trial— professional interest, you know.) Well, he had his regular *alibi* all ready, as clear as clear could be; only you must needs go and mess and bungle the thing up, so that, as I expected all along, he was passed on to me for treatment in due course. You may like to have his opinion—that of a shrewd, though unlettered person. ' It's a real pleasure, miss,' he said, ' to be handled by you. You *knows* your work, and you *does* your work—though p'raps I ses it as shouldn't. If that blooming fool of a mouthpiece of mine '—he was referring to you, dear, in your capacity of advocate—'had known his business half as well as you do yours, I shouldn't a bin here now!' And you know, Enguerrand, he was perfectly right."

"Well, perhaps he was," admitted Enguerrand. "You see, I had been working at a sonnet the night before, and I couldn't get the rhymes right, and they would keep coming into my head in court and mixing themselves up with the *alibi*. But look here, Jeanne, when you saw I was going off the track, you might have given me a friendly hint, you know—for old times' sake, if not for the prisoner's!"

"I daresay," replied Jeanne, calmly: "perhaps you'll tell me why I should sacrifice my interests because you're unable to look after yours. You forget that I receive a bonus, over and above my salary, upon each exercise of my functions!"

"True," said Enguerrand, gloomily: "I did forget that. I wish I had your business aptitudes, Jeanne."

"I daresay you do," remarked Jeanne. "But you see, dear, how all your arguments fall to the ground. You mistake a prepossession for a logical base. Now if I had gone, like that Clairette you used to dangle after, and been waiting-woman to some grand lady in a château— a thin-blooded compound of drudge and sycophant— then, I suppose, you'd have been perfectly satisfied. So feminine! So genteel!"

"She's not a bad sort of girl, little Claire," said Enguerrand, reflectively (thereby angering Jeanne afresh): "but putting her aside—of course you could always beat me at argument, Jeanne; you'd have made a much better lawyer than I. But you know, dear, how much I care about you; and I did hope that on that account even a prejudice, however unreasonable, might have some little weight. And I'm not alone, let me tell you, in my views. There was a fellow in court only to-day, who was saying that yours was only a *succès d'estime*, and that woman, as a naturally talkative and hopelessly unpunctual animal, could never be more than a clever amateur in the profession you have chosen."

"That will do, Enguerrand," said Jeanne, proudly; "it seems that when argument fails, you can stoop so low as to insult me through my sex. You men are all alike—steeped in brutish masculine prejudice. Now go away, and don't mention the subject to me again till you're quite reasonable and nice."

III

Jeanne passed a somewhat restless night after her small scene with her cousin, waking depressed and unrefreshed. Though she had carried matters with so high a hand, and had scored so distinctly all around, she had been more agitated than she had cared to show. She liked Enguerrand; and more especially did she like his admiration for her; and that chance allusion to Clairette contained possibilities that were alarming. In embracing a professional career, she had never thought for a moment that it could militate against that due share of admiration to which, as a girl, she was justly entitled; and Enguerrand's views seemed this morning all the more narrow and inexcusable. She rose languidly, and as soon as she dressed sent off a little note to the Mayor, saying that she had a nervous headache and felt out of sorts, and begging to be excused from attendance on that day; and the missive reached the Mayor just as he was taking his usual place at the head of the Board.

"Dear, dear," said the kind-hearted old man, as soon as he had read the letter to his fellow-councilmen: "I'm very sorry. Poor girl! Here, one of you fellows, just run round and tell the gaoler there won't be any business to-day. Jeanne's seedy. It's put off till to-morrow. And now, gentlemen, the agenda——"

"Really, your worship," exploded Robinet, "this is simply ridiculous!"

"Upon my word, Robinet," said the Mayor, "I don't know what's the matter with you. Here's a poor girl unwell—and a more hard-working girl isn't in the town —and instead of sympathizing with her, and saying you're sorry, you call it ridiculous! Suppose you had a headache yourself? You wouldn't like——"

"But it *is* ridiculous," maintained the tanner stoutly. "Who ever heard of an executioner having a nervous headache? There's no precedent for it. And 'out of sorts,' too! Suppose the criminals said they were out of sorts, and didn't feel up to being executed?"

"Well, suppose they did," replied the Mayor, "we'd try and meet them half-way, I daresay. They'd have to be executed some time or other, you know. Why on earth are you so captious about trifles? The prisoners won't mind, and *I* don't mind: nobody's inconvenienced, and everybody's happy!"

"You're right there, Mr. Mayor," put in another councilman. "This executing business used to give the town a lot of trouble and bother; now it's all as easy as kiss-your-hand. Instead of objecting, as they used to do, and wanting to argue the point and kick up a row, the fellows as is told off for execution come skipping along in the morning, like a lot of lambs in Maytime. And then the fun there is on the scaffold! The jokes, the back-answers, the repartees! And never a word to shock a baby! Why, my little girl, as goes through the market-place every morning—on her way to school, you know—she says to me only yesterday, she says, 'Why, father,' she says, 'it's as good as the play-actors,' she says."

"There again," persisted Robinet, "I object to that too. They ought to show a properer feeling. Playing at mummers is one thing, and being executed is another, and people ought to keep 'em separate. In my father's time, that sort of thing wasn't thought good taste, and I don't hold with new-fangled notions."

"Well, really, neighbour," said the Mayor, "I think you're out of sorts yourself to-day. You must have got out of bed the wrong side this morning. As for a little joke, more or less, we all know a maiden loves a merry jest when she's certain of having the last word! But I'll tell you what I'll do, if it'll please you; I'll go round and see Jeanne myself on my way home, and tell her—quite nicely, you know—that once in a way doesn't matter, but that if she feels her health won't let her keep regular business hours, she mustn't think of going on with anything that's bad for her. Like that, don't you see? And now, gentlemen, let's read the minutes!"

Thus it came about that Jeanne took her usual walk that evening with a ruffled brow and a swelling heart; and her little hand opened and shut angrily as she paced the ramparts. She couldn't stand being found fault with. How could she help having a headache? Those clods of citizens didn't know what a highly-strung sensitive organization was. Absorbed in her reflections, she had taken several turns up and down the grassy footway, before she became aware that she was not alone. A youth, of richer dress and more elegant bearing than the general run of the Radegundians, was leaning in an embrasure, watching the graceful figure with evident interest.

"Something has vexed you, fair maiden?" he observed, coming forward deferentially as soon as he perceived he was noticed; "and care sits but awkwardly on that smooth young brow."

"Nay, it is nothing, kind sir," replied Jeanne; "we girls who work for our living must not be too sensitive. My employers have been somewhat exigent, that is all. I did wrong to take it to heart."

"'Tis the way of the bloated capitalist," rejoined the young man lightly, as he turned to walk by her side. "They grind us, they grind us; perhaps some day they will come under your hands in turn, and then you can pay them out. And so you toil and spin, fair lily! And yet methinks those delicate hands show little trace of labour?"

"You wrong me, indeed, sir," replied Jeanne merrily. "These hands of mine, that you are so good as to admire, do great execution!"

"I can well believe that your victims are numerous," he replied; "may I be permitted to rank myself among the latest of them?"

"I wish you a better fortune, kind sir," answered Jeanne demurely.

"I can imagine no more delightful one," he replied; "and where do you ply your daily task, fair mistress? Not entirely out of sight and access, I trust?"

"Nay, sir," laughed Jeanne, "I work in the market-place most mornings, and there is no charge for admission; and access is far from difficult. Indeed, some complain—but that is no business of mine. And now I must be wishing you a good evening. Nay"—for he would have detained her—"it is not seemly for an unprotected maiden to tarry in converse with a stranger at this hour. *Au revoir*, sir! If you should happen to be in the market-place any morning——" And she tripped lightly away. The youth, gazing after her retreating figure, confessed himself strangely fascinated by this fair unknown, whose particular employment, by the way, he had forgotten to ask; while Jeanne, as she sped homewards, could not help reflecting that for style and distinction, this new acquaintance threw into the shade all the Enguerrands and others she had met hitherto—even in the course of business.

IV

The next morning was bright and breezy, and Jeanne was early at her post, feeling quite a different girl. The busy little market-place was full of colour and movement, and the gay patches of flowers and fruit, the strings of fluttering kerchiefs, and the piles of red and yellow pottery, formed an artistic setting to the quiet impressive scaffold which they framed. Jeanne was in short sleeves, according to the etiquette of her office, and her round graceful arms showed snowily against her dark blue skirt and scarlet tight-fitting bodice. Her assistant looked at her with admiration.

"Hope you're better, miss," he said respectfully. "It was just as well you didn't put yourself out to come yesterday; there was nothing particular to do. Only one fellow, and he said *he* didn't care; anything to oblige a lady!"

"Well, I wish he'd hurry up now, to oblige a lady," said Jeanne, swinging her axe carelessly to and fro: "ten minutes past the hour; I shall have to talk to the Mayor about this."

"It's a pity there ain't a better show this morning," pursued the assistant, as he leant over the rail of the scaffold and spat meditatively into the busy throng below. "They do say as how the young Seigneur arrived at the Château yesterday—him as has been finishing his education in Paris, you know. He's as likely as not to be in the market-place to-day; and if he's disappointed, he may go off to Paris again, which would be a pity, seeing the Château's been empty so long. But he may go to Paris, or anywheres else he's a mind to, he won't see better workmanship than in this here little town!"

"Well, my good Raoul," said Jeanne, colouring slightly at the obvious compliment, "quality, not quantity, is what we aim at here, you know. If a Paris education has been properly assimilated by the Seigneur, he will not fail to make all the necessary allowances. But see, the prison-doors are opening at last!"

They both looked across the little square to the prison, which fronted the scaffold; and sure enough, a small body of men, the Sheriff at their head, was issuing from the building, conveying, or endeavouring to convey, the tardy prisoner to the scaffold. That gentleman, however, seemed to be in a different and less obliging frame of mind from that of the previous day; and at every pace one or other of the guards was shot violently into the middle of the square, propelled by a vigorous kick or blow from the struggling captive. The crowd, unaccustomed of late to such demonstrations of feeling, and resenting the prisoner's want of taste, hooted loudly; but it was not until that ingenious medieval arrangement known as *la marche aux crapauds* had been brought to bear on him, that the reluctant convict could be prevailed upon to present himself before the young lady he had already so unwarrantably detained.

Jeanne's profession had both accustomed her to surprises and taught her the futility of considering her clients as drawn from any one particular class: yet she could hardly help feeling some astonishment on recognizing her new acquaintance of the previous evening. That, with all his evident amiability of character, he should come to this end, was not in itself a special subject for wonder; but that he should have been conversing with her on the ramparts at the hour when—after courteously excusing her attendance on the scaffold—he was cooling his heels in prison for another day, seemed hardly to be accounted for, at first sight. Jeanne, however, reflected that the reconciling of apparent contradictions was not included in her official duties.

The Sheriff, wiping his heated brow, now read the formal *procès* delivering over the prisoner to the executioner's hands; "and a nice job we've had to get him here," he added on his own account. And the young man, who had remained perfectly tractable since his arrival, stepped forward and bowed politely.

"Now that we have been properly introduced," said he courteously, "allow me to apologize for any inconvenience you have been put to by my delay. The fault was entirely mine, and these gentlemen are in no way to blame. Had I known whom I was to have the pleasure of meeting, wings could not have conveyed me swiftly enough."

"Do not mention, I pray, the word inconvenience," replied Jeanne with that timid grace which so well became her: "I only trust that any slight discomfort it may be my duty to cause you before we part, will be as easily pardoned. And now—for the morning, alas! advances—any little advice or assistance that I can offer is quite at your service; for the situation is possibly new, and you may have had but little experience."

"Faith, none worth mentioning," said the prisoner, gaily. "Treat me as a raw beginner. Though our acquaintance has been but brief, I have the utmost confidence in you."

"Then, sir," said Jeanne, blushing, "suppose I were to assist you in removing this gay doublet, so as to give both of us more freedom and less responsibility?"

" A perquisite of the office? " queried the prisoner with a smile, as he slipped one arm out of the sleeve.

A flush came over Jeanne's fair brow. " That was ungenerous," she said.

" Nay, pardon me, sweet one," said he, laughing : " 'twas but a poor jest of mine—in bad taste, I willingly admit."

" I was sure you did not mean to hurt me," she replied kindly, while her fingers were busy in turning back the collar of his shirt. It was composed, she noticed, of the finest point lace; and she could not help a feeling of regret that some slight error—as must, from what she knew, exist somewhere—should compel her to take a course so at variance with her real feelings. Her only comfort was that the youth himself seemed entirely satisfied with his situation. He hummed the last air from Paris during her ministrations, and when she had quite finished, kissed the pretty fingers with a metropolitan grace.

" And now, sir," said Jeanne, " if you will kindly come this way : and please to mind the step—so. Now, if you will have the goodness to kneel here—nay, the sawdust is perfectly clean; you are my first client this morning. On the other side of the block you will find a nick, more or less adapted to the human chin, though a perfect fit cannot of course be guaranteed in every case. So! Are you pretty comfortable? "

" A bed of roses," replied the prisoner. " And what a really admirable view one gets of the valley and the river, from just this particular point! "

" Charming, is it not? " replied Jeanne. " I'm so glad you do justice to it. Some of your predecessors have really quite vexed me by their inability to appreciate that view. It's worth coming here to see it. And now, to return to business for one moment—would you prefer to give the word yourself? Some people do; it's a mere matter of taste. Or will you leave yourself entirely in my hands?"

"Oh, in your fair hands," replied her client, "which I beg you to consider respectfully kissed once more by your faithful servant to command."

Jeanne, blushing rosily, stepped back a pace, moistening her palms as she grasped her axe, when a puffing and blowing behind caused her to turn her head, and she perceived the Mayor hastily ascending the scaffold.

"Hold on a minute, Jeanne, my girl," he gasped. "Don't be in a hurry. There's been some little mistake."

Jeanne drew herself up with dignity. "I'm afraid I don't understand you, Mr. Mayor," she replied in freezing accents. "There's been no little mistake on my part that I'm aware of."

"No, no, no," said the Mayor, apologetically; "but on somebody else's there has. You see it happened in this way: this here young fellow was going round the town last night; and he'd been dining, I should say, and he was carrying on rather free. I will only say so much in your presence, that he was carrying on decidedly free. So the town-guard happened to come across him, and he was very high and very haughty, he was, and wouldn't give his name nor yet his address—as a gentleman should, you know, when he's been dining and carrying on free. So our fellows just ran him in—and it took the pick of them all their time to do it, too. Well, then, the other chap who was in prison—the gentleman who obliged you yesterday, you know—what does he do but slip out and run away in the middle of all the row and confusion; and very inconsiderate and ungentlemanly it was of him to take advantage of us in that mean way, just when we wanted a little sympathy and forbearance. Well, the Sheriff comes this morning to fetch out his man for execution, and he knows there's only one man to execute, and he sees there's only one man in prison, and it all seems as simple as A B C—he never was much of a mathematician, you know—so he fetches our friend here along, quite gaily. And—and that's how it came about, you see; *hinc illæ lachrymæ*, as the Roman poet has it. So now I shall just give this young fellow a good talking to, and discharge him with a caution; and we shan't require you any more to-day, Jeanne, my girl."

"Now, look here, Mr. Mayor," said Jeanne severely, " you utterly fail to grasp the situation in its true light. All these little details may be interesting in themselves, and doubtless the press will take note of them; but they are entirely beside the point. With the muddleheadedness of your officials (which I have frequently remarked upon) I have nothing whatever to do. All I know is, that this young gentleman has been formally handed over to me for execution, with all the necessary legal requirements; and executed he has got to be. When my duty has been performed, you are at liberty to re-open the case if you like; and any ' little mistake ' that may have occurred through your stupidity you can then rectify at your leisure. Meantime, you've no *locus standi* here at all; in fact, you've no business whatever lumbering up my scaffold. So shut up and clear out."

"Now, Jeanne, do be reasonable," implored the Mayor. "You women are so precise. You never will make any allowance for the necessary margin of error in things."

"If I were to allow the necessary margin for all *your* errors, Mayor," replied Jeanne, coolly, " the edition would have to be a large-paper one, and even then the text would stand a poor chance. And now, if you don't allow me the necessary margin to swing my axe, there may be another ' little mistake '——"

But at this point a hubbub arose at the foot of the scaffold, and Jeanne, leaning over, perceived sundry tall fellows, clad in the livery of the Seigneur, engaged in dispersing the municipal guard by the agency of well-directed kicks, applied with heartiness and anatomical knowledge. A moment later, there strode on to the scaffold, clad in black velvet, and adorned with his gold chain of office, the stately old seneschal of the Château, evidently in a towering passion.

"Now, mark my words, you miserable little bladder-o'-lard," he roared at the Mayor (whose bald head certainly shone provokingly in the morning sun), "see if I don't take this out of your skin presently!" And he passed on to where the youth was still kneeling, apparently quite absorbed in the view.

"My lord," he said, firmly though respectfully, "your hare-brained folly really passes all bounds. Have you entirely lost your head?"

"Faith, nearly," said the young man, rising and stretching himself. "Is that you, old Thibault? Ow, what a crick I've got in my neck! But that view of the valley was really delightful!"

"Did you come here simply to admire the view, my lord?" inquired Thibault severely.

"I came because my horse would come," replied the young Seigneur lightly: "that is, these gentlemen here were so pressing; they would not hear of any refusal; and besides, they forgot to mention what my attendance was required in such a hurry for. And when I got here, Thibault, old fellow, and saw that divine creature—nay, a goddess, *dea certé*—so graceful, so modest, so anxious to acquit herself with credit—— Well, you know my weakness; I never could bear to disappoint a woman. She had evidently set her heart on taking my head; and as she had my heart already——"

"I think, my lord," said Thibault with some severity, "you had better let me escort you back to the Château. This appears to be hardly a safe place for light-headed and susceptible persons!"

Jeanne, as was natural, had the last word. "Understand me, Mr. Mayor," said she, "these proceedings are entirely irregular. I decline to recognize them, and when the quarter expires I shall claim the usual bonus!"

V

When, an hour or two later, an invitation arrived—courteously worded, but significantly backed by an escort of half a dozen tall archers—for both Jeanne and the Mayor to attend at the Château without delay, Jeanne for her part received it with neither surprise nor reluctance. She had felt it especially hard that the only two interviews fate had granted her with the one man who had made some impression on her heart, should be hampered, the one by considerations of propriety, the other by the conflicting claims of her profession and its duties. On this occasion, now, she would have an excellent chaperon in the Mayor; and business being over for the day, they could meet and unbend on a common social footing. The Mayor was not at all surprised either, considering what had gone before; but he was exceedingly terrified, and sought some consolation from Jeanne as they proceeded together to the Château. That young lady's remarks, however, could hardly be called exactly comforting.

"I always thought you'd put your foot in it some day, Mayor," she said. "You are so hopelessly wanting in system and method. Really, under the present happy-go-lucky police arrangements, I never know whom I may

not be called upon to execute. Between you and my
cousin Enguerrand, life is hardly safe in this town. And
the worst of it is, that we other officials on the staff have
to share in the discredit."

"What do you think they'll do to me, Jeanne?"
whimpered the Mayor, perspiring freely.

"Can't say, I'm sure," pursued the candid Jeanne.
"Of course, if it's anything in the *rack* line of business,
I shall have to superintend the arrangements, and then
you can feel sure you're in capable hands. But probably
they'll only fine you pretty smartly, give you a month
or two in the dungeons, and dismiss you from your post;
and you will hardly grudge any slight personal inconvenience resulting from an arrangement so much to the
advantage of the town."

This was hardly reassuring, but the Mayor's official
reprimand of the previous day still rankled in this
unforgiving young person's mind.

On their reaching the Château, the Mayor was conducted aside, to be dealt with by Thibault; and from
the sounds of agonized protestation and lament which
shortly reached Jeanne's ears, it was evident that he was
having a *mauvais quart d'heure*. The young lady was
shown respectfully into a chamber apart, where she had
hardly had time to admire sufficiently the good taste of
the furniture and the magnificence of the tapestry with
which the walls were hung, when the Seigneur entered
and welcomed her with a cordial grace that put her
entirely at her ease.

"Your punctuality puts me to shame, fair mistress,"
he said, "considering how unwarrantably I kept you
waiting this morning, and how I tested your patience by
my ignorance and awkwardness."

He had changed his dress, and the lace round his neck
was even richer than before. Jeanne had always con-

sidered one of the chief marks of a well-bred man to be a fine disregard for the amount of his washing-bill; and then with what good taste he referred to recent events—putting himself in the wrong, as a gentleman should!

"Indeed, my lord," she replied modestly, "I was only too anxious to hear from your own lips that you bore me no ill-will for the part forced on me by circumstances in our recent interview. Your lordship has sufficient critical good sense, I feel sure, to distinguish between the woman and the official."

"True, Jeanne," he replied, drawing nearer; "and while I shrink from expressing, in their fulness, all the feelings that the woman inspires in me, I have no hesitation—for I know it will give you pleasure—in acquainting you with the entire artistic satisfaction with which I watched you at your task!"

"But, indeed," said Jeanne, "you did not see me at my best. In fact, I can't help wishing—it's ridiculous, I know, because the thing is hardly practicable—but if I could only have carried my performance quite through, and put the last finishing touches to it, you would not have been judging me now by the mere 'blocking-in' of what promised to be a masterpiece!"

"Yes, I wish it could have been arranged somehow," said the Seigneur reflectively; "but perhaps it's better as it is. I am content to let the artist remain for the present on trust, if I may only take over, fully paid up, the woman I adore!"

Jeanne felt strangely weak. The official seemed oozing out at her fingers and toes, while the woman's heart beat even more distressingly.

"I have one little question to ask," he murmured (his arm was about her now). "Do I understand that you still claim your bonus?"

Jeanne felt like water in his strong embrace; but she nerved herself to answer faintly but firmly : " Yes ! "

" Then so do I," he replied, as his lips met hers.

.   .   .   .

Executions continued to occur in St. Radegonde; the Radegundians being conservative and very human. But much of the innocent enjoyment that formerly attended them departed after the fair Châtelaine had ceased to officiate. Enguerrand, on succeeding to the post, wedded Clairette, she being (he was heard to say) a more suitable match in mind and temper than others of whom he would name no names. Rumour had it, that he found his match and something over; while as for temper—and mind (which she gave him in bits)—— But the domestic trials of high-placed officials have a right to be held sacred. The profession, in spite of his best endeavours, languished nevertheless. Some said that the scaffold lacked its old attraction for criminals of spirit; others, more unkindly, that the headsman was the innocent cause, and that Enguerrand was less fatal in his new sphere than formerly, when practising in the criminal court as advocate for the defence.

KENNETH GRAHAME—*The Yellow Book.*

BROOKSMITH

WE are scattered now, the friends of the late Mr. Oliver Offord; but whenever we chance to meet I think we are conscious of a certain esoteric respect for each other. "Yes, you too have been in Arcadia," we seem not too grumpily to allow. When I pass the house in Mansfield Street I remember that Arcadia was there. I don't know who has it now, and I don't want to know; it's enough to be so sure that if I should ring the bell there would be no such luck for me as that Brooksmith should open the door. Mr. Offord, the most agreeable, the most lovable of bachelors, was a retired diplomatist, living on his pension, confined by his infirmities to his fireside and delighted to be found there any afternoon in the year by such visitors as Brooksmith allowed to come up. Brooksmith was his butler and his most intimate friend, to whom we all stood, or I should say sat, in the same relation in which the subject of the sovereign finds himself to the prime minister. By having been for years, in foreign lands, the most delightful Englishman anyone had ever known, Mr. Offord had, in my opinion, rendered signal service to his country. But I suppose he had been too much liked—liked even by those who didn't like *it*—so that as people of that sort never get titles or dotations for the horrid things they have *not* done, his principal reward was simply that we went to see him.

Oh, we went perpetually, and it was not our fault if he was not overwhelmed with this particular honour. Any visitor who came once came again—to come merely once was a slight which nobody, I am sure, had ever put upon him. His circle, therefore, was essentially composed of *habitués*, who were *habitués* for each other as well as for him, as those of a happy *salon* should be. I remember vividly every element of the place, down to the intensely Londonish look of the grey opposite houses, in the gap of the white curtains of the high windows, and the exact spot where, on a particular afternoon, I put down my tea-cup for Brooksmith, lingering an instant, to gather it up as if he were plucking a flower. Mr. Offord's drawing-room was indeed Brooksmith's garden, his pruned and tended human *parterre*, and if we all flourished there and grew well in our places it was largely owing to his supervision.

Many persons have heard much, though most have doubtless seen little, of the famous institution of the *salon*, and many are born to the depression of knowing that this finest flower of social life refuses to bloom where the English tongue is spoken. The explanation is usually that our women have not the skill to cultivate it—the art to direct, between suggestive shores, the course of the stream of talk. My affectionate, my pious memory of Mr. Offord contradicts this induction only, I fear, more insidiously to confirm it. The very sallow and slightly smoked drawing-room in which he spent so large a portion of the last years of his life certainly deserved the distinguished name; but on the other hand it could not be said at all to owe its stamp to the soft pressure of the indispensable sex. The dear man had indeed been capable of one of those sacrifices to which women are deemed peculiarly apt; he had recognized (under the influence, in some degree, it is true, of physical infirmity) that if you wished people to find you at home you must manage not to be out. He had in short accepted the fact which many dabblers in the social art are slow to learn, that you must really, as they say, take a line and that the only way to be at home is to stay at home. Finally his own fireside had become a summary of his habits. Why should he ever have left it?—since this would have been leaving what was notoriously pleasantest in London, the compact charmed cluster (thinning away indeed into casual couples) round the fine old last century chimney-piece which, with the exception of the remarkable collection of miniatures, was the best thing the place contained. Mr. Offord was not rich; he had nothing but his pension and the use for life of the somewhat superannuated house.

When I am reminded by some uncomfortable contrast of to-day how perfectly we were all handled there I ask myself once more what had been the secret of such perfection. One had taken it for granted at the time, for anything that is supremely good produces more acceptance than surprise. I felt we were all happy, but I didn't consider how our happiness was managed. And yet there were questions to be asked, questions that strike me as singularly obvious now that there is nobody to answer them. Mr. Offord had solved the insoluble; he had, without feminine help (save in the sense that ladies were dying to come to him and he saved the lives of several), established a *salon*; but I might have guessed that there was a method in his madness—a law in his success. He had not hit it off by a mere fluke. There was an art in it all, and how was the art so hidden? Who, indeed, if it came to that, was the occult artist? Launching this inquiry the other day, I had already got hold of the tail of my reply. I was helped by the very wonder of some of the conditions that came back to me—those that used to seem as natural as sunshine in a fine climate.

How was it, for instance, that we never were a crowd,

never either too many or too few, always the right people *with* the right people (there must really have been no wrong people at all), always coming and going, never sticking fast nor overstaying, yet never popping in or out with an indecorous familiarity? How was it that we all sat where we wanted and moved when we wanted and met whom we wanted and escaped whom we wanted; joining, according to the accident of inclination, the general circle or falling in with a single talker on a convenient sofa? Why were all the sofas so convenient, the accidents so happy, the talkers so ready, the listeners so willing, the subjects presented to you in a rotation as quickly fore-ordained as the courses at dinner? A dearth of topics would have been as unheard of as a lapse in the service. These speculations couldn't fail to lead me to the fundamental truth that Brooksmith had been somehow at the bottom of the mystery. If he had not established the *salon* at least he had carried it on. Brooksmith, in short, was the artist!

We felt this, covertly, at the time, without formulating it, and were conscious, as an ordered and prosperous community, of his even-handed justice, untainted with flunkeyism. He had none of that vulgarity—his touch was infinitely fine. The delicacy of it was clear to me on the first occasion my eyes rested, as they were so often to rest again, on the domestic revealed, in the turbid light of the street, by the opening of the house-door. I saw on the spot that though he had plenty of school he carried it without arrogance—he had remained articulate and human. *L'Ecole Anglaise*, Mr. Offord used to call him, laughing, when, later, it happened more than once that we had some conversation about him. But I remember accusing Mr. Offord of not doing him quite ideal justice. That he was not one of the giants of the school, however, my old friend, who really understood him perfectly and was devoted to him, as I shall show, quite admitted; which doubtless poor Brooksmith had himself felt, to his cost, when his value in the market was originally determined. The utility of his class in general is estimated by the foot and the inch, and poor Brooksmith had only about five feet two to put into circulation. He acknowledged the inadequacy of this provision, and I am sure was penetrated with the ever-lasting fitness of the relation between service and stature. If *he* had been Mr. Offord he certainly would have found Brooksmith wanting, and indeed the laxity of his em-ployer on this score was one of many things which he had had to condone and to which he had at last indul-gently adapted himself.

I remember the old man's saying to me: "Oh, my servants, if they can live with me a fortnight they can live with me for ever. But it's the first fortnight that tries 'em." It was in the first fortnight, for instance, that Brooksmith had had to learn that he was exposed to being addressed as "my dear fellow" and "my poor child." Strange and deep must such a probation have been to him, and he doubtless emerged from it tempered and purified. This was written to a certain extent in his appearance; in his spare, brisk little person, in his clois-tered white face and extraordinarily polished hair, which told of responsibility, looked as if it were kept up to the same high standard as the plate; in his small, clear, anxious eyes, even in the permitted, though not exactly encouraged tuft on his chin. "He thinks me rather mad, but I've broken him in, and now he likes the place, he likes the company," said the old man. I embraced this fully after I had become aware that Brooksmith's main characteristic was a deep and shy refinement, though I remember I was rather puzzled when, on another occasion, Mr. Offord remarked: "What he likes is the talk—mingling in the conversation." I was conscious that I had never seen Brooksmith permit himself this freedom, but I guessed in a moment that what Mr. Offord alluded to was a participation more intense than any speech could have represented—that of being perpetually present on a hundred legitimate pretexts, errands, necessities, and breathing the very atmosphere of criticism, the famous criticism of life. "Quite an education, sir, isn't it, sir?" he said to me one day at the foot of the stairs, when he was letting me out; and I have always remembered the words and the tone as the first sign of the quickening drama of poor Brooksmith's fate. It was indeed an education, but to what was this sensitive young man of thirty-five, of the servile class, being educated?

Practically and inevitably, for the time, to companionship, to the perpetual, the even exaggerated reference and appeal of a person brought to dependence by his time of life and his infirmities and always addicted moreover (this was the exaggeration) to the art of giving you pleasure by letting you do things for him. There were certain things Mr. Offord was capable of pretending he liked you to do, even when he didn't, if he thought *you* liked them. If it happened that you didn't either (this was rare, but it might be), of course there were cross-purposes; but Brooksmith was there to prevent their going very far. This was precisely the way he acted as moderator: he averted misunderstandings or cleared them up. He had been capable, strange as it may appear, of acquiring for this purpose an insight into the French tongue, which was often used at Mr. Offord's; for besides being habitual to most of the foreigners, and they were many, who haunted the place or arrived with letters (letters often requiring a little worried consideration, of which Brooksmith always had cognisance), it had really become the primary language of the master of the house. I don't know if all the *malentendus* were in French, but almost all the explanations were, and this didn't a bit prevent Brooksmith from following them. I know Mr. Offord used to read passages to him from Montaigne and Saint-Simon, for he read perpetually when he was alone—when they were alone, I should say —and Brooksmith was always about. Perhaps you'll say no wonder Mr. Offord's butler regarded him as " rather mad." However, if I'm not sure what he thought about Montaigne I'm convinced he admired Saint-Simon. A certain feeling for letters must have rubbed off on him from the mere handling of his master's books, which he was always carrying to and fro and putting back in their places.

I often noticed that if an anecdote or a quotation, much more a lively discussion, was going forward, he would, if busy with the fire or the curtains, the lamp or the tea, find a pretext for remaining in the room till the point should be reached. If his purpose was to catch it you were not discreet to call him off, and I shall never forget a look, a hard, stony stare (I caught it in its passage), which, one day when there were a good many people in the room, he fastened upon the footman who was helping him in the service and who, in an undertone, had asked him some irrelevant question. It was the only manifestation of harshness that I ever observed on Brooksmith's part, and at first I wondered what was the matter. Then I became conscious that Mr. Offord was relating a very curious anecdote, never before perhaps made so public, and imparted to the narrator by an eye-witness of the fact, bearing upon Lord Byron's life in Italy. Nothing would induce me to reproduce it here; but Brooksmith had been in danger of losing it. If I ever should venture to reproduce it I shall feel how much I lose in not having my fellow-auditor to refer to.

The first day Mr. Offord's door was closed was therefore a dark date in contemporary history. It was raining hard and my umbrella was wet, but Brooksmith took it from me exactly as if this were a preliminary for going upstairs. I observed, however, that instead of putting it away he held it poised and trickling over the rug, and then I became aware that he was looking at me with deep acknowledging eyes—his air of universal responsibility. I immediately understood; there was scarcely need of the question and the answer that passed between us. When I did understand that the old man had given up, for the first time, though only for the occasion, I exclaimed dolefully: "What a difference it will make—and to how many people!"

"I shall be one of them, sir!" said Brooksmith; and that was the beginning of the end.

Mr. Offord came down again, but the spell was broken, and the great sign of it was that the conversation was, for the first time, not directed. It wandered and stumbled, a little frightened, like a lost child—it had let go the nurse's hand. "The worst of it is that now we shall talk about my health—*c'est la fin de tout*," Mr. Offord said, when he reappeared; and then I recognized what a sign of change that would be—for he had never tolerated anything so provincial. The talk became ours, in a word —not his; and as ours, even when *he* talked, it could only be inferior. In this form it was a distress to Brooksmith, whose attention now wandered from it altogether: he had so much closer a vision of his master's intimate conditions than our superficialities represented. There were better hours, and he was more in and out of the room, but I could see that he was conscious that the great institution was falling to pieces. He seemed to wish to take counsel with me about it, to feel responsible for its

going on in some form or other. When for the second
period—the first had lasted several days—he had to tell
me that our old friend didn't receive, I half expected to
hear him say after a moment: "Do you think I ought
to, sir, in his place?"—as he might have asked me, with
the return of autumn, if I thought he had better light
the drawing-room fire.

He had resigned philosophic sense of what his guests
—our guests, as I came to regard them in our colloquies
—would expect. His feeling was that he wouldn't absolutely have approved of himself as a substitute for the
host; but he was so saturated with the religion of habit
that he would have made, for our friends, the necessary
sacrifice to the divinity. He would take them on a little
further, till they could look about them. I think I saw
him also mentally confronted with the opportunity to
deal—for once in his life—with some of his own dumb
preferences, his limitations of sympathy, *weeding* a little,
in prospect, and returning to a purer tradition. It was
not unknown to me that he considered that toward the
end of Mr. Offord's career a certain laxity of selection
had crept in.

At last it came to be the case that we all found the
closed door more often than the open one; but even when
it was closed Brooksmith managed a crack for me to
squeeze through; so that practically I never turned away
without having paid a visit. The difference simply came
to be that the visit was to Brooksmith. It took place in
the hall, at the familiar foot of the stairs, and we didn't
sit down—at least Brooksmith didn't; moreover it was
devoted wholly to one topic and always had the air of
being already over—beginning, as it were, at the end.
But it was always interesting—it always gave me something to think about. It is true that the subject of my
meditation was ever the same—ever "It's all very well,

but what *will* become of Brooksmith? " Even my private
answer to this question left me still unsatisfied. No
doubt Mr. Offord would provide for him, but *what* would
he provide? that was the great point. He couldn't provide society; and society had become a necessity of
Brooksmith's nature. I must add that he never showed
a symptom of what I may call sordid solicitude—anxiety
on his own account. He was rather livid and intensely
grave, as befitted a man before whose eyes the " shade of
that which once was great " was passing away. He had
the solemnity of a person winding up, under depressing
circumstances, a long established and celebrated business; he was a kind of social executor or liquidator. But
his manner seemed to testify exclusively to the uncer-
tainty of *our* future. I couldn't in those days have
afforded it—I lived in two rooms in Jermyn Street and
didn't " keep a man "; but even if my income had permitted I shouldn't have ventured to say to Brooksmith
(emulating Mr. Offord), " My dear fellow, I'll take you
on." The whole tone of our intercourse was so much
more an implication that it was *I* who should now want
a lift. Indeed there was a tacit assurance in Brooksmith's
whole attitude that he would have me on his mind.

One of the most assiduous members of our circle had
been Lady Kenyon, and I remember his telling me one
day that her ladyship had, in spite of her own infirmities, lately much aggravated, been in person to inquire.
In answer to this I remarked that she would feel it more
than anyone. Brooksmith was silent a moment; at the
end of which he said, in a certain tone (there is no
reproducing some of his tones), " I'll go and see her." I
went to see her myself, and I learned that he had waited
upon her; but when I said to her, in the form of a joke
but with a core of earnest, that when all was over some
of us ought to combine, to club together to set Brook-

n his own account, she replied a trifle dis-
ly: "Do you mean in a public-house?" I
t her in a way that I think Brooksmith himself
have approved, and then I answered: "Yes, the
d Arms." What I had meant, of course, was that,
the love of art itself, we ought to look to it that
such a peculiar faculty and so much acquired experience
should not be wasted. I really think that if we had
caused a few black-edged cards to be struck off and circulated—"Mr. Brooksmith will continue to receive on
the old premises from four to seven; business carried on
as usual during the alterations"—the majority of us
would have rallied.

Several times he took me upstairs—always by his own
proposal—and our dear old friend, in bed, in a curious
flowered and brocaded *casaque* which made him, especially as his head was tied up in a handkerchief to match,
look, to my imagination, like the dying Voltaire, held
for ten minutes a sadly shrunken little *salon*. I felt
indeed each time, as if I were attending the last *coucher*
of some social sovereign. He was royally whimsical
about his sufferings and not at all concerned—quite as
if the Constitution provided for the case—about his
successor. He glided over *our* sufferings charmingly,
and none of his jokes—it was a gallant abstention, some
of them would have been so easy—were at our expense.
Now and again, I confess, there was one at Brooksmith's,
but so pathetically sociable as to make the excellent man
look at me in a way that seemed to say: "Do exchange
a glance with me, or I shan't be able to stand it." What
he was not able to stand was not what Mr. Offord said
about him, but what he wasn't able to say in return. His
notion of conversation, for himself, was giving you the
convenience of speaking to him; and when he went to
"see" Lady Kenyon, for instance, it was to carry her the

tribute of his receptive silence. Where would the speech of his betters have been if proper service had been a manifestation of sound? In that case the fundamental difference would have had to be shown by *their* dumbness, and many of them, poor things, were dumb enough without that provision. Brooksmith took an unfailing interest in the preservation of the fundamental difference; it was the thing he had most on his conscience.

What had become of it, however, when Mr. Offord passed away like any inferior person—was relegated to eternal stillness like a butler upstairs? His aspect for several days after the expected event may be imagined, and the multiplication by funereal observance of the things he didn't say. When everything was over—it was late the same day—I knocked at the door of the house of mourning as I so often had done before. I could never call on Mr. Offord again, but I had come, literally, to call on Brooksmith. I wanted to ask him if there was anything I could do for him, tainted with vagueness as this inquiry could only be. My wild dream of taking him into my own service had died away: my service was not worth his being taken into. My offer to him could only be to help him to find another place, and yet there was an indelicacy, as it were, in taking for granted that his thoughts would immediately be fixed on another. I had a hope that he would be able to give his life a different form—though certainly not the form, the frequent result of such bereavements, of his setting up a little shop. That would have been dreadful; for I should have wished to further any enterprise that he might embark in, yet how could I have brought myself to go and pay him shillings and take back coppers over a counter? My visit then was simply an intended compliment. He took it as such, gratefully and with all the tact in the world. He knew I really couldn't help him and that I knew he knew

I couldn't; but we discussed the situation—with a good deal of elegant generality—at the foot of the stairs, in the hall already dismantled, where I had so often discussed other situations with him. The executors were in posession, as was still more apparent when he made me pass for a few minutes into the dining-room, where various objects were muffled up for removal.

Two definite facts, however, he had to communicate; one being that he was to leave the house for ever that night (servants, for some mysterious reason, seem always to depart by night), and the other—he mentioned it only at the last, with hesitation—that he had already been informed his late master had left him a legacy of eighty pounds. "I'm very glad," I said, and Brooksmith rejoined: "It was so like him to think of me." This was all that passed between us on the subject, and I know nothing of his judgment of Mr. Offord's memento. Eighty pounds are always eighty pounds, and no one has ever left *me* an equal sum; but, all the same, for Brooksmith, I was disappointed. I don't know what I had expected—in short I was disappointed. Eighty pounds might stock a little shop—a *very* little shop; but, I repeat, I couldn't bear to think of that. I asked my friend if he had been able to save a little, and he replied: "No, sir; I have had to do things." I didn't inquire what things he had had to do; they were his own affair, and I took his word for them as assentingly as if he had had the greatness of an ancient house to keep up; especially as there was something in his manner that seemed to convey a prospect of further sacrifice.

"I shall have to turn round a bit, sir—I shall have to look about me," he said; and then he added, indulgently, magnanimously: "If you should happen to hear of anything for me——"

I couldn't let him finish; this was, in its essence, too

much in the really grand manner. It would be a help to my getting him off my mind to be able to pretend I *could* find the right place, and that help he wished to give me, for it was doubtless painful to him to see me in so false a position. I interposed with a few words to the effect that I was well aware that wherever he should go, whatever he should do, he would miss our old friend terribly— miss him even more than I should, having been with him so much more. This led him to make the speech that I have always remembered as the very text of the whole episode.

" Oh, sir, it's sad for *you*, very sad, indeed, and for a great many gentlemen and ladies; that it is, sir. But for me, sir, it is, if I may say so, still graver even than that: it's just the loss of something that was everything. For me, sir," he went on, with rising tears, " he was just *all*, if you know what I mean, sir. You have others, sir, I daresay—not that I would have you understand me to speak of them as in any way tantamount. But you have the pleasures of society, sir; if it's only in talking about him, sir, as I daresay you do freely—for all his blessed memory has to fear from it—with gentlemen and ladies who have had the same honour. That's not for me, sir, and I have to keep my associations to myself. Mr. Offord was *my* society, and now I have no more. You go back to conversation, sir, after all, and I go back to my place," Brooksmith stammered, without exaggerated irony or dramatic bitterness, but with a flat, unstudied veracity and his hand on the knob of the street-door. He turned it to let me out and then he added: " I just go downstairs, sir, again, and I stay there."

" My poor child," I replied, in my emotion, quite as Mr. Offord used to speak, " my dear fellow, leave it to me; we'll look after you, we'll all do something for you."

" Ah, if you could give me some one *like* him! But

there ain't two in the world," said Brooksmith as we parted.

He had given me his address—the place where he would be to be heard of. For a long time I had no occasion to make use of the information; for he proved indeed, on trial, a very difficult case. In a word the people who knew him and had known Mr. Offord, didn't want to take him, and yet I couldn't bear to try to thrust him among people who didn't know him. I spoke to many of our old friends about him, and I found them all governed by the odd mixture of feelings of which I myself was conscious, and disposed, further, to entertain a suspicion that he was "spoiled," with which I then would have nothing to do. In plain terms a certain embarrassment, a sensible awkwardness, when they thought of it, attached to the idea of using him as a menial: they had met him so often in society. Many of them would have asked him, and did ask him, or rather did ask me to ask him, to come and see them; but a mere visiting-list was not what I wanted for him. He was too short for people who were very particular; nevertheless I heard of an opening in a diplomatic household which led me to write him a note, though I was looking much less for something grand than for something human. Five days later I heard from him. The secretary's wife had decided, after keeping him waiting till then, that she couldn't take a servant out of a house in which there had not been a lady. The note had a P.S.: "It's a good job there wasn't, sir, such a lady as some."

A week later he came to see me and told me he was "suited"—committed to some highly respectable people (they were something very large in the City), who lived on the Bayswater side of the Park. "I daresay it will be rather poor, sir," he admitted; "but I've seen the fireworks, haven't I, sir?—it can't be fireworks *every* night.

After Mansfield Street there ain't much choice." There was a certain amount, however, it seemed; for the following year, going one day to call on a country cousin, a lady of certain age who was spending a fortnight in town with some friends of her own, a family unknown to me and resident in Chester Square, the door of the house was opened, to my surprise and gratification, by Brooksmith in person. When I came out I had some conversation with him, from which I gathered that he had found the large City people too dull for endurance, and I guessed, though he didn't say it, that he had found them vulgar as well. I don't know what judgment he would have passed on his actual patrons if my relative had not been their friend; but under the circumstances he abstained from comment.

None was necessary, however, for before the lady in question brought her visit to a close they honoured me with an invitation to dinner, which I accepted. There was a largeish party on the occasion, but I confess I thought of Brooksmith rather more than of the seated company. They required no depth of attention—they were all referable to usual, irredeemable, inevitable types. It was the world of cheerful commonplace and conscious gentility and prosperous density, a full-fed, material, insular world, a world of hideous florid plate and ponderous order and thin conversation. There was not a word said about Byron. Nothing would have induced me to look at Brooksmith in the course of the repast, and I felt sure that not even my overturning the wine would have induced him to meet my eye. We were in intellectual sympathy—we felt, as regards each other, a kind of social responsibility. In short we had been in Arcadia together, and we had both come to *this*! No wonder we were ashamed to be confronted. When he helped on my overcoat, as I was going away, we parted, for the first

time since the earliest days in Mansfield Street, in silence.
I thought he looked lean and wasted, and I guessed that
his new place was not more " human " than his previous
one. There was plenty of beef and beer, but there was
no reciprocity. The question for him to have asked
before accepting the position would have been not
" How many footmen are kept? " but " How much
imagination? "

The next time I went to the house—I confess it was
not very soon—I encountered his successor, a personage
who evidently enjoyed the good fortune of never having
quitted his natural level. Could any be higher? he
seemed to ask—over the heads of three footmen and
even of some visitors. He made me feel as if Brooksmith
were dead; but I didn't dare to inquire—I couldn't have
borne his " I haven't the least idea, sir." I despatched a
note to the address Brooksmith had given me after Mr.
Offord's death, but I received no answer. Six months
later, however, I was favoured with a visit from an
elderly, dreary, dingy person, who introduced herself to
me as Mr. Brooksmith's aunt and from whom I learned
that he was out of place and out of health and had
allowed her to come and say to me that if I could spare
half an hour to look in at him he would take it as a
rare honour.

I went the next day—his messenger had given me a
new address—and found my friend lodged in a short
sordid street in Marylebone, one of those corners of
London that wear the last expression of sickly meanness.
The room into which I was shown was above the small
establishment of a dyer and cleaner who had inflated
kid gloves and discoloured shawls in his shop-front.
There was a great deal of grimy infant life up and down
the place, and there was a hot, moist smell within, as of
the " boiling " of dirty linen. Brooksmith sat with a

blanket over his legs at a clean little window, where, from behind stiff bluish-white curtains, he could look across at a huckster's and a tinsmith's and a small greasy public-house. He had passed through an illness and was convalescent, and his mother, as well as his aunt, was in attendance on him. I liked the mother, who was bland and intensely humble, but I didn't much fancy the aunt, whom I connected, perhaps unjustly, with the opposite public-house (she seemed somehow to be greasy with the same grease), and whose furtive eye followed every movement of my hand, as if to see if it were not going into my pocket. It didn't take this direction—I couldn't, unsolicited, put myself at that sort of ease with Brooksmith. Several times the door of the room opened, and mysterious old women peeped in and shuffled back again. I don't know who they were; poor Brooksmith seemed encompassed with vague, prying, beery females.

He was vague himself, and evidently weak, and much embarrassed, and not an allusion was made between us to Mansfield Street. The vision of the *salon* of which he had been an ornament hovered before me, however, by contrast, sufficiently. He assured me that he was really getting better, and his mother remarked that he would come round if he could only get his spirits up. The aunt echoed this opinion, and I became more sure that in her own case she knew where to go for such a purpose. I'm afraid I was rather weak with my old friend, for I neglected the opportunity, so exceptionally good, to rebuke the levity which had led him to throw up honourable positions—fine, stiff, steady berths, with morning prayers, as I knew, attached to one of them—in Bayswater and Belgravia. Very likely his reasons had been profane and sentimental; he didn't want morning prayers, he wanted to be somebody's dear fellow; but I couldn't be the person to rebuke him. He shuffled these episodes out of sight—I saw that he had no wish to discuss them. I perceived further, strangely enough, that it would probably be a questionable pleasure for him to see me again: he doubted now even of my power to condone his aberrations. He didn't wish to have to explain; and his behaviour, in future, was likely to need explanation. When I bade him farewell he looked at me a moment with eyes that said everything: " How can I talk about those exquisite years in this place, before these people, with the old women poking their heads in? It was very good of you to come to see me—it wasn't my idea; *she* brought you. We've said everything; it's over; you'll lose all patience with me, and I'd rather you shouldn't see the rest." I sent him some money, in a letter, the next day, but I saw the rest only in the light of a barren sequel.

A whole year after my visit to him I became aware once, in dining out, that Brooksmith was one of the several servants who hovered behind our chairs. He had not opened the door of the house to me, and I had not recognized him in the cluster of retainers in the hall. This time I tried to catch his eye, but he never gave me a chance, and when he handed me a dish I could only be careful to thank him audibly. Indeed I partook of two *entrées* of which I had my doubts, subsequently converted into certainties, in order not to snub him. He looked well enough in health, but much older, and wore, in an exceptionally marked degree, the glazed and expressionless mask of the British domestic *de race*. I saw with dismay that if I had not known him I should have taken him, on the showing of his countenance, for an extravagant illustration of irresponsive servile gloom. I said to myself that he had become a reactionary, gone over to the Philistines, thrown himself into religion, the religion of his " place," like a foreign lady *sur le retour*.

I divined moreover that he was only engaged for the evening—he had become a mere waiter, had joined the band of the white-waistcoated who " go out." There was something pathetic in this fact, and it was a terrible vulgarization of Brooksmith. It was the mercenary prose of butlerhood; he had given up the struggle for the poetry. If reciprocity was what he had missed, where was the reciprocity now? Only in the bottoms of the wineglasses and the five shillings (or whatever they get), clapped into his hand by the permanent man. However, I supposed he had taken up a precarious branch of his profession because after all it sent him less downstairs. His relations with London society were more superficial, but they were of course more various. As I went away, on this occasion, I looked out for him eagerly among the four or five attendants whose perpendicular persons, fluting the walls of London passages, are supposed to lubricate the process of departure; but he was not on duty. I asked one of the others if he were not in the house, and received the prompt answer: " Just left, sir. Anything I can do for you, sir? " I wanted to say " Please give him my kind regards "; but I abstained; I didn't want to compromise him, and I never came across him again.

Often and often, in dining out, I looked for him, sometimes accepting invitations on purpose to multiply the chances of my meeting him. But always in vain; so that as I met many other members of the casual class over and over again, I at last adopted the theory that he always procured a list of expected guests beforehand and kept away from the banquets which he thus learned I was to grace. At last I gave up hope, and one day, at the end of three years, I received another visit from his aunt. She was drearier and dingier, almost squalid, and she was in great tribulation and want. Her sister, Mrs.

Brooksmith, had been dead a year, and three months later her nephew had disappeared. He had always looked after her a bit—since her troubles; I never knew what her troubles had been—and now she hadn't so much as a petticoat to pawn. She had also a niece, to whom she had been everything, before her troubles, but the niece had treated her most shameful. These were details; the great and romantic fact was Brooksmith's final evasion of his fate. He had gone out to wait one evening, as usual, in a white waistcoat she had done up for him with her own hands, being due at a large party up Kensington way. But he had never come home again, and had never arrived at the large party, or at any party that anyone could make out. No trace of him had come to light—no gleam of the white waistcoat had pierced the obscurity of his doom. This news was a sharp shock to me, for I had my ideas about his real destination. His aged relative had promptly, as she said, guessed the worst. Somehow and somewhere he had got out of the way altogether, and now I trust that, with characteristic deliberation, he is changing the plates of the immortal gods. As my depressing visitant also said, he never *had* got his spirits up. I was fortunately able to dismiss her with her own somewhat improved. But the dim ghost of poor Brooksmith is one of those that I see. He had indeed been spoiled.

HENRY JAMES—*The Lesson of the Master.*

NOTES

DR. HEIDEGGER'S EXPERIMENT

HAWTHORNE was born in Massachusetts in 1804, and being appointed to a post in the Customs at Boston and, later, at Salem, was able to devote himself to writing without fear of poverty. His college friend, Pierce, afterwards President of the United States, got him the appointment of U.S. Consul at Liverpool, where he lived from 1853 to 1857. He died in 1864. "Dr. Heidegger's Experiment" was one of a collection of the stories which he had published in his Salem days in the *New England Magazine* under assumed names, and which he issued in 1837 in a volume entitled *Twice Told Tales*. This volume, apart from containing some of his best known stories, such as "Wakefield" and "The Grey Champion," also contained one, "Endicott and the Red Cross," which was later to suggest to him the story which he developed into his most famous novel, *The Scarlet Letter*. Of his other full-length stories, *The House of the Seven Gables* and *The Marble Faun* have survived.

Hawthorne's most noticeable characteristic is the tendency to turn the story into a parable, to leap from the real to the imaginary and back again, and of this tendency "Dr. Heidegger's Experiment" is an excellent example. Eighteenth-century short stories had, like Mrs. Edgeworth's and Hannah More's *Moral Tales*, been sentimental and mawkish: occasionally the tale of terror had intruded, but one and all, whatever their other merits, had been without form or planned construction. Writing in the *Cambridge History of American Literature*, Professor F. L. Pattee sums up Hawthorne's work in the words that he " added soul to the short story and made it a form that could be taken seriously even by those who had contended that it was inferior to the longer forms of fiction. He centred his effort in a single situation and gave to the whole tale unity." It comes to this, that Hawthorne, sombre and humourless though he often is, set the fashion in artistic story-writing and was the first to demonstrate its possibilities as an art-form.

Hippocrates: the most famous of the doctors of the ancient world, a member of a family which was notable for its contributions to medicine. He is said to have been born about 460 B.C., and died more than a century later, c. 357 B.C.

Ponce de Leon: Juan Ponce de Leon accompanied Columbus on his second voyage, and after some years in the West Indies, having heard from the natives of a fountain said to possess the power of restoring youth, toured the islands, drinking of every spring, river or lake that he met: all in vain. In the course of his search he discovered Florida, which he believed to be an island.

THE MASQUE OF THE RED DEATH

No volume of nineteenth-century short stories would be complete if it did not include an example of Poe's work, since he is the most significant figure in the history of the short story. The particular story chosen from the volume entitled *Tales of Mystery or Imagination* will depend on taste: " The Masque of the Red Death " is pure imagination with the added virtue of being a model of English style. Of those more frequently chosen, " The Gold-Bug " is a puzzle; " The Cask of Amontillado " is a highly concentrated thriller: " The Murders in the Rue Morgue " is a forerunner of Conan Doyle; " The Pit and the Pendulum " a tale of horror and suspense. All of them, however, are designed to bring out some definite effect and to present that effect, as he himself says in the passage on the short story from which we have quoted in the introduction, " unblemished, because undisturbed." Though Hawthorne is his superior in sympathy and the depicting of character, Poe's vivid descriptions and balanced plots, in fact his handling of atmosphere, make him the most artistic of all short story writers. In saying this, however, we must not be blind to his limitations. He had no sense of dialogue—one of the things which contribute to the excellence of " The Masque " is the absence of dialogue—and his stories are unreal, not life as it is lived. Later writers surpass him, bringing to their task light and shade, humour and pathos which Poe could never do.

Poe was born at Boston, Massachusetts, in 1809, and from the age of five to that of eleven was educated in London. Most of his life was passed in Virginia, where he became editor of *The Southern Literary Messenger,* in which a number of his tales and his literary criticism—for Poe was a critic of conspicuous ability—appeared. He died in 1849.

Avatar: originally a Sanskrit word meaning " descent " and applied to the appearance of Hindu gods in fleshly form. Poe uses the word to imply " visible sign."

decora: what is called lower down " the movable embellishments ": nowadays applied in the shorter form " decor " to stage furnishings.

Hernani: an early play of Victor Hugo's: " a piece of bombastic melodrama full of the stagiest clap-trap " (Lytton Strachey).

THE SEXTON'S HERO

THERE is very little local colour in Hawthorne: except in a few stories, such as " Mr. Higginbotham's Catastrophe " and those about the past of New England, the scene of the tale might be anywhere. There is some evidence to suggest that Mrs. Gaskell was influenced by Hawthorne: her short story, " Lois the Witch," was a tale of the crusade against witchcraft in his own town, Salem. Mrs. Gaskell was one of the first writers of short stories, however, to rely on local colour for background to the story, a technique which was destined to characterize in a marked degree the work of such later writers as Bret Harte and Ambrose Bierce. Mrs. Gaskell's tales appeared in *Household Words* or other magazines, and their subjects are as varied as the authoress's genius—sometimes humorous, sometimes tragic stories of crime, and more often scenes of domestic pathos as in " The Sexton's Hero." She is fond of portraying acts of duty and devotion, and if she has a weakness, it is that she is an ardent partisan of virtue, determined to point her moral, and disinclined to allow the tale to tell its own story.

Mrs. Gaskell (1810-65) was the wife of a Unitarian minister in Manchester, and is said to have taken up writing at her husband's suggestion to distract her from her sorrow at the death of her only son. She reached the height of her reputation in 1853 with *Cranford*, and died when she had almost completed what is possibly her most finished work, *Wives and Daughters*. She and her husband had a holiday home in the Lake District in close proximity to Grange-over-Sands and Bolton-in-Furness, the scene of " The Sexton's Hero."

Lindal: a village in Furness. Lindal, Cartmel, and Grange, lie in a triangle, with sides about two miles long, on the north side of Morecambe Bay, with Bolton-le-Sands on the south. *Garstang:* ten miles south of Lancaster.

threeped: maintained or asserted.

shandry: a light two-wheeled cart.

beener: a Lancashire word meaning " more nimble " or " clever."

THE ITALIAN PRISONER

THIS story appeared in Dickens's magazine *All the Year Round*, and was reprinted in the collection entitled *The Uncommercial Traveller*, most of the papers of which were not stories but autobiographical essays: it is an exception to the others in this respect, and one of the few short stories from his pen that stands alone and is not incidental to a full-length novel, as, for instance, is " The Convict's Return " in *Pickwick Papers*. Dickens's genius found its expression in the long novel, which gave him scope for the drawing of sympathetic characters, and what Sir Arthur Quiller-Couch called his " broad plenty." It is included here for several reasons: taken as a whole, it shows some kinship with the story-telling of Hawthorne, with which Dickens's visits to America must have acquainted him; it has some indications, especially when the travels of the bottle are described, of his capacity for humorous exaggeration and melodramatic theatricalism; and it possesses some of the elements of which the later short story is to be compounded—local colour, sentiment, and dramatic situations. It has none of the artistic concentration of Poe, but it has Dickens's generous humanity.

Dickens has won so imperishable a place in our literature that it is hardly necessary to enlarge upon his achievements or his career. He was born in 1812 and died in 1870. The pieces included in *The Uncommercial Traveller* commenced to appear in January, 1860, and continued till his death. No. 35 (out of the total of 36 pieces, of which " The Italian Prisoner " is No. 28) is, except for a book review, the last contribution Dickens wrote for *All the Year Round*.

The rising of the Italian people: the Risorgimento, when the Italians, with the aid of the French Emperor Napoleon III, threw off the Austrian yoke and established the Kingdom of Italy under the House of Savoy (1859-60).

Pompeii: the Italian town blotted out by the eruption of Vesuvius in A.D. 79.

one of the vile old prisons: the prisons of the Kingdom of Naples under Ferdinand II (1834-59) were a byword, and his government was described by Gladstone as " the negation of God." Dickens is thinking of such a prison as the Castel dell' Ovo, so called by reason of its egg-shape, which stands on a small peninsula near the harbour of Naples.

Newgate Calendar: a book containing accounts of the principal crimes tried between 1700 and the close of the eighteenth century, when the book was published.

The Imp of the same name: afterwards used as the title of a story in Stevenson's *Island Nights' Entertainments*, the Bottle Imp comes from an early nineteenth-century play, by O. Smith.

Mr. Cruikshank: (1792-1878) a book illustrator who illus-
trated Dickens's own works. He tired of it and turned to
illustrating the evils of drink, for which purpose he
executed a series of eight engravings which he entitled
The Bottle.

lazzarone: a Neapolitan beggar.

Mazzini: the fiery advocate of Italian unity. He lived for
some time in London. He was an ardent Republican.

THE JOURNEY TO PANAMA

ANTHONY TROLLOPE (1815-82) was a born story-teller, a power
he inherited from his mother, and which no doubt accounts
for his renewed popularity in our own day. As a boy he
entered the service of the Post Office and, after seven years
in London, accepted the appointment of postal surveyor in
Ireland, where he remained from 1841 to 1859. In Ireland
he came into contact with the works of the Irish novelists,
particularly with those of Carleton, which he read and re-
read, and his first novel was clearly influenced by them. It
was during his Irish period that he commenced the Bar-
chester novels on which his fame securely rests. Trollope
had a remarkable capacity for making his characters live,
not only in the reader's mind, but apparently also in his
own, which is ample reason why to display the fulness of his
genius he needed a large canvas and was not quite at home
in the short story. From the Maria Edgeworths and Hannah Mores and, indeed, his mother, he inherited the desire
to convey through his story a moral lesson, but he also
brought to it a sense of realism and common sense which
acted as a corrective to the sentimental romanticism of the
earlier age. A modern critic (Dr. Ernest Baker, in *The
History of the English Novel*) says of him: " So far as he
was concerned, the art of fiction stood still: he might have
been a survivor from the eighteenth century." This tale
therefore carries on the English tradition of story-telling
and stands apart from the main stream of development

which in America was revolutionizing the technique of the short story.

Honi soit qui mal y pense: evil be to him who evil thinks.

bourne: a reminiscence of Hamlet's speech " . . . from whose bourn no traveller returns " as a euphemism for " death."

Cerberus: the three-headed dog who in Greek mythology guarded the entrance to the Lower World: hence, as here, used to imply " a vigilant guardian " and particularly apposite in this case, since Miss Viner had three guardians, Mr. and Mrs. Grumpy and their daughter.

BROTHER MORGAN'S STORY OF THE DEAD HAND

ALL Wilkie Collins's novels contain an ingenious plot or puzzle: *The Moonstone,* for example, is the first great detective novel in English. This story is drawn from a collection of short stories, or rather a series of short stories, linked by a common thread, to which he gave the title *Queen of Hearts.* Three old gentlemen tell stories, drawn from their experiences in life, for ten nights, in order to delay the departure of a fair young lady guest until such time as their nephew shall return from the Crimea to claim her as his bride. " Brother Morgan's Story "—he is a retired doctor, the other two being one a retired clergyman and one a retired lawyer—is a first-rate specimen of the type of story in which the plot is supreme and the characters are adapted to fit it. Collins was a friend and collaborator of Dickens in the production of both *Household Words* and of *All the Year Round*: Dr. Baker sums up the difference between them in the words " Dickens applied plot to character, Collins added character to plot." The young guest in the *Queen of Hearts* gives us Collins's view of what the public wanted in fiction, that art which he himself tells us, he had studied " anxiously for some years." " What I want," she says, " is something that seizes hold of my interest, and makes me forget when it is time to dress for dinner; something that keeps me reading, reading, reading, in a breath-

less state, to find out the end." And what the public wanted
—a thriller, with some characterization in the Dickens manner, and a love interest—he tried to give them. *Queen of
Hearts* (1859) is really a serial story, consisting of a number
of short thrillers, with the characterization and the love
interest in the setting: the compass of the short story is not
really wide enough to embrace these three elements of Collins's method.

Collins was born in 1824 and with his friend Charles
Reade is described as belonging to " the Dickens school " of
novelists. His best known short story is " The Terribly
Strange Bed " from *After Dark* (1856), but it is doubtful
whether it is as good as this story: Collins's reputation,
however, rests on his novels *The Woman in White* and *The
Moonstone*. He died in 1889.

TENNESSEE'S PARTNER

WHEN, just after the close of the American Civil War had
united all the States in a sense of common nationhood, Bret
Harte published in the *Overland Monthly*, of which he had
become editor, the story " The Luck of Roaring Camp," he
initiated a new phase in the history of the American short
story. What was new in it was the touch of " local colour,"
the background of picturesque men and women from the
mining areas of the Pacific coast and districts which the
American reader hardly knew, but of which he was eager to
learn. Consequently the story has been described as the
" most influential " ever written in America, for it was the
forerunner of the local colour movement in the eighties
and nineties, of Cable, of J. C. Harris's negro studies, of
Craddock's *In the Tennessee Mountains*, and of Mary Wilkins Freeman. Harte's work, however, in addition to his
development of that local colour which we have noticed in
the work of Carleton in Ireland and Mrs. Gaskell in England, owed something to the theatricalism of Dickens, and
something more to the principles he learnt from Poe—subtle
artistry, the avoidance of excess, description, the working

out of a single effect. While " The Luck of Roaring Camp "
is the most influential, because it was his first success, and
consequently the best known of Harte's tales, " The Out-
casts of Poker Flat " and " Tennessee's Partner " yield nothing to it in charm, and the latter, for the sake of freshness,
is selected for inclusion here. Francis Bret Harte was born
in Albany, N.Y., in 1839, but went to California at the age
of fifteen in the early years of the gold rush. He was suc-
cessively a teacher, a chemist's assistant, and a compositor,
before becoming an editor and reaching fame throughout
the United States. Later he went to Europe as an American
Consul, notably in Glasgow, and died in 1902.

Saleratus: from latin " sal," salt.

iron pyrites: the yellow sulphide of iron, known as "fools'
gold."

bowers: a term from the game of euchre, applied to the
Knave of trumps.

chaparral: tangled brushwood of thorny shrubs or ever-
green oaks.

euchred: scored off (from the game of euchre).

Judge Lynch: the imaginary judge of a self-constituted
court of justice.

buckeye-tree: Californian horse-chestnut.

catafalque: funeral bier, ironically used, since it is rather a
grandiose word.

A RESUMED IDENTITY

OF few short-story writers have there been such diverse
judgments as of Ambrose Bierce. *The Cambridge History
of American Literature*, while paying tribute to his crafts-
manship, is unenthusiastic as to his work on the whole and
gives him a very brief notice: A. G. Ward, on the other
hand, in *Aspects of the Modern Short Story*, obviously gives
him a high place among its exponents and regards the
majority of statements about his work as " perfunctory and
fatuous." Bierce's work is coloured by his detestation of
war as he had seen it during his experience of the American

Civil War of 1861-65; and it would probably be true to say that his stories exercise more appeal to a generation that has known two great European wars than they did at an earlier date. His best story, by common consent, is " A Horseman in the Sky," but it is so well known that it seemed desirable to include here another example of his manner. His work was originally published under the title of *Tales of Soldiers and Civilians*, the tales of soldiers being far more powerful than those of civilians: this story is drawn from a selection of them issued under the title *Can Such Things Be*, a title which is eminently suitable to stories which deal largely with the unreal, with hauntings and hallucinations and uncanny happenings.

Bierce was born in 1838 and fought for the North with the rank of Major in the Civil War. Afterwards he began to write his stories, but found little appreciation of them at the time. He came to London for a short time, but was unsettled and eventually went to Mexico, where he disappeared somewhere about 1914, and his ultimate fate is not known.

caisson: ammunition wagon.

timbre: the quality of a musical note apart from its pitch.

Appomattox: the scene of General Lee's surrender to the leader of the armies of the North, General Grant; this surrender ended the Civil War, in April 1865.

Nashville: the capital of Tennessee.

Murfreesboro: in Tennessee, thirty miles from Nashville: it is situated on a branch of Stone's river.

Federal Army: the Southern states called themselves the Confederates, the Northern are known as the Federals.

THE SIRE DE MALÉTROIT'S DOOR

ROBERT LOUIS STEVENSON, who was born in 1850 and died in 1894, was one of the most melodious writers of English, and whatever he wrote, whether stories or essays, is delightful to read. His reputation as a story-teller is embodied in the name which the natives of Samoa, where he spent his last

years, conferred upon him—*Tusitala*, the teller of tales—
and remembered wherever *Treasure Island* is read and
loved. He wrote a number of short stories, but unfortunately
the best are also the longest, and too long for inclusion here.
Though " The Sire de Malétroit's Door," which he originally
entitled " The Sire de Malétroit's Mouse-trap," has enjoyed
considerable popularity, and had its influence on the school
of writers of whom Harland is the leader, it is not a model
short story, nor did Stevenson himself in later years admire
it very much. It first appeared, as did another story of
medieval France—" A Lodging for the Night "—in the
magazine *Temple Bar*, and writing to Colvin in 1879, the
year after its appearance, Stevenson says, " I am no lover of
either of the things in *Temple Bar*; but they will make up
the volume (a proposed volume of his short stories) and
perhaps others may like them better than I do ": a pre-
diction that came true. It is essentially a story of atmosphere. It sprang from his frequent visits to that part of
France which had been the scene of the bitterest struggle
of the Hundred Years' War and culminated in Joan of Arc's
rescue of Orleans. One imagines Stevenson wandering
round the old-world town of Château Landon and " getting
action and persons to express and realize " the spirit of the
past which he felt around him. So we have the beautiful,
but quite unnecessary to the story, description of the old
town at night with which the tale opens : but if the story
violates the strict principles of unity it is still eminently
readable.

The best of Stevenson's short stories are generally admitted to be "The Beach of Falesa," and "The Bottle Imp,"
both in *The Island Nights' Entertainments*, and " The
Pavilion on the Links," which he himself described as
" grand carpentry."

September 1429: the year of the appearance of Joan of Arc.
England and Burgundy were at the moment in control of
Paris, and Henry VI of England was nominally King of
France, with the Duke of Bedford as regent.

Château Landon: A small and ancient town lying south-east

of Paris, near the fringe of the Forest of Fontainebleau
and not far from Barbizon where Stevenson frequently
stayed. It has quarries of a hard stone capable of taking
a high polish.

Bourges: the headquarters of the dispossessed Dauphin,
afterwards Charles VII of France, who was derisively
called the " King of Bourges."

Leonardo's women: Leonardo da Vinci, painter of the
famous Mona Lisa.

Queen Isabeau: Isabella of Bavaria, wife of the mad King,
Charles VI.

THE THREE STRANGERS

THOMAS HARDY was born in 1840 in the Dorsetshire village
of Upper Bockhampton, and all his life had a weakness for
the rustic superstitions, the grim stories and the creepy tales
which he heard during his childhood. He was trained as
an architect and met with considerable success in his studies,
but gave them up for the joys and the risks of authorship.
His first book was the charming rustic idyll which he called
Under the Greenwood Tree, published in 1872. It was in
Far From the Madding Crowd, published in 1874, that he
first gave the name of Wessex to the district of south England, with which his name is indissolubly linked. Hardy's
Wessex covers a great part of the counties of Hampshire,
Somerset, Wiltshire, and particularly his own Dorset:
Casterbridge is Dorchester, where he ultimately made his
home. *Wessex Tales* was published in 1888, a collection of
short stories written at various earlier times. Nothing in
Wessex Tales is finer than " The Three Strangers," which,
later in Hardy's life, he was induced by Sir James Barrie to
dramatize as a one-act play, entitled " The Three Way-
farers." To the English reader at the end of the nineteenth
century, Hardy and Meredith were the outstanding writers
of fiction of their time, and this story illustrates much that
was best in Hardy's work. The few swift strokes with which

the leading characters, the genial shepherd and his careful housewife, the hangman cheerfully proud of his unpleasant duty, and the debonair sheep-stealer, are delineated, and the knowledge of country ways and humour make this tale what Lascelles Abercrombie in his admirable study of Hardy's work calls it: "the same vision of life which is wrought into larger and more significant form in the novels." The emphasis on "local colour," sometimes unnecessary to the plot, brings it into relation with the work of the "local colour" school of America, and especially that of such a writer as Mary Wilkins Freeman. Hardy was awarded the Order of Merit in 1910 and died at a ripe old age in 1928.

Timon: Shakespeare's Timon of Athens, who withdrew " to the woods " after finding that the friends whom he had lavishly befriended would not extend a helping hand to him in his own difficulties.

Senlac: the Battle of Hastings, literally " lake of blood."

serpent: an old-fashioned wind instrument of deep tone, described as being about eight feet long, and made of wood covered with leather, having three U-shaped turns.

apogee to perigee: from a point in a planet's orbit farthest from the earth to one nearest to the earth.

metheglin: a spiced variety of mead, originally peculiar to Wales.

Belshazzar's Feast: see the Book of Daniel, chapter 5: the reference is to the mysterious writing on the wall.

Timothy Summers: before Sir Robert Peel took over the Home Office in 1822, over two hundred types of offences were legally punishable by death. Before he finally left it in 1830 he had not only established the Police Force but removed over one hundred offences from the list of those for which the death sentence could be pronounced.

circulus, cujus centrum diabolus: i.e. a circle the centre of which is the devil.

skimmer-cake: a small pudding made from the remnants of another and cooked in a " skimmer," i.e. a shallow dish, usually perforated, with which milk was skimmed.

cretaceous: chalky.

THE HOUSE OF EULALIE

HENRY HARLAND was of American birth, but having been educated in Rome and Paris, and having come to London in 1890 when he was twenty-nine, he was during his short life—he died in 1905—more of a cosmopolitan than a citizen of any particular nation. His short stories, probably owing to his French upbringing, betray marked signs of French influence, which shows itself in a sort of impressionism, in a sentimental pathos, which is suggestive of George Sand, and in gaiety and wit combined with an apparently artless and unexaggerated style. Fifty years ago Harland was very popular. To this he owed his appointment as editor of *The Yellow Book*, in which task he was not really successful. " The House of Eulalie " is Harland at his best and has this advantage over his other tales in a French setting—such as " When I am King " and " Mademoiselle Miss "—that its environment, while just as deftly pictured, is pleasanter than the drab realism of the Paris slums in which the other two tales we have mentioned have their being.

colza: cole, a kind of cabbage, the seed of which yields lampoil.

Le bon Dieu sait ce qu'il fait: the good God knows what He is doing.

THE HEADSWOMAN

THIS story belongs to the same year that saw the publication of Anthony Hope's extraordinarily popular tale *The Prisoner of Zenda*, and it is in the same vein of pure romance. It was a vein that had a momentary vogue, and is nearly associated with the contemporary popularity of the highly imaginary historical novel, such as Booth Tarkington's *Monsieur Beaucaire* or Baroness Orczy's *Scarlet Pimpernel*. The stern realities of the 1914 war put an end to this phase of popular taste, but while it lasted it gave rise to a large number of novels and short stories which were far removed from

the realities of life and which were intended only to entertain and amuse. In their light-heartedness and daintiness
they are the literary witnesses of the joy of life of a generation which had freed itself from the trammels of Victorian
propriety and had not yet experienced the deluge.

Kenneth Grahame was born in 1859 and died in 1932.
Two books of his, written with the exquisite delicacy of
feeling evident in this story, have earned him the liking of
several generations of young readers and, indeed, often
of their elders: they are *The Golden Age* (1895) and *The
Wind in the Willows* (1908).

succès d'estime: a partial success, due to public favouritism.

la marche aux crapauds: frog-march.

hinc illæ lachrymæ: hence those tears: the Roman poet is
Terence.

BROOKSMITH

HENRY JAMES was an American by birth who came to London somewhere about 1880 and ended by becoming a
naturalized Englishman. He was born in 1843 and died in
1917. His influence has been so considerable, especially on
English fiction, that no volume of nineteenth-century short
stories could dispense with an example of his art. He is to
his successors what Poe was to the mid-Victorian age, a
leader. Apart from a deep and abiding interest in form,
and the ability to write smooth-flowing English, James's
psychological habit of mind is his most characteristic
quality and the one which exerted most influence on the
future. By this we mean that he was not concerned with
plot, nor with character in the sense that Dickens was concerned with it, but that his tales tended to become studies
of the reactions of the minds of the persons of the story
when faced by crises in their lives. He regards them from
a coldly analytical and intellectual standpoint, recounting
in the minutest detail those words or actions which might
shed light, not on their characters as a whole, but on the
only aspect of it which concerns the immediate problem he

is describing. Thus the reader of " Brooksmith," which has been included because it is an excellent example of James's psychological story, learns little of him except that interest in cultivated talk which was to prove Brooksmith's undoing. James is a finer novelist than short-story writer just because of this tendency to pay more attention to situation than to character, and more to character than to incident, which led him to write at greater and greater length in order to create the impression he desired to give. " Brooksmith " also illustrates other aspects of James's work, a dramatic development of the theme from episode to episode, as in the successive acts of a play, the close attention to detail, and the tendency to impressionism, that is, to leave the picture on the reader's mind, not so much as a completed whole, but as an impression derived from a distant prospect of the scene. Few writers have been so much criticized and at the same time so much praised as James.

Arcadia: a classic land of innocence and simplicity.

salon: a famous institution of eighteenth-century France, noteworthy for the sway that their hostesses exercised over the cultured men and women whom they collected in the drawing-rooms. Englishmen of the time collected in clubs from which women were excluded.

Montaigne: the first great French essayist, translated into English by Florio (1533-92).

Saint-Simon: the Duke de Saint-Simon (1675-1755) wrote *Memoirs of the Court of France under Louis XIV and his Successors*, once a very celebrated book.

Lord Byron's life in Italy: Byron lived in Italy from 1820-23 when he went to help the Greeks against the Turks, and died at Missolonghi. The implication is that the anecdote was a doubtful one.

weeding a little: sorting out the desirable topics of conversation from the undesirable.

Voltaire: French philosopher, dramatist, essayist and novelist (1694-1778). There is a picture of the dying Voltaire.